David S¹
near Lancaste₁
School in Derby₅ₕₘₑ
Durham. After University, he was a ₚ-
Linlithgow, West Lothian and a student at the Episᴄₒₚ
Theological College in Edinburgh. From 1968-1979, he
was Chaplain of St Paul's Cathedral, Dundee and
Anglican Chaplain in the University of Dundee from
1973-1979. Since 1979, he has been Rector of
St Mary Magdalene's Church, Dundee.

Nine detective novels have now been published:

WHO KILLED SOPHIE JACK?
MURDER WITHIN TENT
SLAUGHTER AT THE POLLS
A CHRISTMAS CRACKER
A MISHAP IN MAJORCA
A PROSPECT OF RYE
MURDER ON THE MALLAIG EXPRESS
BURIED IN BAPTISM
FROZEN IN NICE

Copies are available from:

Meadowside Publications
14 Albany Terrace
Dundee DD3 6HR
Telephone 01382 223510

Further details can be obtained from our website:
http://www.crime-fiction.com
Email: meadowsidecrime@btinternet.com

FROZEN
IN NICE

A DETECTIVE NOVEL
BY
DAVID SHEPHERD

MEADOWSIDE PUBLICATIONS
DUNDEE
2008

Meadowside Publications
14 Albany Terrace, Dundee DD3 6HR

© *Meadowside Publications, 2008*

Printed by
Prontaprint,
Dundee, Scotland

*The Characters portrayed in this
novel are all imaginary and bear
no intended resemblance to any
person alive or dead.*

ISBN 978-0-9520632-8-5

Meadowside Crime
is a © imprint of
Meadowside Publications,
Dundee

CONTENTS

The story is set in Nice,
in the South of France,
in May 1990.

1. *Great Expectations*

Inspector Raynes released himself from his partner's tender embrace. He lay back on his pillow and put his hands behind his head.

"By the way," he said, "I've had a letter from Simon."

This snippet of information did not please Mrs May. It showed – all too clearly – that the Inspector's mind was on other – lesser – things. She had hoped that he was still thinking about her. She had arranged this visit to a very expensive hotel to celebrate his forthcoming birthday. Two days of superb food, decent wine, a four-poster bed with all the trimmings. On this night – of all nights – she expected to be the epicentre of his thoughts and desires.

She wondered – and not for the first time – why men always spoilt things. Why did they have such butterfly minds? How could they destroy such a delicate, romantic moment? Could they not block out worldly thoughts and bathe in that deep, sensual glow they had just created?

She could have said something very cutting – but she controlled herself.

The Inspector realized that his interjection had been inappropriate – and was silent.

Eventually, Debbie spoke:

"What was he saying then?"

"He's got a new girlfriend. A Russian. She lives in France."

"Good for him."

Simon was one of Richard's oldest friends. He was an artist with no perceptible morals. One of his recent attachments had involved him in a particularly brutal murder. Raynes had known of his involvement but had turned a Nelsonian blind eye. So Simon had escaped scot-free and another foul-faced crook had taken the rap.

Mrs May turned her head a few degrees to the right and looked at the Inspector.

"Is she rich?"

"Her mother has a villa in the south of France."

"How did he come to meet her?"

"I think they met in some saleroom in Brighton. She was buying Louis Quatorze chairs. Her mother runs an antique shop in Nice."

"Is he going to visit her?"

"He's there now."

Raynes finally unveiled his trump card.

"She's invited him to bring two or three of his friends to stay with them in the villa. He thought we might be interested. Free grub, free accommodation – for a fortnight. All we have to pay for is the flight."

Debbie was about to say: "No, I'm too busy." But the word: 'Nice' had a magic ring. She had once gone to Nice with a wealthy businessman. (His wife had gone to a health farm for a week.) They had stayed at the Negresco on the Promenade des Anglais – probably the best hotel in which she had ever stayed. They had also visited the casino in Monte Carlo where she had done rather well – beginner's luck! But whilst she had been there, she had had time to suss out the local talent. Men were the same the world over – weak, gullible, easily led astray. But in the south of France, they were loaded. It could be a very lucrative visit. It would certainly be a welcome break from Grasshallows where the weather had been grey and wet for several weeks.

So she didn't say: "No". Nor did she reveal her rather sordid calculations. She just smiled sweetly and said: "When do we go?"

Raynes was surprised by her enthusiasm.

"Simon suggested a week on Monday."

"That'd be fine."

Raynes smiled.

"I'll try and make sure there'll be no murders."

Mrs May pulled the sheet higher to cover her breasts.

"I'm sure I'll be able to find something to do – in Nice."

Her words left little room for misunderstanding.

Later, she was able to read Simon's letter in full – a gushing portrait of his new love. She had deep brown eyes, long dark hair, was almost five foot ten inches tall. She had long legs – obviously, at that height! She was a brilliant saleswoman. Possessed a wonderful sense of humour. Had been studying philosophy at university – but had dropped out; she had married some brutal Frenchman and was now taking refuge in commerce. She was called Ludmilla – Ludo, for short.

Anyway, her mother had a large villa on the outskirts of Nice – an old farmhouse, really. It was said that Renoir had painted there with some of his friends. Her mother would be delighted to welcome Simon and all his chums.

The fatted calf would be slaughtered; the best wine brought up from the cellars; the wicked husband – Gaspard – would not dare to show his face.

It was all too perfect. Debbie could see that immediately. Simon was head over heels in love. For him, a holiday in Nice would be the closest thing to Paradise.

She could imagine it all. The relationship would end in tears. Everyone would fall out. The cook would leave just before the guests arrived. The wine would probably be plonk; the food greasy and inedible. There would be cockroaches running all over the floor. Gaspard would arrive on the doorstep to claim his beloved. There might be a duel. Simon would be shot. Richard would happily plunge into the mêlée and try to outwit the local gendamerie.

However, so long as she could 'shop around'; fleece the local talent; drink a few bottles of Pol Roger and recover her famous tan – all would be well. Perhaps Ludo could find some agreeable French slut to entertain the Inspector — whilst she clocked up a hundred thousand francs. Yes. It could be a very profitable holiday for both of them.

She looked again at Simon's letter. The green ink annoyed her. She felt there was something very offensive – something psychologically unhinged – about people who used green ink. Still, that was Ludo's problem. Not hers!

2. *Nissa la Bella*

The flight southward from Luton was troublefree. Unbelievably, the plane had departed on time. Drinks had been served at an early stage in the flight and now the cabin crew were busily dispensing perfumes and spirits. There seemed to be no prospect of lunch.

Through the small side windows, Mrs May observed the jagged peaks of the Alps ten thousand feet below. Seen on a clear day, they looked particularly vicious and nasty. She pointed them out to Richard who was reminded of the intrepid airmen of the 1920s and 30s who had battled against icing and engine failure over these same mountains, terrified to sink lower through the clouds for fear of the enemy beneath.

But today, the sky was cloudless blue. The Mediterranean, just a short distance ahead, was covered by a light haze. The 737 slipped lower, its engines reduced to a mere purr as it positioned itself in the queue to land.

They passed over Cannes, catching a clear view of La Croisette. Then they were out over the water – a deep royal blue. The plane dipped sharply to the left and soon they were running parallel to the shore. They seemed to be flying so slowly that there was a real danger of the 737 falling out of the sky. But only a mile or two ahead was the tiny postage stamp on which they intended to land.

The seat belt sign had been on for the last quarter of an hour but now the matter had become more pressing as the plane continued to lose height, several hundred feet at a time, The sea came nearer. A surprisingly large yacht appeared under their left wing. Then there was a sudden flash of rocks and green grass, and the comforting thump, roar and screech of brakes as the plane hit the runway and proceeded to decelerate rapidly.

Raynes realized that he had been holding his breath.

Debbie packed away her *Hello!* and turned to Richard. "Don't forget your syringe and the heroin capsules!" she said cheerfully.

The woman in the seat next to the aisle looked at the Inspector with horror. To think she had been travelling with junkies!

Mrs May gave her a friendly smile.

"The police were after him in England; but I think we've given them the slip!"

* * * *

Twenty minutes later, having collected their luggage, they were standing outside the airport looking like lost souls.

"He said he would be here."

"Perhaps he's been held up by the traffic."

Mrs May looked at her watch.

"We said 12.30pm."

"He probably expected us to be late."

Mrs May sighed.

Raynes knew that sigh all too well. Debbie was a person who prided herself on her efficiency and good timekeeping. She expected others to maintain the same high standards. Invariably, she was disappointed.

One or two of the taxi drivers began to look at them hopefully.

"It's no use taking a taxi," said Raynes, "because we don't know where we're going."

"He might have given us his phone number."

"I don't think he knew it himself."

"If the worst comes to the worst, we can always hire a car."

Raynes was apologetic.

"I haven't got my licence with me."

"I have."

Debbie had already decided that they would need a car. It would give them – well, her – freedom of movement. And if life at the villa proved totally unbearable, they could always escape.

"We could stay in a hotel overnight," she said helpfully. "And then, tomorrow morning, you could go round the antique shops and seek out this Russian beauty. Something to do with angels, wasn't it?

"La Grotte de Seraphim. . . "

Mrs May sighed again.

"I've had enough 'grotte' for one day."

Raynes persuaded her to give Simon another five minutes.

"You know what he's like. . . "

"Completely irresponsible!"

But still nothing happened.

Debbie insisted on going to the Avis desk and hiring a small car. The negotiations were almost complete when a familiar voice greeted them:

"My darlings! You must forgive me. I'm so sorry I'm late; but I was busy painting her ladyship and tempus simply fugit."

They had been joined by a small middle-aged man with a slightly balding head and protuberant olive-coloured eyes. He was wearing a flowery open-necked shirt and a pair of beige-coloured shorts which looked too big for him.

"Brackles!"

"What are you doing here?"

"Same racket as you. Free booze. Free nosh. Chaperoning impoverished young artists." He smiled apologetically. "But not doing it all that well."

"Where is Simon?"

Brackles shrugged his shoulders.

"Who knows? Cavorting on a yacht in Cannes harbour? Drinking cocktails in the Grand Casino in Monte Carlo? She's got him wrapped round her little finger. Sex is a terrible thing!"

Raynes laughed.

"I've never heard you say that before."

Brackles grimaced horribly.

"You've not met Signor Spumante. . . "

"Signor who?"

"Come on, let me treat you to a cappucino; and whilst you're waiting for your car, I'll fill you in."

Brackles stirred his coffee.

"The Villa Rose is a fine old place. More farmhouse than villa. It has an incredible number of rooms. You're in Honeymoon suite No 2. No. 1 is spoken for. There's a good-sized pool. Excellent food. Immaculate service. A wine cellar to die for. And it's all paid for by selling junk.

"Her ladyship lives surrounded by quite a crowd of hangers-on – people like us. I don't know whether they're there to protect her – or to entertain her; but she enjoys good company. She likes to play *la grande hôtesse*. And she does it rather well. By contrast, her daughter is rather pale meat. Lovely girl – but much quieter. Her mother spoils her rotten. Indulges her every whim."

"Are you painting the daughter?"

"No, the mother. Much more challenging. When I arrived, she said to me: 'Monsieur Brackles, I hear that you are a great artist. Your friend, I expect, will be fully occupied; but I should like you to do something useful and worthwhile during your holiday. I commission you to paint my picture.'

"She thought for a few moments and then she said: 'I should like to be painted as a Russian Empress. The last of the Romanovs.' 'No problem,' I said. 'As long as I have an unlimited supply of Courvoisier, I shall do anything you want.' So a deal was struck. And I must say the picture is coming along rather well."

(Brackles was not renowned for his modesty.)

"No horses, this time?" said Raynes mischievously.

"No. But we have a small lion cub – not a real one – nestling at her feet. I invented that – but she was delighted. You see, she's called Leonie. And she's very much a lioness guarding her den, protecting her brood, fending off the riff-raff. When she roars, everyone runs for cover. I made sure the lion cub had her eyes. She loved that."

"Did you bring your paints with you?"

"No. She ordered them from a shop in Nice. And a huge canvas. 'I shall place it in my boutique,' she said. 'It will impress *mes clients*.' I dare say they'll all want copies," Brackles added optimistically.

Debbie was more interested in Simon.

"Is he really in love with her daughter?"

Brackles shrugged his shoulders.

"Who knows? Simon is always in love with someone. *Toujours les dominatrices*! He loves to grovel. That's probably why women get tired of him. They long for a real man."

Brackles thrust out his chest and uttered a low gorilla-like growl. "A real man," he repeated.

"D'you think it's her money that attracts him?"

The artist shook his head.

"Simon's not really interested in money. As you know, he likes beauty. That's why he loved doing your picture. He simply adored you."

"That wasn't the real me."

"It was how he saw you. And, believe me, Ludo is a beautiful girl. She could be a top class model. But, like her mother, she's been bitten by the bug of commerce. The over-powering attraction of filthy lucre. She could flog a Napoleon III escritoire, riddled with woodworm, to any gullible Eskimo without blinking an eyelid."

Raynes looked at Debbie.

"Be careful not to buy any furniture from her."

Debbie smiled.

"I've got a bed – what more do I need?"

Brackles chuckled.

"Perhaps a Madame de Recamier chaise longue?"

"What's that?"

"Never mind. It's just that she's a rattling good sales – woman. I take my hat off to her."

"What does she see in Simon?"

Brackles laughed.

"What a question! Perhaps she likes the bohemian in him?

The penniless muppet living in a garret, eating sparrows?"

Debbie winced.

"Well, some women like that sort of thing."

But clearly Mrs May did not.

"So what are we supposed to do?" Raynes asked.

"Enjoy yourselves! Enjoy yourselves to the full. Appreciate the food. Swim in her pool. Treat it as if it were your own. Go and see the Roman monument at La Turbie before it crumbles into dust. Spend your last sou at the gaming table. Plunder the Galeries Lafayette! Dance naked under the trees at midnight. All the world loves a lover!"

Raynes was still suspicious.

"This *dame formidable*. . . she won't expect me to make love to her?"

Brackles' eyes twinkled.

"Your French accent is improving. No, you're quite safe. She is fully occupied with her slimy Italian gigolo. . ."

"Signor Spumante?"

"Yes. He is forever at her side, cutting her toenails, massaging her back, slapping on the suncream. It's quite revolting. He's at her beck and call twenty-four hours a day. He drives her car. Carries her shopping. Is the butt of her jokes. And he is insanely jealous of his position."

"Jealous?"

"Yes. When I started doing her ladyship's picture, he insisted on staying in her room to make sure we didn't get up to any hanky-panky. She kept sending him away for more brandy, but I'm sure he was watching us through the keyhole. I think I've satisfied him that I have no designs on La Grande Duchesse; but I know that if I laid a hand on her, he would kill me."

"It sounds fascinating."

"Actually, my dear, he's called Camille Calvoressco. Possibly even Count Calvoressco! But everyone calls him 'Spumante' behind his back. But they'd never dream of saying it to his face." Brackles raised his hands in a gesture of dramatic horror.

"My darlings, if we did that, the truffles would really hit the crème brulée!"

Brackles pushed away his cup and saucer.

"Now, I'm sure your car will be ready for you. I shall drive round to the compound and you will do your best to follow me through the traffic." He paused. "And who is driving? You? Quel horreur!

"I shall give you the address and the telephone number in case you get lost. But, if you do, remember! You have only to stop and ask any Niçois – or Niçoise – the way to the Villa Rose. They will be delighted to direct you. La Grande Duchesse is already a living legend!"

3. *The Best of all Possible Worlds*

Brackles drove slowly out of the airport so that Debbie could keep up with him. He headed east – along the Promenade des Anglais. He kept to the nearside lane until he reached the harbour, where he turned sharp left. Debbie stuck grimly to his tail, ignoring red traffic lights and angry blasts on the horn from infuriated motorists. More than once, Richard shut his eyes. It was better that way.

But they managed to circumvent the port without accident or injury and climbed the Boulevard Carnot, heading for Mount Boron. The road skirted the headland but Brackles again turned sharp left down a tree-lined lane. An unpretentious gateway led to a drive bordered with rhododendrons. The drive twisted and turned, moving ever upwards, and finally emerged on a grassy hillside with a fine view over Nice and the Baie des Anges.

"What a splendid view!" said Debbie.

"Keep your eyes on the road!"

The warning was timely. The driveway was extremely narrow and the hillside fell away sharply to the left. However, just round the corner, they reached their destination – a large collection of stone buildings surrounding a central courtyard.

As Brackles had said, it was more farmhouse than villa but with all the additions and extensions, it amounted to quite a substantial building. Stone lions guarded the front porch.

Debbie switched off the engine.

"It looks rather nice."

"Very secluded."

They got out of the car. Brackles joined them.

"You did very well."

"I could never have made it on my own."

"We're lucky we made it at all."

"Grumpy old man!"

Brackles helped them get the luggage out of the car.

"Bonjour, Messieurs et Madame!"

"Ah, Sylvie."

Raynes looked to his right. A slim young woman in her late thirties with dark hair and very clear eyes. She was wearing a sleeveless black dress and carrying a clipboard.

"Sylvie's the housekeeper. She speaks excellent English."

Everyone shook hands.

"Monsieur and Madame Raynes, you are in the *Chambre des Petits Cygnes*."

"All the rooms are called after pieces of music by Tchaikovsky," explained Brackles. "I'm in the *Rococo* apartment. Simon and Ludo are in *Swan Lake*. Our hostess is in the *Romeo and Juliet*."

Raynes smiled.

"And what about Signor Spumante? Is he in the *Nutcracker*?"

"No, he's in the *Pathétique*."

Sylvie laughed.

"Oh, Monsieur, you are too cruel. He is in the *Capriccio Italien*."

Brackles picked up Debbie's suitcase.

"Well, let's get you up to your room. Where is the *Chambre des Petits Cygnes*?"

Sylvie clasped the clipboard closer to her bosom.

"Follow me. I will show you."

17

Richard picked up his luggage and followed the others through the porch and into the main hall. The first thing that caught his eye was the chandelier. Even though it was lit by electricity rather than candles, there was no doubt it was 'the real thing'. Raynes could guess that it had come from some chateau or a Bourbon palace.

The rest of the furnishings had the same exalted pedigree. Cabinets, tables, mirrors, pictures, silk hangings and oriental carpets. . . The word 'Bokhara' instantly sprang to mind. A great bowl of fresh gladioli stood at the foot of the staircase. Everything shone. A huge silver kettle – possibly a samovar; but perhaps not! It looked like a kettle. The stair rods – pure brass. More pictures – they must be worth a fortune.

Of course, being in the antiques' trade, their hostess could probably pick up such things for a song. But it was nonetheless a treasure house. The Inspector hoped she had everything well-insured.

Compared with the beauty of the house through which they were passing, he was conscious that Debbie and he were mere travel-stained peasants. He felt quite humbled by all the wealth and good taste which surrounded them.

Debbie, of course, could carry it off. Nothing would embarrass her. She was used to dealing with people of every class, taste and culture. She could always play the part that was required of her – be it slave girl or contessa. He wondered how she would cope with their hostess? Had she brought a suitable evening dress?

All these thoughts ran through his mind as they made their way up to their room. It had a massive door. When the door opened, the first thing he saw was a huge four-poster bed with fluted oak pillars the size of small trees. Once again, there were two beautiful pictures on the wall – ballet dancers – "Reproduction Dégas," he said to himself. But almost immediately he dismissed the unworthy thought. They were bound to be genuine.

It was a very feminine room. Soft pinks and lace; large bottles with gold stoppers; white curtains with immense tassels; another smaller chandelier; heaps of towels; a deep, deep carpet into which one's feet would sink. And the bed – king-sized, if not truly Napoleonic – just waiting to be explored.

Sylvie smiled.

"You like it?"

"It's marvellous," said Raynes.

"Better than mine!" said Brackles. "I've got a rather poor Seurat. I feel like touching it up. I'm sure the Grand Duchess would never notice."

Sylvie laughed nervously.

"Madame is very proud of her pictures."

"She has excellent taste," said Brackles graciously. "I just think it was one of Seurat's off-days. His mistress must have left him. Or he'd discovered he'd caught the clap. Perhaps both!"

"Is the room haunted?" asked Debbie.

"*Hanté*," Brackles translated.

"*Mais, non!* Madame would never have bought *une maison hantée*." She smiled. "But if she had, she would have brought in a priest . . . "

". . . to perform an exorcism?"

"Just so. She would have dealt with it. . . ."

". . . as she deals with everyone! I don't think any self-respecting ghost could survive the pace round here. If he wasn't earning his keep, he'd have been sent straight to purgatory. Do not pass 'Go'. Do not collect £200."

Sylvie interrupted Brackles' flights of fantasy: "It is not an old part of the house. It is quite new. But Madame had it built in *style ancien* wiz the old stones and the old. . . *ardoises*. I do not know the word."

"Slates?" suggested Brackles.

"Just so, Monsieur. So there are no ghosts to frighten Madame." She looked reassuringly at Debbie.

Brackles looked thoughtful.

"I should think the cellars are probably the oldest part of the building. La Grande Duchesse has a wonderful selection of wine. The Hungarian Tokay we had last night was out of this world. We shall have to go and see if she has a few more."

Sylvie blushed very sweetly.

"I can assure Monsieur that there are no ghosts in the cellars. . . "

". . . but plenty of spirits!"

Brackles laughed.

"Come on," he said, "we must let these people get settled in. They must've been on the road for hours. Must be completely knackered. I shall be down at the pool." He turned to Sylvie. "Which reminds me. . . Could one of your underlings find me another bottle of brandy? The last one's right down to the dregs." He smiled apologetically. "A man has to drink to live."

"Perhaps a bottle of iced champagne for Monsieur and Madame?"

"That would be perfect."

* * * *

"I still can't see why she invited us."

Richard was roaming round the room whilst Debbie was emptying the contents of their suitcases into deep drawers.

"She probably likes company."

"She knows nothing about us. We could be complete crooks!" He laughed cynically. "Most of Simon's friends are crooks!"

"It's probably not much fun living on your own – especially if you're rich. If you've got a large house, you might as well fill it."

"I don't know." Raynes looked suspiciously at two large mirrors built into the wall. "Do you think they're two-way? She could be watching us. . . filming us! D'you remember that scene in *From Russia with Love*? When James Bond was having it off with that bird in the honeymoon suite? She was a Russian!"

"If it gives them pleasure. . . "

"Yes, but just think! If they sent the film back to our Police Committee; that'd be embarrassing." He took an icon off the wall and looked at its back.

"What are you doing?"

"Seeing if it's bugged."

He picked up the telephone and inspected it.

"I think you're completely paranoid."

Mrs May was casting Richard's dark-blue Y fronts into a bottom drawer. How much more ridiculous he would look in canary yellow! She must try and find a pair in Cannes. That would discourage any midnight cameramen.

The Inspector had now gone into the bathroom and was trying out the shower. In the process, he drenched the right arm of his shirt. Debbie looked at him despairingly.

"Take it from me; it's bug free. If there were any such things, Brackles would have found them by now. He's even worse than you." She paused. "You'd better change that shirt and put on a pair of shorts. Look the part. Pretend you're enjoying it. Once you've had a couple of glasses of champagne, you'll be beyond caring. Just remember! The drinks are free!"

Mrs May started stripping off.

Raynes looked at her with pleasure.

"I'm putting on my new bikini."

"So I see." He laughed. "And so will everyone else."

Debbie tore off the price tag.

"I don't see why we shouldn't bathe in the nude if we want to. It's a private pool. I expect the staff are used to it. You could do it too." Her eyes narrowed maliciously. "I'm sure it'd give Sylvie a thrill."

Mrs May had a capacity for perceiving other people's unspoken thoughts. This time, she had clearly hit the nail on the head. Richard looked sheepish. He muttered: "Well. . . Mm. . . " and wandered back into the bedroom to look for his shorts. Where had she put them?

Debbie looked at her face in the mirror to see what was needed. At this time of day, there was no need for sun-tan lotion. Just a spot or two of moisturizing cream and a touch of Chanel. After all, it was France!

She slipped into her gold sandals; and looked at Richard wandering around the room in beige-coloured shorts, still looking for a belt.

"You don't need a shirt," she said. "Just take a towel down with you. You look quite manly without it." She smiled wickedly. "You could always ask her if she'd like to join us for a threesome. . . "

"Who?" he asked absent-mindedly.

"Sylvie!"

Raynes breathed a sigh of relief.

"I thought you were meaning Leonie. . . "

Debbie shrugged her shoulders.

"Well, make it a foursome! You're always boasting!"

4. *At the Villa Rose*

Debbie swept down the staircase, her multi-coloured chiffon wrap flowing behind her. Clearly, she felt at home. Richard followed her, slowly and more thoughtfully, out on to the broad terrace which encompassed the swimming pool, where Brackles was reading a crumpled copy of the *Daily Mail* which he had picked up at the airport.

He flung his paper to one side and rose to his feet.

"My dear! You look simply gorgeous."

Debbie smiled happily.

"What a lovely place!" she said. "And what a splendid view."

She walked over to the stone balustrade and looked down at the trees and bushes twenty feet below. The hillside fell away so steeply that she couldn't even see the driveway or the grassy slope. Beneath the tree line was the city of Nice, basking in the late afternoon sun with the distant shadow of the Cap d'Antibes reaching out into the Mediterranean and the grey-pink massif of the Esterel.

"Ernst is bringing you a bottle of champagne," said Brackles. "He has absolutely no sense of humour. Never laughs. Never smiles. I think in a previous incarnation, he must have been a guard at a concentration camp or one of those thugs who protected General de Gaulle."

Almost on cue, a tall, bald-headed man strode on to the terrace with a silver bucket, tinkling with crushed ice, a green and gold bottle bobbing in its watery depths. He placed the stand between the two white, wooden deckchairs and returned to the house to collect the glasses and a bottle of brandy for Brackles.

Raynes noticed that his grey, soul-less eyes raked over Debbie's body. Perhaps white-slaving had also been his portion. It would be unfortunate if any woman got into his clutches. Brackles was right. The man was a brute.

But good manners had to be displayed.

"Merci, Ernst."

"Messieurs, Madame. . ."

The slight hint of a bow and he was away, back into the house.

"Formidable, eh? I call him King Kong."

"I'm sure he must have some redeeming features."

"A mother who loves him. . ."

"I doubt it."

The Inspector lifted his glass.

"To our invisible but generous hostess!"

"Long may Simon's affair last."

Debbie gulped down half her champagne and then looked at it with some surprise.

"That's the real thing!"

"What else d'you expect? Leonie only stocks the best stuff. Her wine cellar's a bit like Fort Knox. Keeps it all under lock and key. I haven't managed to work out the combination." Brackles laughed. "But I will."

"It must be wonderful to have so much money."

"I think it's a family business. She's the third generation. Came over after the revolution. The Russians have always had a soft spot for Nice. There's a splendid Orthodox church – if you're interested. Founded by Tsar Nicholas II. . . "

Brackles looked at Debbie and Richard guzzling their champagne. No, they weren't interested.

Debbie's mind was concerned with more material matters.

"I shall marry an elderly French millionaire! Very elderly," she added.

Brackles smiled sadly.

"I expect if you hang round Leonie for long enough, you're bound to meet one or two." He looked at Debbie's elegant figure as she lay back in the well-padded, white sun-lounger. "But I'm sure it'll be a great loss to all your admirers. Particularly Richard. . . "

Debbie sniffed contemptuously.

"He can always find someone else. He's not particular. Anyway, I'm thinking of increasing my charges after the summer. I think there should be a premium on experience."

She looked at Richard mischievously.

Raynes did not rise to the bait.

Instead, he sipped at his champagne, enjoying the ice-cold tingle as it trickled down his throat.

"Must have been maturing for quite a long time," he said. He took the bottle out of the bucket. "1964? Must have been a very good year."

"Just drink it!" said Debbie. "Don't go on about the dates. You'll never drink stuff like this again!"

Raynes quickly helped himself to a refill. The bottle was more than half empty. Mrs May was certainly making the most of her opportunity.

"If you need another bottle, Ernst will bring you one."

It was almost too good to be true.

Raynes sank back in his seat.

"Antiques," he said. "A wonderful racket. Buying in junk; selling it to dealers and collectors; you can hardly lose."

Brackles stuffed the remains of the *Daily Mail* into his pocket.

"We were talking about it the other night. Apparently, the

business really took off during the war. The White Russians and the Jews left the country in droves. They were willing to sell their furniture and pictures for a song – just to get their hands on ready cash. They couldn't take any of their possessions with them. Leonie's grandad lashed out dollars and filled his warehouse with goodies. Apparently, he hid the best stuff in caves – hence the name of the shop – La Grotte de Seraphim. Russian version of Aladdin's cave.

"But he didn't trust his son. Thought he might blab to the Nazis or the Vichy police. So he confided his secrets to his little grand-daughter. Gave her the details of where the loot was stored. As a child, it meant nothing to her. But when she grew up, she went hunting and found where the caves were. By that time, Grandad had long since snuffed it and her dad wasn't making all that much of the business. She bided her time. Once she got her hands on the shop, she rolled out the treasures one by one. They funded further purchases. Since that moment, she's never looked back.

"In fact, she told me that the descendants of some of those refugees actually bought back their old family pictures – and furniture. They were delighted that the stuff had survived the war. Hadn't been filched by Goering and his chums. . . "

Brackles looked at Richard and Debbie to see if they were taking in the full flavour of Leonie's remarkable success – but both of them were fast asleep. The flight, the sunshine and the champagne had all taken their toll. La Grotte de Seraphim had been a lullaby which had sent both of them to the Land of Nod.

Brackles sighed. He took out his *Daily Mail* and turned up "Your Star Sign". He looked up Sagittarius:

"At the moment you have Venus in your communications zone and Mars in your relationship zone. This means that you really are in the right place at the right time to let people know how you feel. Old friends may desert you but new friends offer romance and excitement. The clearer you keep your head over the next few weeks, the better your life will be."

Even if it was complete crap, it was encouraging. For, as

the horoscope reminded him: The great thing about being a Sagittarian is "your endless optimism!" That, at least, was true.

* * * *

When Raynes finally surfaced, he became conscious that the number gathered round the pool had increased. There were now five of them. They had been joined by Simon and a tall, willowy young woman with long, dark brown hair and very expensive leather boots. They had drawn up chairs and were making unflattering comments about the "sleeping beauty".

It seemed that Debbie had awoken some time earlier and changed into something warmer and more comfortable. For the sun was going down in a great ball of fire; the city of Nice was a rich shade of purple and the Villa Rose almost lost in the twilight.

Simon did the introductions;

"Dick, this is Ludo. Ludo, this is my old university mate, Dick Raynes. He gets me to paint naughty pictures."

Hands were shaken.

Raynes said to Ludo: "Simon described you perfectly. I can see why he was so ecstatic."

"Love is blind!" said Brackles.

"It's very kind of you to invite us down here. It's the most beautiful place."

"You can thank Maman. She loves company. The more people she has round her table, the happier she is."

"And where have you been?" asked Brackles, looking pointedly at his watch.

"Monte Carlo," said Simon. "Aboard a most exclusive yacht. Almost a small destroyer – but much better kitted out."

"We were working," said Ludo. "Working very hard."

She gave Simon a soft kiss on his cheek.

"Selling a picture to a trillionaire who had absolutely no idea about art. Ludo was flogging him a Braque but he'd never heard of him. We had to show him a catalogue from an exhibition in Paris to make him realize its value. I think he's only bought it for show."

Ludo smiled.

"He said he had this small alcove in his main cabin. He couldn't think what to put there. He was wandering round Maman's boutique when he saw it. 'That would fit perfectly,' he said. So we rushed over to Monte Carlo before he could change his mind. Simon was wonderful."

"In what way?" asked Raynes.

"I convinced him of its authenticity. Talked about the age of the canvas; the quality of the oil paint; the artist's idiosyncrasies; the era when the picture had been painted; its current value on the market."

"I didn't think you knew anything about Braque," said Brackles suspiciously.

"I don't really. But there were certain generalities I could expand on."

"Was it actually a genuine Braque?"

"I don't know. And neither does he. By the time he sells the ship – painting included – he'll have completely forgotten about it. The next owner will probably toss it overboard. I think our secret will be safe."

"You're a complete conman!" said Brackles. "I hope you never have to meet the real artist in the after life."

"Maman will be delighted with the sale. The picture has been hanging around for a very long time."

"It'll certainly cover the cost of the holiday," said Simon apologetically. "We can drink Leonie's champagne with a clear conscience."

"Thank God for that!" said Debbie.

The tall figure of Ernst emerged from the house.

"The canapés and drinks are being served in the small salon in fifteen minutes time, Madame."

"Thank you Ernst."

"Time to get dressed for dinner," said Simon. He looked at Richard. "None of your sloppy provincial outfits," he said, "Have you got a black tie and a cummerbund?"

27

Raynes bristled.

"Never travel without them."

"Well, don't let the side down!"

As they moved towards the house, Debbie pulled Richard to one side. She whispered: "Who is Braque?"

"I haven't the foggiest idea! So long as the food and the booze are good, who cares?"

5. *La Belle Epoque*

Raynes did not disgrace the party – and neither did Debbie.

She was wearing a deep pink, figure-hugging concoction which blatantly emphasized her physical charms. Ludo was in a long blue dress with a short train which swirled across the floor and suggested Balenciaga. Other women were in red and grey satin.

Leonie herself was resplendent in dark emerald green which recalled la belle époque of Napoleon III. In the absence of a sash or a badge of the Legion d'Honneur, she wore an immense diamond brooch which discouraged the ungodly from looking too closely at her magnificent cleavage.

Like her daughter, Leonie was tall and statuesque. Richard could understand how Brackles could depict her as a Romanov Empress. Probably more beautiful and compelling than the real thing. And yet, she must be in her late fifties. Quite a woman!

In the course of the next half hour, Raynes discovered the value of mirrors in a room. Everywhere you looked there was colour and movement. The constant flutter of dresses, seen from so many different angles – one mirror reflecting and multiplying the images from other mirrors. The mixture of red, green, grey, pink and blue, contrasting so sharply with black and white – provided a more vivid display than any arrangement of flowers. This was a living tableau. Who needed pictures with such a kaleidoscope of colour?

The only touches of eccentricity were Brackles' red bow tie

and a tall, grey-haired man in a lounge suit and a pale blue silk tie.

"Who is that?" he asked Simon.

"A distinguished American historian. Julius D. Foster. A thundering bore. Make sure you don't sit beside him at dinner. Leonie avoids him like the plague."

"Why did she invite him?"

Simon chuckled.

"His wife's a reporter for some highly-respected heritage magazine. *American Antiques* – or something like that. She's their European correspondent. She's been having a field day discovering Leonie's artistic treasures. They'll all be featured in forthcoming articles in her magazine. Thereby boosting sales."

"I see."

"She's also proved quite a hit with the local photographer. Before she arrived, he was having rather a lean time. Now, I imagine, all his Christmases have come at once."

Simon pointed out the photographer who was chatting up Debbie.

"I wonder what they're talking about?"

"I think I can guess."

"Never stops, does she?"

"A true professional."

The Inspector realized now – if he hadn't realized it before – the attractions of Nice for Mrs May. No wonder she had agreed so readily to the holiday! She had already calculated percentages and profits. He didn't imagine that the young photographer would attract her all that much but he could be a gold mine of local information. Contacts, places, prices. Within a few minutes, she would have a complete picture of the demi-monde which she would then exploit happily for the rest of the holiday. The photographer would supply her with names and phone numbers and get a percentage of the take.

She was always very particular about that.

Richard shook his head sadly.

"Are we all phonies?"

"Speak for yourself!" said his friend.

"I mean – that picture!"

"Well, it's made us all very popular with the management. Welcomed us with open arms. Netted her nearly a quarter of a million. . . "

"Francs?"

"Pounds!"

"I can't believe it."

"Neither can I."

"That should help your love life!"

"Immensely."

Raynes looked around the gilded chamber.

"Are you ready to inherit all this?"

"Any day."

Richard could not help but admire Simon's unbounded optimism. He was sure it would all end in tears. And then back to the garret in Rye, painting endless reproductions of Henry James' house for the tourists at £20 a time. He suppressed the unworthy thought. Let him enjoy it while he could.

Ernst bustled about with the wines and spirits whilst one of the maids circled the room with a tray of canapés which were soon consumed. The Inspector noticed that Mrs Foster seemed to be the only guest drinking tomato juice. Presumably it was one way of maintaining her excellent figure. Raynes was so busy looking at her shapely bottom that he failed to see her husband coming towards him with an outstretched hand.

"I don't think we've been introduced. I'm Julius D. Foster. And I think you're the policeman we've been expecting."

The Inspector decided to eat humble pie.

"Yes, that's right. Richard Raynes."

"Great to meet you."

Raynes did not like Americans – brash Americans – at the best of times; and he was not particularly sure that he liked historians either. People who regurgitated stale facts culled from other people's works and then garnished them with wild hypotheses based on totally improbable evidence. Thus – General Patton was gay and Winston Churchill's grandmother had been a Red Indian.

But he subdued his prejudices.

"What does the 'D' stand for?" he asked politely.

"Dominic."

"With a 'c'?"

"Is there any other way to spell it?"

Raynes smiled. "I seem to remember there was a singing nun who called herself Dominique – with a 'q'."

"No. My mum and pop came down on good plain Dominic."

"And the world has never forgiven them!" thought Raynes. He smiled in a friendly fashion. "Are you down here doing some research?"

"Not in Nice itself. In Cannes. . ." Raynes had unwittingly opened the floodgates. "I'm doing a little monograph for my publishers on Napoleon's return from Elba – cocking a snook at you Brits. You thought the war was over, but the Eagle returned. He gave you guys the slip and sailed back to France. Landed on a beach just near Cannes and then began his heroic march back to Paris. . ."

". . . and Waterloo," said Raynes.

"Yea. His troops sure let him down there. But, in Cannes, he got a real warm welcome. They camped out under the stars. People flocked to his colours. Gee, it must've been great to see him return. The Frenchies were so impressed that they built a damned great church on the site. There's a huge plaque on the wall – put up in 1932. I was down there this afternoon getting it photographed professionally."

"With . . . ?" Raynes nodded towards Mrs Foster's bright young friend.

"Yea. Arnaud's a real useful guy. We did lots of shots. Plenty of the church; some of the registers. They've got some really old photographs. Long time since they've seen the light of day."

"How long will your book be?"

"Gee, I don't know. How long is a piece of string? Probably 60,000 words. More if they'll print it."

"And a huge bibliography?"

"Of course. When you think of the thousands of books that have been written about 'Old Boney'. He was a real special guy." A longing look appeared in Mr Foster's eyes.

"Gee, I'd have loved to meet him."

Raynes decided it was time to puncture the balloon.

"We 'Brits' don't see him in quite the same light."

"Of course not. He was your enemy."

"He was everybody's enemy. He was a dictator. A tyrant. A mass-murderer. He invaded other people's countries. Carted off their treasures. Just like Hitler and Goering. He killed hundreds of thousands of his own people. Bled the French dry. I can't see why people admire him. 'La Gloire. . . ' It's crap. Like Hitler, they should have put him on trial for crimes against humanity. All his statues should be reduced to rubble – melted down. They should teach children the truth about him. He was a psychopath!"

Mr Foster's hero was unfortunately one of the Inspector's *bêtes noires*. It was one of his strongest reasons for disliking the French; that they continued to venerate such a monster.

"And it's people like you who sustain that legend. All you historians drooling over him. Saying he built wonderful roads. Established the metre as a universal instrument of measurement! The man was a complete crook! Put that in your book! Tell the truth for a change!"

Raynes' final words were said so forcefully that they were heard by everyone in the room. There was an embarrassed silence and then a flurry of comment.

"Oh, God!" said Simon to Ludo. "Dick's blown it!"

Brackles looked heavenwards.

"How to win friends and influence people!"

"My boyfriend doesn't like Napoleon," Debbie told Arnaud. "He thinks he was a complete *****."

Ernst broke into a rare burst of laughter; slapped the Inspector on the back; said; "Bravo!" – and then remembered that he was no longer a member of the Baader-Meinhoff gang, but simply a butler.

Sylvie, watching from the sidelines and about to announce that dinner was served, murmured: "Quelle passion!"

Leonie looked somewhat shell-shocked at such venom being poured out under her roof.

"Who is that man?" she demanded.

Signor Spumanti wrung his well-manicured hands.

"It is that wretched English policeman whom Simon brought over. Together with his 'horizontale'. They are a disgrace to society. Un embêtement. You should eject them immediately."

"But who was he talking about?"

"L'Empereur. . . "

Signor Spumanti's voice quavered with the reverence due to a deity.

Leonie's face relaxed.

"Eject him? Certainly not. I quite agree with him."

Minutes later, the lady of the house descended on the two protagonists and rescued the somewhat shaken Julius D. Foster.

"I'm afraid I have been failing in my duties, Monsieur Raynes."

"I apologize for being so loud-mouthed and offensive."

"They are your sincerely held views?"

"They are."

"They are views which I share." There was a warm twinkle in Leonie's eyes. "You see – although I was born and have lived most of my life in France – my father sent me to a school in England after the war. I have sent Ludo to the same school. There I have seen my country through English eyes. I understand how you English feel. *Je suis toujours sympathique*."

She looked to the right where the American historian was downing a third glass of neat whisky.

"Julius is a very insecure man."

"But I am told he has a very talented wife."

Leonie nodded.

"Amelie is a great friend. An enormous help to my

business. You must not be too hard on him. Outside his research, he has very few pleasures. I try to encourage him."

The same point was being made by the photographer to Debbie: "He is a very sad man. He has very few friends. I am told. . . " He put his finger to his lips. ". . . I am told also that he is impotent."

Mrs May looked thoughtfully at the American who had slammed down his glass on the table and was walking a little uncertainly towards the dining room.

"Impotent?" she said to herself. "We can certainly do something about that."

6. *Les Caves du Vatican*

When Raynes awoke, the sun had already been warming up the Côte d'Azur for over three hours. Its gentle light had long since penetrated the white silk curtains of the rear bedroom at the Villa Rose. The clock on the bedside table said 9.45am.

When he opened his eyes, the first things he saw were the two fluted pillars at the bottom of the bed. They were quite unnecessarily huge. The wooden beams around the top of the bed and the canopy did not require such massive support. However, he had to admit it was a very large and comfortable bed and he had slept well. He turned to his left, looking for Debbie; but her side of the bed was empty. She must already have gone downstairs for breakfast. It was her favourite meal.

With some reluctance, he threw back the covers and sat on the edge of the bed. His feet did not touch the floor. He detected a slight hangover from the night before. It did not feel too bad; like a morning mist, it would soon evaporate.

He made his way into the bathroom, shaved and brushed his teeth. He decided not to wear shorts. A sober blue shirt and dark blue trousers would look smart – but casual. Black sandals. Where was his watch?

He pulled back the curtains and looked into the courtyard.

Mrs Foster was getting into her car. She was wearing a loose white pleated skirt. He imagined that she was off for another happy day with her photographer. Oh! She had got out of the car again. Had she forgotten something? No, she was looking in her boot. He watched the twists and turns of her body with quiet pleasure.

Slowly, he wandered along the corridor and down the stairs. He felt more part of things this morning. He stopped to look at one or two of the pictures he had not noticed so far. In the distance, he could hear the sound of a vacuum cleaner. People were at work. Perhaps he was too late for breakfast?

In the main hallway, he picked up the local newspaper, *Nice-Matin*. It had a nice picture of a yacht on the front page with four people in life-jackets looking blissfully happy. The only word he recognized was "Mitterand". It did not inspire him to look any further than page one.

As he strolled into the dining room, he realized he was very much on his own. There were bowls and plates, cereals and croissants, a strong smell of coffee – but he was the only guest. He wandered over to the window and looked out over the pool to the distant city. Nice looked pinky-orange in the morning light. He was looking forward to exploring it.

"Monsieur?"

He was no longer alone.

"Sylvie?"

"You have slept well?"

"Extremely well, thank you."

"Madame has gone into town." (Better not to say: 'with Arnaud.') "Would you like café? *Deux croissants*?"

"That sounds perfect."

Raynes moved over to the table. He was not used to being waited on hand and foot; but these people took it for granted.

Within a minute, Sylvie had returned – and fussed over him, making sure he had *le sucre, la beurre*. She even poured his coffee.

"*Du lait*, M'sieur?"

"No, I prefer it black."

At least he had recognized one word.

"And where is everybody?" he asked.

"Simon and Mademoiselle have gone to a chateau near Grasse. An old lady is returning to England. She has lived there for many years. Her family wish to sell the chateau and its contents. They are inspecting it this morning. After that, they will have a picnic lunch and go painting."

"I saw Amelie getting into her car."

"She is going down to the boutique. Madame is also at the boutique. Monsieur Camille has done his usual twenty lengths in the pool. Every morning, he swims a kilometre before breakfast."

"And where is Mr Foster?"

"He has gone to survey La Grande Route Impériale."

Raynes looked blank.

"The road which Napoleon has taken from Cannes to Grenoble – through the mountains – on his way to Paris."

"I see." The less said about Napoleon the better.

"And Brackles?"

"He is still asleep. He drank too much last night. He was quite *ivrogne*. He loves so much the brandy. He will sleep till 11.00am. After lunch, he will paint Madame."

Raynes felt a little selfish, eating and drinking on his own.

"Would you like a cup of coffee?"

Sylvie looked over her shoulder before she replied. She was clearly thinking of what the rest of the staff were doing at that moment. Most of them were working in distant parts of the villa.

"Yes, I will join you. But I must make a fresh café."

She returned from the kitchen with a small café au lait. She settled down at the table. She crossed her legs, looked at Richard and said: "So you are an inspecteur?"

Raynes nodded.

"A real inspecteur?"

"Yes. Very real. I look after the police in a small university town in England."

"Do you have many murders there?"

"Some."

"And do you always catch the murderers?"

"Yes," said Raynes modestly. "I think I could say that I do."

"What is your most famous murder?"

Raynes was spoilt for choice.

"Well," he said, "last year, someone killed our member of Parliament."

"Votre deputé? Quel horreur!"

"It was after his victory party. He had only just been elected. The same night. He was found hanging from the staircase. His neck was broken."

"And who did it? His wife?"

"Well, she had good reasons for wanting to kill him. But it was another person who did it. Someone very jealous and angry."

"Ah, *la jalousie*." Sylvie sipped at her coffee. "You have the jealousy, Monsieur, for Madame?"

"She is not my wife."

"I know. She told me. But you love her very much?"

Raynes could not really deny it.

"I'm very fond of her. But she is very independent. Goes her own way. I have no control over her whatsoever."

He smiled sadly. "I don't think men are capable of controlling women. They will always go their own way."

Sylvie's eyes twinkled with laughter.

"You are quite right, Monsieur. *Les femmes sont totalement incontrollables. Toujours*." She looked more serious. "And Madame has gone . . . shopping?"

"Yes. She has gone shopping. And she will find exactly what she wants."

"And you? You are très isolé?"

"At the moment, yes. But I am sure I will soon find something to do."

Sylvie nodded.

"Madame Leonie has plans. . . "

"Does she?"

"She wants to speak to you before the lunch."

Raynes wondered whether perhaps he and Debbie were

being asked to leave. For bringing the establishment into disrepute. Surely not? Sylvie seemed to guess his thoughts.

"It is something good. Something that could make Monsieur a lot of money."

Sylvie finished her coffee and picked up the cups and plates.

"And what would you like to do this morning, M'sieur?"

Only one thought came into the Inspector's mind.

"I would like to see your wine cellar."

Sylvie was clearly surprised.

"Les caves?"

"Brackles tells me Madame has a wonderful collection of wines. The stuff we have been drinking is superb. I would love to see it."

"Les caves are extremely cold."

"I would imagine so."

"You must wear un pul – perhaps two."

She seemed to think over the request.

"First, I have a few things to do – in the kitchen. I must see the staff. In half an hour perhaps. . ." She looked at her watch. "At 11.00am, we shall visit *les caves*."

* * * *

Raynes went upstairs to find his thickest juniper. When he packed, he had expected to be mostly in the sunshine. He had not expected to be needing warm clothes. So he took Sylvie's advice and put on two pullovers.

By 11.00am, he was waiting in the main hallway, admiring a highly decorated Chinese plate, when Sylvie arrived wearing a sheepskin jacket and a pair of boots, carrying a large bunch of keys.

"You will freeze!" she said.

"It's the best I can do."

Raynes followed her out into the hot sunshine. They walked across the courtyard and into an empty garage. Beside the far wall, there was a steep ramp leading down to a stout wooden door. Sylvie selected a large old-fashioned key.

"These were the caves of the original farmhouse."

They entered a short passage which led this time to an iron door and an alarm. Before he could take in the numbers, Sylvie typed in the combination. Then she used two keys on the mortice locks.

"Brackles said it was like Fort Knox."

"It has to be. There are many valuable wines down here. Many millions of francs."

"Might take quite some time to shift them."

"Yes," said Sylvie thoughtfully. "You would need many men."

As they entered the cellars, Sylvie switched on the lights and checked the temperature control on the wall. She adjusted it slightly.

Ahead of them stretched rows of metal racks – each one containing two hundred and forty bottles. Raynes did a quick count.

"How many bottles are there?"

"Je ne sais pas."

Even despite the sheepskin jacket, she shivered a little.

"I do not stay long. I collect the bottles and run. Normally, I send Ernst."

"He has cold blood already!"

Sylvie laughed.

They walked down the alleyways between the racks. The curved roofs were extremely low – just a few inches above their heads.

"These are the Burgundies. . . the Bordeaux. . . These are all Medoc. . . . Here we have the Italian wines. They have to be drunk quickly. And here we have the Moselles. . . the Champagnes. . . The Hungarian Tokays." It was almost a tour of Europe.

Raynes noted that the Champagne bottles were heavily crusted with dust. He rubbed the dust off one label to see what date it was. 1894 – truly vintage.

Further along, there were the ports, the sherries, Maderia

and the great liqueurs of France. Sylvie pointed out the dull looking bottles containing Calvados.

"It is from La Normandie," she said. "I am Normande. From Honfleur. Perhaps you know it?"

"I've been there once. Lots of boats."

"C'est très jolie."

As they returned nearer to the door, there were two large oak barrels.

"*Le cidre*," she said. "It is pumped in from the outside."

By now, the chill of the cellars was getting to Raynes. His legs felt particularly cold. He had kept his hands in his pockets.

"You have seen everything?"

"Yes, thank you. It's marvellous. No chance of drinking Madame dry. Most of them'll still be here when she's gone."

Sylvie looked at him quizzically.

"Then perhaps Simon will drink it?" She laughed. "They are very sweet together."

"I don't know how long it will last," said Richard cynically. "Ludo's a very rich woman and he's just a poor artist."

"She needs a lot of love."

Raynes couldn't help saying: "Don't we all?"

Sylvie once again checked the temperature control and switched off the lights. Once through the iron door, she locked the doors and switched on the alarm. Then she turned to Richard: "Would you warm me up a little?"

The dark little passage between the two doors was made for lovers. Sylvie opened her sheepskin jacket and snuggled close to the Inspector. He felt the warm body under the black cotton dress. It was warmer than he might have expected. He pressed himself close to her and put his hands on her hips. This was an unexpected pleasure.

Since he had received such a pressing invitation, he bent his head down to hers. Let us see, he said to himself, what the Normans are like as kissers. They had already proved themselves successful as conquerors in 1066. Was this the moment to witness another Norman conquest?

Her lips parted immediately and the next five minutes were sheer bliss. He stroked her body with great tenderness and she undid her blouse. So he caressed her small breasts and, feeling she wanted more, ran his hands up the inside of her thighs. It was almost a textbook seduction. He could hear her murmuring with pleasure.

But then she pushed him gently away.

"*Ça suffit*, Monsieur. Enough." She said it so softly, he was not offended.

"I have to prepare the lunch." She giggled. "Bangers and mash!"

Even Raynes laughed.

"We must meet again – when Madame goes shopping!"

Raynes thought this would provide quite a few opportunities.

She gave him a final kiss and hug and then they were out through the wooden door on the way up the incline into the garage.

"I shall go first," she said. "You wait two minutes. It is better no one should see us."

So already there was a sense of conspiracy between them. Richard knew how much Mrs May despised amateurs, but he could not fault Sylvie. She seemed quite perfect – and even the sudden ending of their passion was redeemed by her gentleness and the promise of further love-making.

He waited for a couple of minutes and then walked quietly and thoughtfully across the courtyard and back into the house.

7. *Venus Fastened on Her Prey*

Leonie looked at the Inspector for several minutes before she spoke.

"Simon told me you were a police officer."

Raynes nodded.

"A famous police officer."

Raynes shrugged his shoulders. Who was he to judge?

"I have never heard of you. But, never mind, you may be able to help me."

The Inspector felt glad he was not a dentist or a chiropodist; people would be for ever asking him to look at their teeth or their corns. Perhaps the Grand Duchess would be asking him to track down a missing picture or foil a persistent shoplifter? But no such luck.

"There is a man who is causing me a lot of trouble."

Leonie's eyes became as glacial as a Siberian icicle. "His name is Gaspard de la Nuit. You have heard of him?"

Raynes shook his head.

"Has Simon not mentioned him?"

"No."

"Or Ludo?"

"Neither of them."

"I am surprised. He was her husband. It was a great mistake." Leonie sighed deeply. "She was young and naive. She believed he was her Prince Charming. She believed everything he said. But of course he was a con man. A crook. He was only after my money. That was why he married her. He expected that I would provide her with a splendid dowry – and then he would spend it. But I gave him nothing!"

Leonie's words showed her blistering contempt for the repulsive creature which had crawled out from under the manure heap.

She had seen through him right away. His honeyed words cut no ice with her. He might deceive her daughter, but he would never deceive her. She had tried to prevent the marriage but – voilà! They had run away to Italy – to Napoli – where some corrupt priest had married them. The priest was reported to be in the pay of the Mafia. It was said that had poisoned the Host and given it to their political opponents. Of course, he had been shot – in the confessional; where else? But it had been too late to save Ludo.

The knot had been tied – perfectly legally – and he had taken her to Capri for their honeymoon. Ludo had said that he was a good lover.

"But. . . " She shrugged her shoulders.". . . of what importance was that? You English have a saying: 'Fine words grease no broccoli. . . '"

"Fine words butter no parsnips?" suggested Raynes.

"Precisely! However good he was between the sheets, he was useless in every other way. He had no job. He could not maintain my daughter in the standard to which she was accustomed. He expected to live in my house, eat my food, drink my drink, spend my money. He used her as a weapon against me. My own daughter! He hoped to divide us; but he did not succeed."

Raynes nodded.

The picture was not unfamiliar.

"When he could not get his way with her, he stole my pictures, my ivories, a beautiful set of Japanese miniatures. That was stupid! The man to whom he sold them knew that I was a keen collector of Japanese miniatures. He brought them straight to me. I recognized them immediately. I could not believe it. I said that I would need to check my collection to see whether I already had these items. Of course, I discovered they had gone. I confronted Gaspard. He denied it. I threw him out of the house. Sadly, Ludo went with him. She still believed in him, you see."

A tear ran down Leonie's cheek.

"They ran away to Paris. I put the police on to him. I did not hear about them for six months. Then he was arrested. He had treated my daughter shamefully. He had used her to rob people of their money. Together, they would go to expensive

43

hotels and prey on vulnerable old women. He would pose as a financier – and Ludo would vouch for him. Together, they would invite their victims to invest in some wild scheme – an animal sanctuary, a fitness club, a fashion magazine. The profits would be out of this world. And the suckers fell for it – every time!

"Fortunately, he was caught. He was jailed. At his trial, all his previous crimes were revealed. Even Ludo was shocked. She was fined many thousands of francs for her part in his crimes. I paid it, of course. I could not let my daughter be sent to jail. Gaspard was put away for six years."

Leonie's eyes glinted with scarcely suppressed anger. "But in December, he was released. Once again, he is free."

"And living in Nice?"

"You have guessed it, Monsieur. He has returned to his old haunts. Once again, he has been trying to contact Ludo – but I have sent her to England to buy furniture – where she has met Simon. But do not doubt it, he is in the wings, waiting like a spider, to catch her in his web. I tell you, Monsieur, I am frightened. He is a dangerous man. He will stop at nothing. He seeks revenge – on me and my daughter. He may kidnap her and demand *l'argent*. Or he may attack us here – or in the shop. We are not safe. I watch. I look over my shoulder. I carry a pistol in my handbag. But one cannot be vigilant twenty-four hours a day. He can choose his moment."

She smiled a grim smile.

"And that is why I am glad you are here. You will find him. And you must kill him! You know how to do these things properly. No clues! No body! The police baffled. You return to England. End of story."

Raynes had been following her exposition carefully – but the ending had taken him by surprise. He had imagined that she would ask him to investigate. To provide a little discreet surveillance. Perhaps to set a trap which would cause Gaspard to fall foul of the local police. But the invitation to become an assassin was certainly unexpected.

"I shall pay you a million francs!"

Raynes did a quick calculation. One hundred thousand pounds. He was sure Debbie would urge him to take it. She would agree with Leonie that Gaspard was better dead; and the money in the Inspector's pocket. But Raynes had some principles – not many, it was true – but he had never set out to kill anyone. And even though Ludo's ex-husband was an unpleasant blot on the landscape, there was no justification for killing him.

Certainly he could think of a few easy ways of disposing of him. Electrocution was the most effective. Drowning. Being caught in the propellers of a speedboat. Messy – but unlikely to provide any direct evidence of murder, especially if the local sharks got to him first. Yes, it could be done. He could certainly provide a few helpful ideas; but he would not himself wield the dagger.

Leonie looked at him.

Her eyes watched him with eager anticipation.

She hoped for a spark of enthusiasm – even of greed. But although the Inspector looked interested – and smiled, he shook his head.

"There are other ways of dealing with him."

"Are there?"

Raynes nodded.

"Thieves quarrel. Normally over money. Sometimes over women. All we have to do is to set one crook against another. Then we phone the police. Gaspard will probably be on parole. If he breaks his parole, the gendarmes will quickly shove him back in jail."

"But I would prefer him to be killed."

"I quite understand that. But I am sure that can be arranged."

"Would you arrange it?"

"I would first have to find out where he is."

"I can tell you."

Raynes realized that he faced a very determined woman. He uttered a word of caution. "Remember," he said, "I speak very little French."

45

"I realize that. I will send someone to help you. Someone who can speak perfect French and English."

For a moment, Raynes' heart leapt up. Was she proposing to send Ludo with him? What would Simon say? But it was too good to be true.

"I shall send Camille. The villains do not know him. He will say that your mother was one of those deceived by Gaspard in Paris. She has now died and you have discovered that your heritage has been plundered. You want to meet the man who has done this dastardly deed. You naturally want your money back. You do not know that Gaspard has been in jail. You think he is living a life of luxury in some villa. You are willing to pay for information. Camille will provide you with the money. Once you find him, you will know what to do."

It seemed that Leonie had planned out his mission very carefully. He was being given a minder and a translator. The cover story was plausible. He was being sent into the lion's den and if he came out alive, he would be suitably rewarded. He would have earned his keep.

The one thing he didn't like about the plan was the choice of escort. Camille would not be the most pleasant of companions. He looked and sounded like an autocrat – let alone an aristocrat. He would put up the backs of the criminal fraternity and make his investigations more difficult.

Raynes wondered if Leonie had ulterior motives in sending Signor Spumante with him. He would be out of the house – and in the Inspector's company – for several hours at a time.

Leonie would therefore be free to have a roll in the hay with Brackles without the Count spying on them. And if Gaspard killed Camille. . . well, she would have killed two birds with one stone. And the Inspector would provide an admirable witness.

There was a long pause whilst Raynes considered his hostess' plan. The plan was all right, but not Signor Spumante. He would be like an albatross around his neck.

"I would prefer Sylvie."

"Of course you would. But she is busy this afternoon."

Leonie was very much mistress of her own domain.

"You will go with Camille. He will do exactly what I tell him to do. The car will be ready at 2.30pm."

8. *Le Noeud de Vipères*

So he was fated to spend the afternoon with Signor Spumante. He must remember to call him Camille. He might be an ageing gigolo but Leonie obviously trusted him. Raynes could be sure he was acting in her best interests.

When he told Brackles where he was going – and with whom – Brackles laughed heartily.

"Greater love hath no man than this; that a man should drive away his deadly rival and leave the coast clear for his friend! Don't bring him back too quickly. Give me time to put my brushes away!"

So, at 2.15pm, Raynes was out in the hot sunshine, standing beside Leonie's rather battered estate car.

Camille emerged from the house ten minutes later. Clearly, he was in a bad temper. He was being sent on a fool's errand. Why couldn't the policeman speak French like any other civilized being? Why couldn't he conduct his own interviews? Why involve him?

He got into the car and fiddled with the ignition key.

"I'm not used to this car," he said. "I normally drive my own. An Alfa Romeo. . . " he added. "But this one has the carnet – so we can park anywhere."

Having got the car moving, Camille had no problem negotiating the tight bends and the long drive. Soon they were racing down the Boulevard Carnot as if they were taking part in the Monte Carlo Rally.

"Where are we going first?" Raynes asked politely.

"The Cafe Austerlitz."

"Is it a pleasant place?"

"No. It is what you English call 'the pits'."

"And why are we going there?"

"That's where Gaspard used to work."

"Five years ago?"

"I've no idea how long ago it was. I've only known Madame for two years. It was long before my time."

"So you don't know what Gaspard looks like?"

"No."

"Are there any photographs?"

"I've never seen any. I gather they've all been burnt or binned."

Raynes was taken aback.

"So we might end up talking to Gaspard without knowing it was him?"

"That's your problem! You're the policeman."

"And you're my translator."

There was clearly no love lost between them.

Raynes reflected that this was a far cry from Maigret, lighting up his pipe and slipping into familiar haunts, meeting old friends and receiving helpful advice: "Anyone seen a chap calling himself Simenon?"

Here they were both strangers – standing out like sore thumbs. Having no plan of action – not even a photograph. Spumante's manner was scarcely likely to be ingratiating and it would be difficult to bully someone at second hand. They would probably end up quarrelling in front of the crooks. It was a complete contradiction of his normal methods of policing. It was bound to end in disaster.

"Here we are."

An undistinguished cafe – like a thousand other French cafes on a sunny afternoon. A few tourists sitting out front drinking coffee or light beers. A dark interior.

"Who are we looking for?"

"A Madame Jourdan."

Camille approached a woman manning the espresso machine in a magisterial manner.

"Madame Jourdan?"

"*Elle est morte.*"

Camille translated:

"She says she's dead."

"When did she die?"

Camille managed to look concerned as he posed the question.

"Apparently, last year. She was shot."

"By her husband?"

"She doesn't know."

"Will you tell her we are looking for someone called Gaspard? Gaspard de la Nuit? Has she ever seen or heard of him?"

A lengthy dialogue continued between Camille and the woman. She wanted to know who it was asking the questions and why he couldn't speak for himself? Camille explained that he was an Englishman whose elderly mother had been tricked out of a lot of money by the said Gaspard.

Raynes tried to look hurt and anxious.

Camille then put his question.

"She thinks he was the person who shot Madame Jourdan."

"He couldn't have done. He was in jail at that time."

Camille tried to explain why Gaspard couldn't possibly have killed anyone at that time. The woman shrugged her shoulders.

"Ask her if he's been here lately?"

The woman shook her head.

"Are there any other members of the staff who have been here longer than she has?"

More discussion. Even a name.

"Pierre."

But where was Pierre?

Tuesday was his day off.

So much for the Cafe Austerlitz.

Raynes congratulated Camille on handling the interview so well. Too bad the woman was so unco-operative.

"Who's next?"

"A flat in the Rue Sébastien. No 112."

49

"Which flat?"

"H. Third floor."

As Camille drove the car through the back streets of Nice, Raynes began to see what a large city it was. There was a huge hinterland which the tourists never saw. They stuck to the Promenade, the fancy shops, the railway station, the airport and the restaurants in the Old Town. This was the other side of the picture.

"No 112."

A grim building, six floors high with a solid oak front door.

"And what's the connection?"

"Gaspard used to live here. Madame thinks it is possible he might still be here."

Raynes allowed himself a faint burst of optimism. Soon extinguished.

He pressed the button 'H'. No reply. He tried several other buttons without success. However, flat 'M' responded. There was a sudden buzz – and they were in. A dark passage. An even darker stairwell and several flights of very steep steps.

However, as they reached flat 'H', they noticed the door was partially open. An unpleasant face peered out.

"It's all right," said Camille. "We're not the police."

The door opened a little further.

"My friend is looking for someone called Gaspard."

Raynes noted the immediate glint of recognition in the man's eyes.

The man spoke quickly.

"He says he doesn't know anyone called Gaspard."

Raynes said: "I think he does. Ask him if we may come in."

Anticipating – rightly – that the answer would be "No", Raynes put his foot in the doorway.

"Vous êtes les flics?"

"No. We're not the police. My friend is an Englishman who wishes to ask you a few questions."

The man could not think of any connection between Gaspard and England so he opened the door and let them in.

The reason for his reluctance to let them in was soon

apparent. Down the passage were hundreds of boxes of electrical equipment – obviously new – obviously stolen. Had he and Camille been the French police, the man would have been arrested immediately.

As they walked down the passage, Raynes cast his eyes into various rooms. Despite the squalor of the staircase, the flat seemed to be clean and well-furnished. There was no sign of any lodger.

Once they had reached the kitchen, Raynes turned on the heat.

"I believe that Gaspard stayed here some years ago?"

The man claimed that he had no knowledge of anything that had happened there in time past.

"I think that Gaspard returned here recently. In February or March? Is he still here?"

The man shook his head.

"No Gaspard!"

Raynes looked at Camille.

"I think he's lying. In fact, I know he's lying. Tell him that if he doesn't come clean, we'll let the police know about all that stuff in the passage!"

Camille translated forcibly.

The man looked helpless.

Raynes gave him one of his menacing looks.

"The truth!" he said. And then remembered another word from his schoolboy French. "La verité!"

The man wrestled with his conscience. He was cornered against the chest freezer by two very forceful figures who were determined to get answers to their questions. Why should he defend the absent Gaspard? What did he care about him?

"He was here," he muttered.

"When?"

"In March and early April. But he has gone."

"Where?"

The man shrugged his shoulders.

"And what was he doing here?"

The man was about to say he didn't know; but he caught the look on the Inspector's face. Raynes looked pointedly at the gas cooker and one of its lighted rings. The message was clear. If he didn't cooperate, the man wouldn't hesitate to give his hand, arm or back a roasting. The Inspector turned up the flame.

The man's resistance collapsed like a pricked balloon. Bit by bit, they got something approaching the truth.

When Gaspard came out of jail – which he thought had been in December – he had stayed with friends in Paris. But he had had very little money and it took him several weeks to regain his confidence – even to go out. He had tried one or two con tricks in Paris to see if he still had the knack. But then he had decided it would be safer to leave Paris and return to Nice where he had previously lived and worked.

He had arrived late in February, stayed at the flat and made his plans. These centred mostly on his ex-wife. He said that she was rich. Very rich. He planned to meet her secretly – and work his charm on her. But if he didn't succeed he would kidnap her and hold her to ransom. Her mother would pay up – especially if he threatened her with something really nasty.

He had been up to her house once or twice. He had sent letters; but there had been no reply. Then he heard that her mother had spirited her away – to England, it was said.

His next plan was to burgle the house. The mother had many valuable treasures. Even one of them would be a fortune to him. He boasted that he knew a way into the house avoiding the alarms. He had laid his plans; but then he had gone.

"When?"

"About a week ago."

And where had he gone?

The man didn't know. He assumed that he had gone back to Paris to get some extra help. Gaspard had spoken of it as being a "five man job."

That seemed to be the sum of his knowledge. He said that Gaspard had talked freely about his plans for the attack on the house; but he thought he was still organizing his team. When they were ready, they would strike hard. Yes, they would probably have guns.

Was that all?

He thought so.

If they gave him money, would he tell them when Gaspard came back to the flat?

"*Ça depend.*"

It depended on the amount promised.

Camille offered 50,000 francs.

The man suggested a hundred would be better. Camille gave him a contact number. And that was it.

Raynes made sure that the man led them to the door – and that he was first out of the flat. He was sure that if they turned their backs on him for a moment, he would attack them.

But Raynes was wrong. All the man wanted to do was to get these two busybodies out of the flat. Then he had the problem of shifting and finding another home for all that electrical equipment as quickly as possible.

He was glad he hadn't told them about Gaspard's suitcase and clothes which were still lying in the spare bedroom.

Gaspard certainly hadn't gone back to Paris. He was still somewhere in Nice – probably shacking up with some bird. Wasn't there a girl who had worked in a hairdresser's?

He had forgotten her name.

* * * *

But Leonie had remembered.

Her name was Danielle and she worked in the Salon Marianne in the west end of the city.

The shop did not seem all that busy. Camille and Raynes made their way in and asked if they still had a girl called Danielle working for them. The manageress stubbed out her cigarette and pointed to a sulky-faced blonde.

"Voilà, Messieurs!"

So they sat down with Danielle in a small smoke-filled room at the back of the shop.

"Do you know Gaspard de la Nuit?"

She did. Was he in any sort of trouble?

No. But this Englishman wanted to meet him.

"Why?"

It was a private matter concerning his mother. Once again, Raynes managed to look sad and anxious.

"We believe he has been in Nice since the end of February."

"He was in prison."

"We know that."

But had he been in contact with her?

Yes, he had.

"Was he staying with her?"

No. She had married during the time Gaspard had been in prison Now she had a husband and a small baby. She showed Camille her wedding ring.

But had she seen him?

Yes, several times. He'd come to the shop; and they'd been out for a couple of drinks. Coffee, she added. (In case they got the wrong idea.)

Did she know where he was staying?

Rue Sébastien. She thought it was no. 112.

Had she seen him in the past week?

No.

Did she think he had gone back to Paris?

She had no idea. But she had been very disappointed not to get a card on her birthday. He had always remembered her – even when he had been in prison. She was hurt.

Had he told her what he was doing in Nice?

She looked embarrassed.

Not really. He had said it was a big job. A really big job. She didn't think he'd done it yet because he had said it would be front page news in all the newspapers. And there hadn't been anything yet, had there? Except that man rescued from his sinking yacht?

Raynes remembered the picture in that morning's *Nice-Matin*. That hadn't been Gaspard, had it?

She laughed.

No, he hated the sea.

But she was frightened of him being sent to prison again. He was such a nice bloke. They had known each other for several years.

Once again, Camille offered her a phone contact and a small reward for putting them in touch with him; but she wouldn't cooperate.

"No," she said. "That's his business. He's got to deal with it himself. I've got my husband and family to think about. I don't want to get involved in all that."

* * * *

So that was Danielle.

The final name on the list was Bruno Polanski – a secondhand piano dealer, who had his shop not far from the Salon Marianne.

Monsieur Polanski's shop was seriously uninviting. The blue paint had faded in the hot sunshine and all that one could see through the windows was a large Bluthner upright – with a cat sleeping on the piano stool. The ivory keys were deep yellow and the copy of *Rosamunde* on the music desk looked so ancient, it might well have been a first edition. But if it had been, Monsieur Polanski would have sold it.

"This gentleman is what you English call a 'fence'."

Raynes immediately thought of the Japanese miniatures. They got out of the car and walked over to the door. The cat opened its eyes. Visitors? At this time of the afternoon?

Surprisingly, the door opened and an invisible bell rang in the back regions. The cat decided to leave the piano stool and stalked off into the darkness.

Behind the Bluthner stood a remarkably ugly Steinway baby grand and a Yamaha which someone had attacked with paint stripper.

Raynes imagined that they were being looked at and assessed by the owner of the shop. Were they crooks? Did they have something to sell? Or had they come to duff him up?

They must have seemed harmless for Monsieur Polanski bustled happily into the shop.

"Messieurs! Bon après-midi!"

He was a small bald-headed man – immaculately dressed – with a red handkerchief blossoming from his top pocket. He was clean-shaven and had a pair of thick, black-rimmed spectacles.

Camille had now got his story about Raynes' mother almost word-perfect and he rolled out his request for information about Monsieur Gaspard de la Nuit.

Monsieur Polanski drew back at the mention of his name. Surely the young man was in jail? And had been for quite some time? His reaction suggested that Monsieur Gaspard was very much ancient history.

Raynes watched his reaction with interest.

No, said Camille, Gaspard was no longer in jail. He had been released in December and had been in Nice since late February. Had he not been to see Monsieur Polanski?

"Mais non!"

"Mais oui," said Raynes. Was it not possible that Gaspard might have been hoping to sell some rather hot property as quickly as possible? Had he not asked Monsieur Polanski if there was some particular item he might be anxious to buy?

The shop-owner made a gesture towards the Yamaha. He was simply a purveyor of secondhand pianos.

Raynes muttered the words: "Japanese miniatures."

But even before Camille could translate his words, the Inspector noted the man's reaction. He obviously understood English.

Raynes decided to take over.

"We are aware that Monsieur Gaspard is planning a major operation – possibly against the Villa Rose. He has talked about it to his friends. In the past, he has brought stolen goods to you. You will remember the Japanese miniatures, which you tried to sell back to Madame Leonie. It seems likely that he will come to you again. Perhaps you have already given him an advance? He is rather short of money."

In case Monsieur Polanski had not taken in the full import of Raynes' words, Camille produced a full translation.

Monsieur Polanski did not make any comment. Instead, he asked rather nervously: "Are you from the police?"

"No," said Camille. "We are friends of Madame Leonie."

"Ah, I see."

Raynes was determined to get an answer to his question. He smiled politely.

"Have you seen Gaspard lately? In the last two months?"

His eyes held the piano dealer in a vice-like grip. Lie – if you dare! Monsieur Polanski decided to lie – but in French.

No, he had never seen him. He had no dealings with the criminal fraternity. He did not deal in stolen goods. He never had. He may have received something from a friend – without knowing where it came from. But Monsieur Gaspard – of whom he had heard – was no friend of his. He would not receive a warm welcome at his shop.

All his life, the Inspector had had the remarkable gift of knowing when a person was telling a lie. Usually, one had to listen very carefully to catch the subtle nuance, but here the lie was quite blatant. Perfectly obvious – even in French. It annoyed him.

"These men," he said, "are planning an attack – with guns – on the Villa Rose. If Madame Leonie is killed – or severely injured – in the attack, we shall immediately suggest to the police that you be taken in for questioning. You will not escape."

Monsieur Polanski was unwilling to discuss the matter any further.

"Messieurs, I must ask you to leave. Now!"

Raynes ignored his request.

"We are trying to prevent this attack from taking place. All we want to know is whether Monsieur Gaspard has been to see you – whether he has taken you into his confidence. You can help us to protect Madame Leonie. If you refuse to help us, we shall know that you are personally involved in the plan to attack the Villa – and we shall have to go to the police."

Camille tried to give a translation of the Inspector's words but Monsieur Polanski brushed him aside: "I know what he said."

He seemed very upset and walked backwards and forwards, up and down the shop, looking extremely agitated. The cat sidled back into the shop and watched them unblinking from beside a red velvet curtain.

The uncertainty lasted for several minutes.

Then Monsieur Polanski spoke:

"Messieurs, I am in a very difficult position. You will understand. . . " He flashed a meaningful look at Camille. "I do not care for Madame Leonie. I do not like her business methods. But I do not want her to be hurt.

"You are right. Monsieur Gaspard has been to see me. He has told me of his plans. He has asked me to sell some of the items he proposes to steal. He has made his plans very carefully. Everyone at the Villa Rose is in great danger. I can say no more.

"If he comes to me again – before the attack – I shall warn him that the police know about his plans. That may deter him." He looked at the Inspector. "I will try to stop him; but I have promised to buy certain items. The price has been agreed."

Raynes spoke very quietly.

"And you have already given him some money in advance – to help him organize his attack?"

Monsieur Polanski sighed deeply.

"I have. I have. I know I should not have done it."

Raynes wondered if he could offer him some incentive – some prospect of reward – which would encourage him to co-operate further.

"I am sure Madame Leonie would be willing to refund that advance, if you can prevent this attack taking place. I am sure she will be deeply grateful for your help."

* * * *

"She'd never give him a sou!" said Camille contemptuously when they had left the shop. "He's a dirty little crook. Always was; always will be."

"Well, at least he admitted he was involved. And he promised to try and stop Gaspard."

"I wouldn't listen to any of his promises. He's the sort of man who'll wriggle out of anything – and then stab you in the back."

"We can only try."

Raynes had to admit that he was now feeling more charitably disposed towards Camille. He had proved an extremely useful colleague. He had done a good job of translating. They had obtained positive results.

In a rare moment of generosity, he said: "I think we deserve a drink after all our efforts. Can I treat you to something?"

Camille smiled a wry smile. Victory was in sight. He was tired of being patronized by this smug Englishman who thought he was the greatest sleuth on God's earth. With a contempt worthy of Brackles' most damning portrayal of Signor Spumante, he said: "I shall be delighted to accept your generous offer, Monsieur Raynes. A bottle of Roederer '29 at the Hotel Negresco would suit me just fine."

Raynes had no idea what sort of wine the Roederer was – and certainly no picture of the Hotel Negresco in his mind; but when he saw the doorman wearing his top hat and the five stars on the brass plaque beside the door, he began to realize that this might prove to be a rather expensive invitation.

9. *A La Recherche du Temps Perdu*

They sat down in the ornate surroundings of the cocktail bar. They gave their order. Clearly, the order was questioned because some more superior person came to check that they had indeed ordered the Roederer '29 – and also to make sure they were the sort of people who could afford to pay for it.

"Yes, indeed," said Camille expansively. "We're in a mood to celebrate. My colleague is treating me."

The eyes of the superior person turned to Raynes. There was inevitably some suspicion. He did not look quite the sort of person who would be lashing out hundreds of pounds on a bottle of champagne. But there was also respect.

Raynes gave a friendly nod as if it was a matter of little consequence. He knew he was going to be stung – badly – but he was determined that Signor Spumante should obtain absolutely no *schadenfreude* from the experience. But, by George, he would suffer for it! Raynes sat back in his deep, comfortable chair and plotted his revenge. It must be infinitely sweet – and horribly expensive.

The silver wine cooler arrived first. Then a generous selection of nibbles. And, finally, an exceedingly dusty bottle of the very special vintage, handled with enormous reverence by the wine waiter. It was very like the other ancient bottles he had seen that morning in Leonie's wine cellar.

"Yes," he said, "that's fine."

(Just like those other bottles of Roederer '29 he was in the habit of drinking in top hotels around the world!)

Before they had dusted down the bottle and begun the traditional ritual of opening and pouring the champagne, Raynes surreptitiously checked that he still had his small wallet containing his Visa cards in his pocket. What was his limit? £4500?

The champagne was poured into a pair of beautiful glasses. The waiter hovered at their side until Signor Spumante had sipped the heavenly liquor.

"Perfect!" he said. "Just perfect!"

Raynes sipped from his glass. It had a remarkable taste – very full, very rich, deliciously sparkling – even after all those years. It was wonderful to think that such stuff had been produced in some glorious summer – over sixty years ago – long before the depression, the world war, the atom bomb, the jet engine or the first supermarket. It had been gathered in and transmuted into pure gold. It had been buried deep in chalk pits; hidden from the Germans; treasured more highly than gold bars in the Bank of England; preserved just for him to enjoy on a May afternoon, on the promenade in Nice, in the year 1990. What a pity Debbie was not there to share it.

"That's the real stuff!" she would have said.

And so it was.

Raynes drank his first glass with infinite slowness.

"It is lovely," he said.

"Sheer perfection," said Camille.

He too was enjoying a rare experience; but he was now beginning to suffer the first twinges of conscience – realizing that when the policeman saw the bill, he might have a sudden heart attack or run screaming out of the hotel.

That would certainly spoil the afternoon. It might even mean that he would have to foot the bill. It was his turn to reach for his wallet. Oh dear! He had left it at the villa in case they met any pickpockets. That could prove embarrassing. But surely the policeman would survive the shock? He was a young man. In his forties, probably. He looked healthy. By now, he must realize he was in for a large bill. Obviously, he was being "a good sport" – something the English were renowned for. Le "stiff upper lip". Having settled back to enjoy the champagne – and being in no mood to chat to his tormentor – Raynes looked round the cocktail bar to see what the other drinkers were consuming. There were one or two others enjoying champagne. Some were drinking beer. One was drinking Coca-cola! It seemed like blasphemy.

He looked over to the main bar where a businessman was enjoying a close tête-a-tête with a blonde. Her dark blue dress had a generous slit and he was gently stroking her thigh.

Raynes knew that thigh! He also knew that dress!

He froze. The sight caused him more embarrassment than ordering the bottle of Roederer '29. That was Debbie May fully engaged with one of her sordid customers – though the Inspector had to admit the man looked very clean, handsome and rich. (Of course he was rich!) Raynes reflected that what she was making out of this deal would probably cover the cost of the Roederer '29.

Once he had got over the shock of seeing her there, he wanted to laugh. Fancy both of them ending up in the same bar! He tried not to stare in Debbie's direction in case Spumante noticed. But he had finished his first glass and was beginning to hanker for a second.

Raynes let him wait whilst he thought of some way to embarrass Mrs May – giving her a taste of her own medicine – upstaging her no less.

He caught the waiter's eye.

"Could we please have a third glass?"

Signor Spumante looked surprised. Had the policeman cracked his glass? He hadn't noticed.

Whilst the waiter was bringing the third glass, Raynes took out his Biro and wrote a few words on a white napkin. When the man returned, he said: "Would you be kind enough to pour my colleague a second glass? And when you have done that, would you please pour an extra glass for the lady in blue at the bar – and give her this note?"

"Certainly, sir."

However eccentric their tastes might be, the staff at the Negresco were used to catering to the needs of the rich.

Spumante picked up his glass and, with some curiosity, followed the path of the waiter through the maze of chairs and tables up to the bar.

The waiter coughed apologetically – unwilling to disturb the couple who were so deeply engaged in their own affairs – and placed the champagne glass in front of the lady.

She looked surprised.   She was already drinking

champagne. Why the interruption?

"A message for Madame."

He handed over the folded napkin.

"A higher bid?" suggested her companion jokingly. "Am I going to have to raise my offer?"

Mrs May opened the napkin.

The message read:

Please remember not to be late for dinner. Hope you enjoy the champagne. It's the real stuff! R.

Mrs May looked across the room.

Good God! It was Richard and that creep, Signor Spumante. Both of them gave her a friendly wave. How embarrassing! However, Debbie was used to awkward situations. She encountered them every day. She shrugged her shoulders.

"Oh," she said, "it's just one of my exes. He isn't half as rich as you. And I'm sure you're a much better lover."

(Oh, the treachery of it! But business is business – and it pays to flatter!)

"What's that stuff he's sent up to you?"

"I haven't the vaguest. Champagne, obviously."

She sipped at the glass.

"Gosh! It's the real thing!"

The businessman summoned the wine waiter.

"What's in that glass?"

"Roederer '29, sir."

The businessman was a little abashed. Even his generous expense account could hardly embrace such a luxury. A man who could treat his ex-mistress to such delights was certainly to be respected – if not admired.

His first reaction was to get her away from the bar before she demanded more of the stuff – or before she ran away – back to him.

"Drink up," he said, "and let's get on with the main course."

Raynes did not see them go. The bill had arrived and was as staggering as he expected. Actually, it was even more than

63

he had expected. Double, in fact.

He looked at Signor Spumante with the utmost malice. He presented his Visa card, signed the credit note and sat back, feeling more happy than he could have predicted. Something of the sunshine of 1929 had touched his heart. With enormous pleasure, he threw back the last drop.

10. *L'ésprit de l'escalier*

"He did what? That's outrageous! And you paid for it?"

Raynes nodded.

He had been acquainting Brackles with Spumante's treachery. "You should have walked away and left him to pay the bill."

"It did cross my mind."

"You're not going to take it lying down?"

"Of course not. I've been trying to think of some subtle way to humiliate him. . . and to make him pay." Raynes stared across the peaceful waters of the pool. The sun was setting and the villa was lit up with a rich orange glow.

"He's got plenty of money, hasn't he?"

"Loaded, I should think. But humiliating him? He's such a shit already; it's difficult to see how he could sink much lower."

"Something that might embarrass him in Leonie's eyes. . . "

"Screwing Sylvie – or one of the maids?"

Raynes winced inwardly.

"Screwing Ernst?"

"Much better. But I don't think our German friend is interested in women."

"I can't see him being interested in Spumante."

"No."

"That photographer fellow. . . ?"

"Arnaud?"

"Yes. Arnaud. He might be able to do some trick photography. Using Spumante's face and someone else's body. It's been done before."

Raynes shook his head.

"Not very convincing. We need to make him do something that he thinks is sensible. Something that he thinks his lady friend would want him to do. Something that goes terribly wrong. Embarrasses her acutely. Makes her thoroughly angry. Costs him a packet. And leads to him being thrown out."

"I wouldn't do anything to embarrass Leonie."

"Passion still blossoming?"

"It did this afternoon."

"Good for you."

"You've no idea what a relief it was – to know that creep was elsewhere. Leonie was so much happier. So much more relaxed. So. . . frivolous. We got on like a house on fire. Can't you take him out every afternoon?"

"Well, that depends on Leonie. She provided the names and addresses of the people we went to see. There's only one we have to go back to. If she can come up with a few more names, I'm willing to keep on hunting for Gaspard. But no more drinks at the Negresco."

"I should think not."

Brackles downed the last of his brandy.

"And where's your good lady? I haven't seen her all day."

Raynes laughed sadly.

"She was at the Negresco."

"As well? At the same time? Did Spumante see her?"

"I'm afraid he did. So now he's got a hold over me. Imagine him leaning across the supper table – in front of everyone, saying: 'And how much did you make from your boyfriend; the one I saw you with this afternoon?' How would she cope with that?"

Brackles was diplomatic.

"I think she might do rather well. She's good at delivering one-liners. I think she might say: 'Well, not as much as I normally do. You must remember to bring your wallet next time. We English girls expect to be paid more for escorting horrible old men!"

Raynes laughed – to cover his embarrassment. And changed the subject.

"When can we hope to see your picture?"

"In a few days. It's in Leonie's boudoir and that's where it has to stay. Under wraps. Under lock and key. It's basically finished; but, as you know, I can spin out the final bits till kingdom come. Finishing it would spoil things."

"And she's happy with it?"

"Ecstatic!"

"Better be careful Spumante doesn't attack it."

"He wouldn't dare."

"But, as you said, he's insanely jealous. Most of the time he was with me, he was biting his nails and muttering to himself. He could be quite destructive."

"Well, if he did attack it, I could do it all over again."

Brackles tapped his head. "It's all in here." He reflected quietly. "It might be no bad thing. It would prolong the pleasure. Spumante would definitely be thrown out. You could have your revenge. And I could have . . . "

". . . The Grand Duchess?"

"Yes." Brackles beamed happily. "Mark you," he said confidentially, "I've got another admirer. Amelie Foster. She wants me to do a nude. Style of Renoir. . . Goya. . . or Boucher. She hasn't made up her mind yet. But of course I'll have to see the goods before I make a final decision." He smiled broadly. "Her husband knows nothing about it. She's thinking of renting a room from Arnaud."

"The photographer?"

"Yes."

"A very useful chap."

Raynes started thinking about him. A fixer. A go-between. A source of useful information. A man who could provide spare rooms for private assignations. A man who could doctor photographs. Yes. A very useful chap.

His thoughts were interrupted.

"Do you think Debbie'll be home in time for dinner?"

"I should think so. Food is her No 2 pleasure. I don't think she'd want to miss one of Leonie's banquets."

"It's going to be quite a profitable holiday for her."

"For both of you."

"And what do you get out of it?"

"I'd settle for a murder. A nice juicy murder. You know who!"

"I'll do my best to arrange it."

11. *The Leper's Kiss*

Camille was reporting back on his afternoon with Raynes. Leonie was having her hair done by Célestine. In the background was Brackles' painting – not under wraps, not under lock and key; but very prominent. Such paint – such little paint – as had been added to the picture during the afternoon was drying rapidly.

Leonie looked at the mirror. Camille looked fixedly at his mistress.

"We went to the cafe; but Pierre was not there. It was his day off. Then we went to the Rue Sébastien – a horrible place. Vile, in fact. That was where he had been staying in February; but the man didn't know where he was now. The house was full of stolen goods. Boxloads of electrical equipment all the way down the passage."

"Are you sure he's not still there?"

"The policeman searched the rooms."

(He didn't; but Leonie would never know.)

"Then we went to see the hairdresser – as you suggested, Madame. Danielle. Rather a poor sort. She said she had known him for several years. But now she is married and has a child. She was expecting to receive a card from him on her birthday – but nothing arrived."

"Has she been in touch with him since he left prison?"

"Yes."

"That is important."

"We also went to see Bruno. A very pompous little man.

There we had more success. To start with, he was not very forthcoming. He said he knew the man; but he had not seen him recently. He knew he had been in jail; but he declared that he would have no further dealings with him. Then he ordered us to leave the shop."

"You left?"

Leonie looked at him with some surprise.

"No. The policeman refused to leave."

"Why?"

"He said that Bruno was a liar. He was sure he had seen Gaspard. And not only seen him; but also done a deal with him. He said that he had an instinct about this. And he was right. It appeared that Bruno had agreed to sell items stolen from this house. He even admitted that he knew an attack had been planned."

Leonie looked at the mirror.

"Céléstine, stop listening to Monsieur Camille. Continue with my hair."

"Pardon, Madame."

Leonie turned to Camille.

"What made Bruno talk? How did Monsieur Richard make him change his story?

"He said that if there was an attack, you might be hurt – or even killed. If he knew these things, he must speak – or the police would regard him as a party to the crime."

"Very true."

"Monsieur Bruno said he did not like you. . . "

"The feeling is mutual."

". . . but he did not want to be involved in any physical attack on you. He could see what it would involve. So he was compelled to tell the policeman what he knew. He said he had not only agreed to buy your property; but also had given the man money to assist him to prepare the attack."

Leonie felt very glad she had sent Monsieur Richard to see Bruno. Camille would never have got him to admit to anything.

"There is one thing which will annoy you, Madame. The

policeman said he was sure that if Bruno helped to prevent the attack, you would be more than willing to repay him the money he had given to the man. I knew that you would not be willing to do this; but the policeman insisted. It was very impertinent of him to speak thus without your authority."

"How much money had he given him?"

"I do not know."

"And what is Bruno going to do now?"

"He is going to tell Gaspard (the name slipped out) that the police already know about his plans. That they are waiting for him. That he will not escape. Bruno will try to stop him."

Leonie relaxed perceptibly.

"I think that may be money very well spent. You must leave me to judge. We must ask Monsieur Bruno precisely how much he has paid out."

"I felt it was very ill-advised to commit you to paying anything to such a man. He would deceive even his own grandmother."

"Of course, he would." Leonie nodded in agreement. "But he has betrayed his colleagues. When they find out – as they will – they will be very angry with him. They may even kill him. He will need my money to escape." She smiled at her courtier. "You have achieved much good this afternoon. Tomorrow, you will return and see Pierre. He knows the man better than anyone else. After that, I have a few more contacts who must be approached. Tonight, my lawyer, Maître Duclos, is coming to dinner. I will discuss the matter with him."

"As you wish, Madame."

"And was that everything, Camille?"

She felt he was bursting to say more.

"Not quite, Madame." He licked his lips. "We went for a drink together, the policeman and I, after our visits. We went to the Negresco."

Leonie raised her eyebrows.

High living indeed!

"And you will not believe what we have seen! We have seen that woman which that policeman has brought here

69

'prostituting' herself in the public bar of the hotel! She was with some man. I don't know who he was. Even the policeman was surprised. But he sent her a glass of wine. He was condoning her shame. I was disgusted!"

By now, all thought of hairdressing had left Céléstine's mind. Like Leonie, she was listening to Camille's every word.

"Céléstine, will you please leave us."

"Madame."

When the maid had left the room, Leonie turned on Camille: "What you have said will be reported throughout the servant quarters. You have brought shame and humiliation on two of my guests.

"I value the help of Monsieur Richard very highly. He is a famous English detective. He will protect me. He will protect all of us from Gaspard. I know nothing about his friend; but she is a very beautiful girl – full of spirit and adventure. If she wishes to go with other men, that is her concern. . . their concern – not ours!"

Her voice softened. "I will also have you know, Camille, that there was a time in my life when I had very little money and I could not ask my father for more. I too have prostituted myself with several men. Without their help, at that difficult moment, I should not be here today."

"Madame. . . !"

"Camille, you have said too much. You must go!"

12. *Batterie de Cuisine*

"Madame, we are all in great danger!"

Sylvie looked up from the kitchen table where she was inspecting the marinade for the duck. Had the cook put in enough port? What on earth was the girl talking about?

"Monsieur Camille is saying that there will be an attack on the house by Monsieur Gaspard. Madame Leonie may be killed. The house ransacked. What will become of us?"

All work in the kitchen stopped.

Célestine was normally a quiet, balanced person. She did her job well and was greatly valued by the lady of the house. Sylvie had never seen her so distressed.

"Tell us – but more slowly," she said.

"Madame has heard that Monsieur Gaspard has been released from prison. He has returned to Nice. He is in need of money. He is living with criminals and he is already planning to sell Madame's treasures through a fence. A Monsieur Bruno. This man has already chosen the pieces he wishes to buy and he has paid money to Monsieur Gaspard to assist the attack."

Célestine sounded almost breathless as she delivered her story.

"Monsieur Camille and Monsieur Raynes have spent the afternoon hunting for him. They have visited many horrible people and discovered his plans. He will attack this house with many men – and Madame Leonie may be killed." She sat down, put her head in her hands and wept. "And we may be killed also."

Sylvie looked at Ernst.

"I don't think they will dare attack this house. Ernst will break their necks. Probably with great pleasure!"

A broad smile came over Ernst's face. He went through the motions of putting someone's head under his arm and breaking their neck. This demonstration was followed by a very realistic crack.

"But they will have guns!" insisted Céléstine.

"Ernst has a gun."

Ernst nodded.

"I must do more practice. I am, as they say, a little rusty."

The atmosphere in the kitchen simmered down.

"I do not like this marinade," said Sylvie to the cook. "You must put in more port. It must be stronger. Beaucoup plus fort, you understand?"

"Yes, Madame."

When everything was once more under control, the canapés delivered to the small lounge and Ernst gone upstairs to supervise the drinks, Sylvie took Céléstine to one side.

"You do not have to be anxious," she said. "Monsieur Raynes is a famous English detective. He has solved many murders. He has come here specially to protect Madame. The fact that he has spoken to Bruno and discovered the plot, means that the police will be told and Gaspard will be arrested. We shall be quite safe.

Céléstine looked relieved.

"But there is another thing. . . "

"Another thing?"

"Yes. I did not tell the others. . . But Madame Raynes. . . she has been seeing other men. This afternoon, her husband has seen her 'prostituting' herself in the Negresco."

Sylvie was not surprised. In fact, she was vaguely amused. Nice is no more than a very large village. Everyone sees everything. Everyone knows everyone. To go to such a well-known hotel – of course she would be seen. Perhaps she wanted to be seen?

To Céléstine, she said: "Madame Raynes is not Monsieur Richard's wife. She is his. . . friend. She is a very independent lady. Very much *une femme du monde*. She probably needs the money." She put a finger to her lips. "You must not repeat this to anyone else. You understand?"

"Yes, Madame."

A few minutes later, Sylvie followed Ernst up to the small lounge to make sure everything was ready for the cocktail party and the dinner.

Tonight, Leonie was one of the first to arrive. She swept across the room in a magnificent silver and black dress.

"Madame Sylvie," she said. "Has Céléstine spoken to you?"

"She has spoken of her fears that there may be an attack on this house and Madame's jewels may be stolen. But I have calmed her fears. She is now more composed."

"And did she speak. . . " She looked round to make sure Debbie was nowhere near. ". . . of Monsieur Richard's friend?"

"Only to me, Madame. But I have told her she is not his wife. That she is a very independent person and that Monsieur Camille was doubtless exaggerating. She has been told to keep the information to herself."

"Thank you, Sylvie. You have – as usual – been most discreet. Camille was very foolish to say what he did in front of the child. The trouble is that he does not like Monsieur Richard. He does not understand how important it is to gather information; and he must learn to help the Inspector – not hinder him."

"I like Monsieur Richard. He is *très drôle*."

Leonie gave her a knowing smile.

"*Soyez discrète, ma petite!*"

Her eyes caught sight of her lawyer entering the lounge.

"Monsieur Duclos! *Quel plaisir!*"

She turned to Ernst.

"Ernst. Deux Manhattans, *s'il vous plaît*."

13. *Les Fleurs du Mal*

Amelie had also been discovering some interesting things about Mrs May.

She had started work shortly after 10.00am in La Grotte de Seraphim. Work consisted mainly of selecting one or two of Leonie's latest purchases and then consulting some large reference books which claimed encyclopaedic knowledge of French paintings and French antiques since 1500. From their detailed descriptions, it was possible to date the piece, pinpoint the area from which it came and perhaps even identify the cabinet-maker or painter.

It was she who had discovered the Braque painting. It had been hanging in an upstairs room when her eyes had lighted upon it. Of course, it might have been a forgery or one of the painter's juvenile throwaways – but all the reference books pointed to it being a genuine Braque and Leonie was willing to go along with her.

The previous afternoon, Ludo and Simon had sold it to the so-called 'trillionaire' yachtsman for £250,000 – a piece of very sharp practice. Leonie had been delighted with the sale and promised her 5% – £12,500. After all her efforts, she felt 10% would have been more appropriate; but even five per cent would cover her holiday expenses.

She was busy looking for another 'winner'.

The Louis Quatorze chairs which Ludo had found in Brighton had only just been delivered; but Amelie was not entirely convinced they were genuine. She was sure they were late-Empire reproductions. She examined the woodwork, the seat covers, the hessian underneath, the filling (one of the chairs was badly torn). None of it added up to a genuine find.

Of course, they could be restored nicely – and sold for a good price; but there was nothing special about them.

Leonie left Mrs Foster very much to her own devices. She was busy dealing with her customers, ushering them into her beautiful saleroom with its highly polished furniture, handsome pictures and elegant clocks ticking on the wall, emitting the most fascinating chimes every quarter of an hour. There was something for everyone – providing you had money. Large table lamps dotted about the room gave even the poorest table surface a certain sheen.

Really promising customers would be given a full tour of the establishment. They would be treated to coffee, chocolate or even Earl Grey in antique Limoges china. "Not a full set, I'm afraid. . . the rest was destroyed during the Revolution!"

By 12.00 noon, Amelie had examined seven different items. An escritoire had excited her – and possibly a child's head done in bronze. She thought it might be an early Mestrovic. He had been a student in Paris.

But now it was lunchtime and she had promised to go round to Arnaud's to collect the photographs he had taken yesterday in Cannes for her husband. She was sure they would be ready. But her real reason for going round to the photographer was that they should be able to spend a little time on his sheepskin rug. He was rough but she enjoyed it.

So, in her loose, white pleated skirt, she strode through the Old Town, stopping to buy a couple of baguettes and a bottle of St Emilion Grand Cru. That should brighten up the afternoon.

But perhaps she had arrived too early? A couple of slim nymphettes were baring their breasts and buttocks in a series of erotic poses against a backdrop of purple and pink gauze.

The poor dears looked frozen. Their nipples were as hard as buttons and they looked as if they could do with a few platefuls of spaghetti carbonara to fatten them up.

The girls looked rather annoyed when she appeared. Had she interrupted something? Surely he couldn't be interested in them? She was sure Arnaud preferred mature women.

He ushered her into his office, explaining that he would be another twenty minutes. So she settled down on his large leather sofa – with its soft sheepskin rug, ate one of the baguettes and drank half the bottle of wine. She comforted herself with the constant clicks of the camera and the ease with which he drove them away.

She didn't see the hundred franc notes he stuffed into their hands; or his whispered order: "Come back at three o'clock. I shall be free then." At least he had bought himself time. His teeth tore into the baguette. He swigged down the St Emilion. He locked the doors of the studio and gave Amelie a satisfying half hour on the sofa. But then it was back to business.

As she straightened her pleated skirt and looked at herself in the mirror ("Did she once again look like a lady?"), he went for her husband's photographs.

"I hope he will like them. I have made several enlargements."

She looked through them. They were excellent.

"He will be delighted."

She opened her handbag.

He protested: "It is nothing. It is on the house. . . "

He looked at himself in the mirror.

". . . But you can tell me something. That woman I sat next to at dinner last night. . . "

"The inspector's wife?"

"His wife? For his sake, I hope she is not!"

He laughed.

"Why?"

Amelie was puzzled.

"Last night, before dinner, she asked me some extraordinary questions. About rich people in the city. Their bad habits. Their perversions. She expected me to know. . . "

"You probably do."

"Well, of course, I do."

"And you gave her the information she wanted?"

"Of course, I did. She's promised me a ten per cent cut on every successful contact that I arrange for her."

"I'm sure she wasn't being serious."

"Ma foi, she was! When I came down to breakfast, she was waiting for me. She offered me a lift into town and she sat here whilst I made the calls. What is more, she gave me two thousand francs on account."

"So what's she doing?"

"She's meeting one of the city councillors – at home – at 10.30am. As we speak, she's dating a lawyer. Later this afternoon, she's got a Canadian businessman lined up. She's also taken a number of telephone calls for tomorrow. She's a professional hooker!"

"She's very pretty."

"Lovely woman, but she won't let me touch her. All I'm getting is ten per cent commission."

Amelie felt rueful that Arnaud was getting a better deal than she was getting from Leonie. But she reflected that Mrs May would not be earning £250,000 so she would still be making more than Arnaud.

She eyed the photographer.

"I have a rather naughty request."

Arnaud's eyes sparkled.

"Not for you, sweetie! I want a little room somewhere. That artist – Brackles – he's the one who's painting Leonie, he wants to paint me. A nude. Can't do it in the house. Leonie would be most upset. Have you anywhere we could go?"

"There's always 112 Rue Sébastien."

"Oh no. I couldn't go there. I might meet *him*. That'd be terribly embarrassing."

Arnaud smiled a twisted smile.

"I think he might enjoy it."

Amelie ignored his salacious jibe.

Instead, she asked: "Has he come back from Paris yet?"

"I don't know."

14. *Le Lièvre et La Tortue*

Raynes had begun to fear that Debbie might not return in time for dinner. That would mean further public embarrassment. But, as the first guests arrived for the cocktail party, he heard her car pull into the courtyard.

At last!

She raced up the stairs, burst into the bedroom. Threw her handbag into a chair, tore off her clothes and rushed into the bathroom. It was perhaps one of the quickest showers on record. The shower was no sooner on than it was off. There followed ten seconds of frantic towelling and then the sounds of sprays and creams being slapped on.

She returned to the bedroom; flung open a drawer and whipped out some pink underwear. She had already selected a long red dress and her gold sandals. She straightened the dress in front of the mirror.

She looked at Richard.

"What are you staring at? Zip me up!"

"I'm just marvelling how quick you can be when you put your mind to it."

"Practice!" she said. "I couldn't remember where I'd left the car."

"The Negresco?" suggested Raynes maliciously.

"No. It was one of those little streets beside the Palais de Justice. You have to get there early to get a place."

"I'm surprised you got one at all."

"Arnaud lent me his parking carnet."

"How kind of him!" said Raynes sarcastically.

"Now don't be nasty about him!" said Debbie. "He's been a great help. He knows everybody." She looked round the room. "Where is my make-up bag? God! My hair looks awful! I need my brush."

Raynes provided all the items requested.

"There's no need to rush. There's another thirty minutes before dinner."

"Now you tell me!" She calmed down. "Actually, I'm longing for a gin. Too much champagne." She smiled. "That was good stuff."

"It was the best."

Debbie opened her jewel box and put on a gold necklace and a gold bangle. She rearranged the rings on her fingers.

"Can you find my small white handbag? It's in one of the cases."

Raynes looked at her larger handbag.

"I think you should probably hide your money. We discovered today that Gaspard is planning to rob the house. He's after Leonie's objets d'art, but I think he'd probably seize any money that was going."

Debbie stuffed the days takings into a large purse and looked round the room seeking a safe hiding place.

"Under the wardrobe? Or on top of the four poster?"

"He wouldn't think of the four poster."

Debbie tossed the purse up on to the canopy over the bed.

"He'll have to climb for it," she said. "What a bloody nuisance! Are we going to be held up at gunpoint?"

"I hope not. We've spent the afternoon hunting for him. The Grand Duchess has offered me a million francs if I kill him."

Debbie's eyes sparkled – as he knew they would.

"But that's wonderful! That would pay for one visit to me each week for the next ten years!"

"At the new rates, I presume?"

"Oh, don't be so mean! I bring you endless comfort and joy."

"And to thousands of others!" He shook his head sadly. "This afternoon was very embarrassing. I'm sure Spumante will take great pleasure in spreading the news far and wide. In fact, I bet it's round the house already."

Debbie did not look dismayed.

"I'm not bothered. Why should you be? We'll never see any of these people again. Why shouldn't we grab what we can, whilst we can?"

"Your philosophy – in a nutshell."

"It works." She looked at Richard thoughtfully. "You said you were looking for Gaspard?"

"Yes."

"You don't know where he is?"

"No."

Triumphantly, Mrs May delivered a full hand of trumps.

"Tomorrow," she said. "I shall be seeing an inspector of police. Thanks to Arnaud," she added, "who knows everyone. I shall ask the inspector to help you find Gaspard. Then you will be able to kill him."

Raynes was delighted with her proposal; but he drew the line at murder.

"If Gaspard gets killed, the inspector will know exactly who did it. I should be arrested before I could leave the country."

Mrs May smiled.

"But you'd do it so well. So elegantly. You're much cleverer than the people down here." Debbie was well-versed in the art of flattery. "You wouldn't do anything stupid like biffing him over the head with a champagne bottle. You would lace his drink. . . Smother him with a lace pillow. . . Electrocute him. . . You always say that's the best way. No proof. We could bury him miles away in some remote mountain gorge. I'd help you. It'd take them months to find him. Probably never. By that time, you'd be miles away. . . and a million francs better off."

Raynes smiled gratefully.

"I think you've solved one of my problems. We only need to find him – not kill him. If your police inspector can help, I'm sure the Grand Duchess would be delighted."

Debbie smiled.

"I have my uses."

"You do."

"Thank you. Now, for God's sake, get a move on and let me get at that gin!"

15. *Terre des Hommes*

If the Inspector had hoped to repeat the pleasures of Tuesday morning – and spend more time in Sylvie's company, he was sadly disappointed.

First of all, Brackles rose unexpectedly early for breakfast. He told the Inspector that Amelie would be taking him to see a flat she had found where he could do her painting. She was collecting a canvas on the way back from the station.

"The station?"

"She takes her husband to the station every morning to catch the train to Cannes. He's exploring the treasures of the local library. More about 'you know who'."

"Oh," said Raynes. "I wondered where he was."

"A very single-minded fellow." Brackles laughed. "Mind you, he may have found a sizzling piece of crumpet in one of those designer shops. They go for the older man. Think they must be retired film stars. . . "

Raynes shook his head.

"I doubt it. Julius is impotent. Someone told me."

"That's not true. He was telling me about some bird he met in Paris when his wife wasn't around. Can't remember her name. . . But he's certainly not impotent."

"Probably fantasizing," said Raynes.

"He had some very colourful memories. Colourful but disgusting. I think his parents would be ashamed of him."

Raynes stayed chatting to Brackles until Amelie arrived to collect him. At first, she did not see Raynes.

"Darling, I'm ready for anything! Let's go!"

Then she saw the Inspector – and the smile was wiped off her face.

Richard was not put out.

"I'm sure it'll make a splendid birthday present for dear Julius!" (And then he wondered why people hated him.)

Even Brackles looked a little shocked.

* * * *

Soon after they had gone, Signor Spumante arrived – not in the best of moods. Leonie wanted them to go out and see three other known contacts – including Pierre whom they had missed the previous day.

His mood was not perhaps greatly improved when Raynes said cheerfully: "I think it's your turn to pay for drinks at the Negresco!" And, to twist his tail even further: "I'm told they have this absolutely gorgeous wine which contains tiny flecks of gold. Quite cheap, I believe. Much cheaper than the Roederer. I thought I'd let you know before we start."

But Camille was not in the mood for pleasantries.

"I'm not proposing to stop for any drinks. I must get back."

Raynes immediately guessed that he wanted to be back in the house before Brackles returned to paint his official picture. With studied contempt, Raynes said: "Oh, I'm in no hurry."

* * * *

That same Wednesday morning, Bruno Polanski left his cat in charge of the shop. He was not expecting any customers. The demand for secondhand pianos in Nice was not great. Certainly, he had no desire to entertain unexpected visitors such as those who had called on him the previous afternoon.

The bullying Englishman and the snobbish, aristocratic toerag. A most unpleasant combination, bearing exceedingly bad news. That scheming Russian bitch had heard that Gaspard was back in town. She knew what he was after. She knew he would try to get in touch with her daughter. She knew that, after being in prison, he would be desperate for money.

Rather than wait for a full-scale attack, she had decided to track him down herself. Of course, he should have realized that they would come to him first. After the Japanese miniatures fiasco, he was a marked man. They knew of his connection with Gaspard. If they were going to employ any local "fence", it would obviously be him. He was the best "fence" in the city. At least, he was . . . But publicity was the last thing any "fence" wanted.

So, as he walked along the pavement, he was cursing himself for getting involved. But the list of 'goodies' had been mouthwatering. He knew exactly where he could sell them. He would make a huge profit. But perhaps he had been too greedy? The person who had drawn up that list of treasures knew what they were doing.

The thought occurred to him that perhaps it was the Russian bitch herself? He might have been caught in a classic sting. He had paid out good money to Gaspard but he would never see it again. The whole thing would have to be called off; or he and the others would end up in jail.

It was very distressing.

So he had decided to come and see Pierre. Pierre would know where Gaspard was. He could talk to him. Persuade him to call the whole thing off. It was too hot. Pierre would know what to do. Failing that, he would just leave. He had a visa for Brazil. He could have a holiday on the Copacabana. Drown his sorrows in sin. He turned into the Cafe Austerlitz.

Pierre watched him as he walked up to the bar. Bruno looked a broken man. So they had been to him as well.

"'Jour, Monsieur."

It didn't pay to be too friendly until he was sure the coast was clear. Bruno might have been followed.

"Un café, s'il vous plaît."

Pierre set the coffee machine in motion and casually walked to the front entrance of the cafe. He wiped a couple of tables and looked around. Bruno seemed to have come alone. He went back to the machine and poured out a black coffee. He carried it over to the table.

"Ça va bien?"

Bruno shook his head.

"I had a visit yesterday. Two men. . . "

"They were here too."

"You spoke to them?"

"No. I was off. But they'll be back."

"They know all about it."

"You told them?"

"Of course not! But they knew about the guns. They even knew I'd given Gaspard money."

"They weren't from the police?"

"No. One of them was an Englishman."

"It was probably the daughter's boyfriend. He's English."

"Well, I don't know who he is; but he's sharp. We've got to warn Gaspard. They're waiting for him. Even if he gets the goods, they'll come straight to me. This business has cost me a lot of money and I'll never see it again."

Pierre didn't care a damn about Bruno's money; but he was very upset at their plans running into the buffers. This had had all the makings of an easy heist. Gaspard knew his way into the house. He knew where all the stuff was kept. He knew how the alarms worked; how they could be disconnected.

The idea was to get the stuff to Bruno within the hour – and by the time the crime was reported, it would be on its way to Paris. The proceeds would have made all of them a lot richer – and Pierre had been looking forward to it.

He blamed Bruno. Even if it wasn't his fault, he would still blame Bruno. He despised him – because he wasn't a hard man. He was a weakling. Gaspard should have known better than to involve him. Once bitten. . .

Bruno looked up.

"Will you speak to Gaspard?"

Pierre wondered how much he should say.

"I haven't seen him since last Wednesday."

"Has he gone back to Paris?"

"I don't know where he's gone."

"D'you think he's going to do it on his own – without us?"

"I hope not."

"That bitch's daughter'll give him everything he wants. He won't even need to break in."

Pierre stared into middle distance. He didn't know what to do. Up to last Wednesday, Gaspard had been in the cafe every lunchtime – every evening – full of plans and ideas. He had been on top form. He and Pierre were old buddies. They'd pull this one off together.

But then – nothing.

He had wondered whether he had been arrested by the police. Sent back to prison. But surely they would have heard? A friend of his in the gendarmerie had checked the records. They hadn't lifted him. Had he had an accident?

Perhaps, as Bruno suggested, he might have already done the job and never told them. Today, he could be in Miami, enjoying the fruit of his spoils – leaving him and Bruno in the shit. If he had, he'd kill him!

"If he does come in, will you speak to him?"

"Bien sûr. I will speak to him."

Bruno finished off his coffee.

Two men walked into the bar.

Pierre's stomach muscles tightened. But then he realized who they were – and he relaxed.

"Bonjour, Messieurs."

"'Jour."

The Englishman looked down at Bruno.

"How nice to see you again. Have you been warning your friend?"

Camille did not bother to translate.

Raynes looked at Pierre.

"We enjoyed our visit yesterday. Bruno told us so much."

Bruno exploded. "That's a lie. I didn't tell you anything."

Camille obliging translated both remarks.

Pierre nodded in a surly fashion. It confirmed his opinion of Monsieur Polanski.

Bruno stood up.

"I'm going . . . "

"You're not going anywhere," said Raynes, blocking his way and pushing him back into his seat.

Pierre did not have to be told that this man was a policeman. Whatever his nationality, they were all the same. Same attitude. Same ruthlessness.

"Can we help you. Messieurs?"

"Yes," said Camille. "We came here yesterday but you were having your day off. We're looking for a friend of yours called Gaspard."

Pierre looked at the empty restaurant.

"He's not here."

"Are you expecting him?"

The answer was "Oui" but Pierre said: "Non".

"Do you know where he's living at this moment?"

Pierre again said: "Non".

Raynes smiled.

"112 Rue Sébastien?"

So they knew his address. Why ask?

"He's not there."

Pierre knew that.

Bruno said: "He could have left the country."

"If you warned him," said Raynes.

"I haven't."

Raynes had listened for a lie – but he hadn't heard one. Monsieur Polanski must be speaking the truth. Perhaps neither of them knew where he was. The crooks were as puzzled as they were.

"D'you think he's gone back to Paris?"

"Could've done."

Pierre's answer did not sound like a cover-up. His very uncertainty suggested that they were all looking for a needle in a haystack. Like the Jackal, Gaspard had gone to ground.

Monsieur Bruno asked: "Has the theft happened yet?"

When Camille translated, Raynes laughed.

"You think he might try it on his own?"

Pierre said to Camille: "He wouldn't be doing it on his own. He'd get the daughter to help. She was his wife. She'll help him."

Camille was livid.

"How dare you make such a suggestion against Madame's daughter? A poor innocent child who was led astray by a filthy con man!"

He didn't bother to translate so Raynes was a little confused by the sudden outburst of anger.

"She's not innocent," sneered Pierre. "She was in the same game as he was. Ripping off the punters. She only saved her skin because her mother paid for an expensive lawyer to defend her."

"And you think she would go back to working with him?"

"Bien sûr," said Pierre. "She drew up the lists. . . "

"What lists?"

"The lists of items to be stolen."

"She would never have done such a thing! Steal from her own mother!"

"She's done it before!"

Pierre seemed to know more about the characters in the Villa Rose than Camille. Raynes asked him what they had been saying.

"This man says Ludo may have given Gaspard information about her mother's valuables. He thinks she may be hand in glove with Gaspard. They may be planning to do the robbery together. I have told him such a thing is unthinkable!"

Raynes raised his eyebrows.

There was a thought! He hadn't considered it; but it was eminently possible.

But Camille was having none of it. He defended Madame Leonie and her daughter most vigorously.

"They're both crooks," said Bruno.

Raynes thought Camille was going to hit him.

He decided it was time to intervene.

"So neither of you have seen Gaspard?"

Pierre said nothing.

In English, Bruno said: "He hasn't seen him since last Wednesday."

Raynes spirits lifted. His fellow-conspirators didn't know where he was. They were already falling out. That was a good sign. He smiled at the two villains.

"Well, gentlemen, I think you have told us all we need to know. When Monsieur Gaspard does appear, please tell him that we are waiting for him. Madame, her daughter – and all her friends."

"Friends?" said Pierre. "She hasn't got any friends! She buys friends. Fair weather friends. Some of her 'friends' are really her sworn enemies. As she will discover."

Pierre turned on his heel and returned to the bar.

16. *La Vie Parisienne*

As they got back into the estate car, Raynes asked: "Where next?"

"Some fancy woman."

Raynes cheered up. So far, Gaspard's friends had seemed a very sordid bunch – and rather dirty. A bit of class would be welcome.

They drove out to the western suburbs of Nice – almost as far as Cagnes. A quiet lane of houses.

"Who are we seeing?"

Camille consulted his notes.

"Madame Yolande de Brieuc. A fashion designer. She has a couple of boutiques."

"In Nice?"

"No. In Paris and Cannes."

Raynes immediately thought about Julius Foster. They walked up to the front door and rang the bell. A woman in a purple blouse and white cotton trousers opened the door. She had very dark hair, a thin brown face and sharp eyes.

"Oui?"

"We are friends of Gaspard," said Camille.

His opening gambit proved immediately successful. They were invited into the house and ushered into the lounge. The floors were polished wood, the furniture minimalist – four modern chairs surrounding a glass coffee table, which bore one book: *Renoir*. The walls were uniformly beige and bare. There was nothing to look at except Madame Yolande.

"Do you know where he is?"

"No, we were hoping you could tell us."

"I have not seen him since Wednesday morning. He spent the night here. It is most unusual that he does not phone."

"Do you think he has had an accident?"

"No. I am sure the hospital would have told us."

She wrung her hands anxiously.

"We wondered whether he had gone back to Paris?"

"No. My husband is there. He would have told me. He is coming down tomorrow night."

She seemed a very nervous sort of woman.

Raynes had no idea what Camille was saying but the Italian waved a hand in his direction.

"Mon ami, Monsieur Richard. . . "

(It must have taken him quite something to describe the Inspector as a friend!)

Raynes smiled in a friendly fashion.

"You met Gaspard in Paris, I believe?"

"Yes. He stayed with us for two months."

"After he came out of prison?"

She nodded.

Yolande asked him how he came to be involved with Gaspard.

Without a shadow of hesitation, Raynes said: " I know his wife, Ludo."

Yolande sighed deeply.

"She is making it very difficult for us. All the time, she is with that Englishman – a painter, I am told. They are going everywhere together. Her mother sent her to England. On Monday, they were in Monte Carlo; yesterday in Grasse. She is trying to keep her out of the way. Gaspard was hoping to see her last week. They had planned to meet here – but she was unable to get rid of that *boudin*."

Camille took great pleasure in translating her words. He thought Raynes would be surprised to hear his friend, Simon, described as *un boudin* – a black pudding!

Raynes wanted to laugh; but he realized that, in the circumstances, they were walking on a knife edge. At any moment, she might discover that they were friends of Leonie.

Replying to Camille, he suggested a way of maintaining their cover as friends of Gaspard:

"I think we ought to tell Madame Yolande why we are here. We are extremely worried about Monsieur Bruno. We think that he has revealed details of the burglary to Madame Leonie. He has got cold feet and is frightened of the police. We thought that we should let Gaspard know that his plans may have been betrayed and the police will be waiting for him."

Putting the blame on Bruno seemed to work. Madame Yolande put her hands to her head and groaned.

"Ma foi! Why did we choose him? There are much better people in Paris who know how to deal with these things. Bruno – he is an amateur."

Camille translated faithfully.

Raynes tried to make it more difficult for Monsieur Polanski. "I think he is worried about his money. He has given Gaspard an advance and he is worried that he will lose it."

"Perhaps he will. It is no concern of ours."

"Do you think it would be safer if the raid was called off?"

Madame Yolande bristled with anger.

"Called off? Never! There is a fortune in that house. We have decided that the attack will happen this weekend. The longer we leave it, the more people will hear about it." She smiled. "You English have a saying: 'The fortune is to the brave!' We shall succeed – even without Gaspard. You will see." She smiled. "But thank you for the information. My husband will know what to do with Bruno."

The interview seemed to be over. Camille and Raynes stood up. As they made their way to the door, the telephone rang. With every fibre in his being, Raynes knew that it was Pierre.

"Au revoir, Madame."

"Au revoir, Messieurs."

The scream of anger could be heard – even out on the pavement. Raynes looked across the roof of the estate car at Camille. "Well done, Monsieur."

* * * *

Raynes was of a mind to travel on to Cannes – either to see what Mr Foster was doing or to have a look at Madame Yolande's shop. He thought there might be a connection between the two. The French woman seemed very well informed about Ludo's movements. He thought it might be worth checking.

But Signor Spumante was anxious to return to the Villa Rose. He was worried about Brackles. Within the past week, he had seen this wretched Englishman worm his way into Leonie's affections. He could not believe it. That she should be attracted to someone so worthless. True, the man was a great painter – he could not deny that; but he was undoubtedly an alcoholic. A complete waster. And Leonie was enjoying his company. They were laughing; teasing each other; sharing secrets together. They would soon become lovers – if it had not happened already. Their looks and glances said it all. Camille felt that he must defend Madame against such scum.

On the journey back through Nice, Raynes was deep in thought. The visits to Pierre and Madame Yolande had set him thinking.

He had assumed that Ludo and her mother were of one mind when it came to Gaspard. But a new picture was emerging. Gaspard had renewed his charm offensive on the daughter. He had sent her letters. They had been on the phone. They had even been planning to meet at Madame Yolande's home. Ludo was in a position to tell the enemy all about her mother's prized possessions; which items were worth taking. She could give them details about the alarm system – even the security code. The fortress had been breached from within.

Gaspard had been planning to see his ex-wife last Wednesday. But his letters or his phone calls must have been intercepted. Leonie had wisely kept her daughter busy, making sure that she was out of town, constantly in Simon's company. But, by inclination it seemed, Ludo was a member of the enemy camp. Pierre had said that she had stolen things from her mother in the past. In fact, a very unpleasant picture was emerging. As Pierre had said: "Some of Leonie's friends are her sworn enemies." It was sad to think this might include her own daughter.

17. *Marrons Glacés*

He was still thinking through these things when Brackles returned from his painting expedition.

"What a dump!" he said.

"That's no way to speak about a lady."

"The flat!" he said. "The flat! It looked absolutely vile. The stairwell was so dark, it was positively dangerous. But once you were in the flat, it was fine. Quite bright and comfortable. We set ourselves up in the sitting room. I've done the preliminaries."

"You mean you've pinned the canvas to the wall and set up your paints. I can't imagine you had time to do much more – with such an eager lady!"

"Ah, there you're wrong. We sorted out the lighting. Decided on the pose. I sketched out a few ideas. In fact, I took a leaf or two out of Simon's book," he said apologetically.

"You mean you've copied his painting of Debbie?"

"The other way round. It suited her better."

"You'd better not tell either of them. They'll be furious."

"I shouldn't have told you."

"It's all right. I won't say anything." Was nothing sacred? But to get back to Amelie: "Did she like it?"

"Of course. I got to work immediately. As you know, I work much quicker than Simon. Within the hour, we'd got the general lay-out. I had to move her head a bit. Arrange her legs and so on."

"I bet you enjoyed it."

"I did."

Brackles opened his box of paints to check that he had all

his brushes and oils ready for his next picture. That he had left nothing at the flat.

"And now," he said, "I've got to get ready for the next bout."

"Spumante's determined to be in the background."

"Thank heaven for that. I don't think I could manage two such demanding females in one day."

"You managed to have her?"

"Couldn't refuse. Art. . . real art. . . demands touch, taste, all the senses. . . I worked for two hours. She was so delighted, I got my reward. We retired to the spare bedroom and she quite literally let herself go. I tell you. That woman's a cracker. A volcano of passion. She left me like a limp rag. Phew!"

"And where is she now?"

"She's gone back to the boutique."

"And the picture?"

"It's still in the flat. Waiting for the next sitting. I wouldn't dream of bringing it back here. There would be fireworks. Leonie would give me the boot."

Brackles reached into his back pocket.

"By the way, I've got something here for you." He smiled. "I think you'll be surprised. Small world and all that. Whilst her ladyship was in the bathroom, putting herself together – so to speak – I had a mooch round the flat. There was a suitcase – unlocked. So I poked around to see what it contained. Frilly underwear? Porn? You never know. But guess what I found."

He produced a French passport.

"No?"

"Very much yes."

Raynes looked at the name: "Gaspard de la Nuit". He looked at the photograph and details.

"This is the Holy Grail."

"Thought so."

"He can't leave the country without it."

"I thought you'd like to have it."

Various pieces of the jigsaw came together.

"I take it you were in No 112 Rue Sébastien?"

"Is that what it's called? I didn't notice. I was too busy picking my way through chicken giblets and greasy onions. It was a hole."

"Flat H?"

Brackles nodded.

"And were there still boxes of electrical equipment in the hallway?"

"Not a sausage, mate!"

"And Amelie has the key? How very interesting!" He smiled. How would she explain that? He looked up. "And the rest of Gaspard's things are there?"

"Just a suitcase. Mostly clothes from the looks of it."

"You've been a great help. A really great help."

Raynes put the passport into his pocket.

"You'll forgive me plaigarizing Simon's painting?"

"Of course."

Brackles picked up his box of paints and brushes.

"Well, once more into the breach, dear friends!"

"I think you need a brandy."

Brackles groaned.

"Two – at least."

18. *The Red and the Black*

Raynes walked out on to the patio and went over to the balustrade. He was feeling quite pleased with himself. Within two days, he and Spumante had visited most of Gaspard's friends and caused much confusion in their ranks. But, knowing the dangers he faced, and the lady he was up against, Gaspard had gone to ground. He must have other contacts whom Leonie did not know, with whom he was now staying.

He had been stupid to leave his passport in No. 112 Rue Sébastien. Without it, his escape route was blocked. But was he now living under another name? Did he possess a forged passport?

Raynes thought about the American historian and his wife. What was he really doing in Cannes? Amelie had been a fashion reporter before she moved on to antiques. Yolande and her husband ran a fashion boutique in Paris. Did they know each other? Amelie had the run of Leonie's villa and her shop. She was capable of recognizing valuable antiques. She was just the person who would know what was worth stealing. And what was her connection with Gaspard's flat? Why had she taken Brackles there?

The Inspector began to wonder if he should phone his colleague, Detective-Constable Carlisle, in Grasshallows and ask him to contact Interpol and find whether they had anything on these two American globetrotters. Was she really a reporter for a genuine American magazine about antiques; or was it all a big con?

And what about Ernst – that silent, sullen denizen of the servants' quarters, who looked as if he too was an ex-jailbird? Where did his loyalties lie?

The Inspector was still wrestling with these problems when a faint smell of perfume made him realize that he was not alone on the patio.

"You have not eaten, Monsieur Richard."

"No, I'm all right."

"You have had nothing since breakfast. I think you should have a coffee and a sandwich."

Raynes considered. Yes, he supposed he was hungry. And who was he to refuse any temptation?

"Well, I'm not doing anything else."

"Good. Madame is having her picture painted by Monsieur Brackles. As always, Monsieur Camille is watching them. Mademoiselle and Monsieur Simon have returned to the chateau. And Madame Raynes is. . . "

". . . still shopping!"

Sylvie laughed.

"So we can have coffee together?"

"That seems a very good idea. You're not busy?"

"No. I have the afternoon off. All the servants have

Wednesday afternoon off. We shall eat in my room. It is on the top floor."

She pointed to one of the attic windows overlooking the pool.

"Does it have a name?"

Sylvie chuckled.

"Of course it has a name. All the rooms have a name. . . But you will never guess. . . "

"I should have thought it was perfectly obvious. 'The Queen of Spades'!"

"Oh, no. Monsieur! The Queen of Hearts!"

* * * *

Actually, it was called *The Little Russian* – as Raynes discovered when he arrived at the door of Sylvie's room under the villa's high eaves. She followed him with a flask of coffee and two baguettes.

"The door is open, Monsieur."

All doors, it seemed.

Sylvie's room, as one would have expected, was very neat and tidy. No silk or lace but a penchant for blue and white stripes, with dark blue velvet curtains and an expensive-looking Persian carpet on the floor. Her bed had one of those round, roly-poly type pillows, much beloved by the French, but always, in Raynes' experience, too small, saggy and uncomfortable. On the bed was her collection of Norman dolls – about eight of them. On the wall was a Manet: "Evening in the harbour at Honfleur". It was quite small, but it was the most beautiful picture he had seen in the house. He hoped that Gaspard had not got that picture on his list.

They munched their baguettes and drank their coffee. After lunch – if it could be called lunch, Sylvie produced a bottle of Calvados and two glasses.

"We shall toast your success."

They clinked glasses.

The Calvados was extremely strong – and not exactly

pleasant. Certainly, it was not sweet. But it created a warm, burning sensation in Richard's throat and stomach which seemed to radiate outwards towards the rest of his body.

"Mm," he said.

"It is from my uncle's farm. He makes it from les pommes. You see. No label."

Raynes had assumed that it was one of Leonie's vintage liqueurs, filched from the cellars; but it seemed that in her own quarters, Sylvie drank her own poison. It was pretty powerful stuff. He looked into her large grey eyes.

Did passion beckon?

No!

"First, we do business."

Raynes was momentarily disappointed. But his disappointment turned to amazement as Sylvie produced Debbie's purse.

"It is a great mistake to put this on the canopy of your bed. It is where many guests hide their money. Every day, the staff clean your room. They check the bed. It is much better to put it behind the mirror. There is a hidden cupboard. I will give you the key."

"I hope Gaspard doesn't know about it?"

"Gaspard knows nothing. Your money is quite safe."

She gave him the purse and the key.

"There are two locks – on the left. You look for the little holes."

She chuckled.

Then she went over to her small chest of drawers and came back with a sheaf of paper.

"I think you were asking if there is a list of valuable items in Madame's house. I think you will find here a full list. It is for the insurance. . . " she explained.

She handed it to the Inspector.

He glanced through it. It was a photocopy – he could see that. Obviously, she wouldn't trust him with the original. But it was a long list, with the items listed room by room. Sylvie looked at him eagerly.

He thought that perhaps she was bursting with passion. But no. As he thumbed through the pages, he noticed small ticks beside various items. He looked more closely. They were all small moveable things – like pictures, silver, clocks, china, the gold buddha in the small lounge.

"Vous remarquez. Monsieur?"

Raynes nodded.

"This is what they are after."

"They have taken Madame's list. They have copied it. This is their. . . shopping list. There are one hundred and sixty seven items they have selected. If you look at the valuations, you will see that they are worth more than ten million francs!"

Raynes nodded again.

"And where did you find this list?"

"I think you know."

"In Madame Foster's bedroom?"

"The same. It was in her brief case. I had already searched her room – twice. But, last night, while you were at dinner, I have got Ernst to open her case. I had the curiosité. A woman's curiosité!"

"I'm not surprised," said Raynes. "It was only this morning that I realized she could have links with Gaspard. I think she met Madame Yolande in Paris. I think she may have met Gaspard at her house."

"It is very dangerous."

"Yes. She has the freedom of the house. She spends most of the day in Leonie's shop. She takes photographs – with Arnaud. She knows a great deal about Leonie's property."

"That picture. . . "

"Yes, that was very clever." Raynes could see it now. "She found something worth a lot of money and drew Madame's attention to it. So Madame could sell it for a good price. You would not think she was in the enemy's camp. She is helping Leonie."

"Yes. And Madame is giving her five per cent."

Raynes calculated.

"£12,500. Yes, she's done rather well out of that picture.

And she has covered her tracks. If Gaspard does not succeed, she can rob Madame herself."

"That is what I think."

"Does Madame know about this list?"

A guarded expression came over Sylvie's face.

"No. I have not told her."

"It is a copy?"

"Yes, it is a copy."

"And where does Madame keep the original?"

"In her safe."

"And who has the key to the safe?"

"Only Madame."

Raynes' eyes narrowed.

"And who knows where Madame keeps the key?"

"I know. But there is one other person. . . "

"Yes," said Raynes. "Ludo. . . And she is more friendly with Gaspard than her mother knows."

"She is torn – both ways."

For several minutes there was silence.

"And what are you doing with that list? Are you going to put it back in Mrs Foster's brief case?"

Sylvie smiled.

"It is a copy of a copy. She will never know. Everything is as it was."

She went back to her chest of drawers and put the list away.

"Tiens, Monsieur! We have spent too long on the business. The time is passing. We have better things to do."

Without a moment's warning, she drew up her black dress and pulled it over her head. She was wearing a bright cherry-pink bra and pants. She went over to the bed and started to remove her Norman dolls.

"Do you want me to lock the door?"

"It is already locked, Monsieur. You cannot escape!"

There seemed to be very little to do except enjoy oneself. Raynes took off his clothes and joined Sylvie on the bed.

Sylvie looked at Richard's body with some interest.

"It is not enough for Madame Raynes?"

"I'm afraid not."

Sylvie's eyes flashed and her dark hair tumbled over her shoulders.

"It is enough for me."

* * * *

They spent a couple of hours of vigorous love-making with two pit stops for extra doses of Calvados. During that time, Raynes felt he had explored most of Normandy. Sylvie, the housekeeper, was lying glutted with passion. She was smiling with her eyes closed.

"Have we come to the end of the Bayeux tapestry?" he asked teasingly.

"For today," she said. "But I must have more. We must make sure Madame Raynes does a lot of shopping."

"I think we can count on that."

Raynes gave her a final, gentle kiss and rolled off the bed. With some reluctance, he pulled on his shirt.

Sylvie sat on the edge of the bed and looked at her toes. She stretched once or twice – and yawned.

"And now I have to organize the dinner," she said. "It is the wild duck."

"Le mallarde imaginaire?" suggested Raynes.

(She did not get the joke.)

And then it happened.

As Raynes picked up his trousers, the French passport dropped out of his pocket.

Sylvie saw it immediately and pounced on it.

She was a fast mover.

"You have found this?"

"Yes, I have found it – in the course of my travels."

He realized immediately that he could not say that Brackles had found it in the flat because he wouldn't want Leonie to know that he had been painting Amelie or having it off with her in Gaspard's flat.

Very casually, he said: "I found it yesterday when we were

in the Rue Sébastien."

"Monsieur Camille said nothing about this."

"He didn't know."

She looked at the photograph and all the details.

"C'est authentique."

"I thought so." Raynes smiled. "Now he cannot escape."

Sylvie laughed and handed back the passport.

"You must hide this. Put it in your secret place – with Madame's purse – behind the mirror."

"To which you have the second key?"

Sylvie grinned.

"Of course."

She picked up her black dress and pulled it over her head, She put on her black sandals. Raynes once more felt aroused – knowing she was wearing no underwear. But perhaps the moment of passion had passed?

"Perhaps Madame Raynes will be so enchanted with Gaspard – be so impressed with his good looks – that she will want to marry him? Then I can marry her policeman!"

It was a nice idea but Raynes immediately dismissed it.

"Gaspard is too poor for her."

Sylvie said proudly: "I cost you nothing!"

"I know. It's wonderful."

Sylvie unlocked the door.

"Now you are free to go. Monsieur."

"Thank you," he said. "It was lovely."

They gave each other one last kiss.

Force of habit caused him to ask her one final question. It was the sort of thing he did at the end of most interviews – just as he was going through the door. It was pure instinct.

"I don't suppose you know where Gaspard is?"

He looked into the big grey eyes. Beautiful. Irresistible.

"Non, Monsieur."

For the first time, he suspected that Sylvie could be lying.

19. *Le Blé en Herbe*

Mrs May unlocked the handcuffs binding the French inspector to the brass bedstead. He rubbed his wrists which were a little sore; but sighed happily. He had enjoyed his hour in paradise.

If Mrs May had any literary pretensions, she might have remembered the words of a famous French philosopher, who said; "Man was born free; but everywhere he is in chains."

Sadly, Debbie was only interested in profit – another few thousand francs into her bank account. But this morning, she had a final favour to extract.

As the French inspector pulled on his shirt, she asked: "I wonder if you could do something to help me?"

"Bien sûr."

"One of the people I know here in Nice is looking for someone – but he seems to have gone missing. Do you think you could find him?"

The inspector looked down at his naked partner with her rich golden hair and her small chubby arms. He calculated that this might be a convenient way of meeting her again – perhaps at a slightly cheaper price!

"What's the person's name?"

Debbie managed to look embarrassed.

"I'm told he's a criminal. A thief. Anyway, he's been in jail. But, " she said optimistically, "he comes from Nice. I'm sure you'll know him."

The inspector's face was encouraging. There was little he didn't know about the criminal fraternity in Nice.

"He's called Gaspard." She looked up hopefully. "Gaspard de la Nuit. . . Does that ring a bell?"

The inspector laughed.

"I know all about him. But he doesn't come from Nice. He comes from Marseilles. That's where they all come from." He tapped his nose. "They smell the money. They come running."

"And Gaspard?"

"Very slippery. Very difficult to pin down. Here today – gone tomorrow. Many of his victims are too embarrassed to speak to the police. He has promised them – how do you say – a quick buck? They do not like to admit they have been conned. And once he has made the killing, he moves on. To Lyons. . . to Paris."

"But now he is back in Nice."

"So I have heard. But I am told he is lying low. He has his friends. They are protecting him. They always do."

The inspector was curious. "Why is your friend interested in him?"

Debbie had been carefully briefed. She was not to say anything about the Villa Rose or the expected attack.

Leonie's name was not to be mentioned.

"He is an Englishman. His mother has recently died. He was expecting her to leave him a lot of money but, when she died, he discovered that most of her savings had gone. She used to come for her holidays in Nice – and he thinks that she had put all her money into some scheme – and Gaspard has deceived her."

"He would deceive anyone." The inspector's eyes narrowed. "When did this happen?"

Debbie managed to look uncertain.

"Five or six years ago."

"Not recently?"

"No."

The inspector shook his head.

"He will never see his money again."

"He's heard that Gaspard has been in jail."

"That is true. Is he seeking revenge?"

"I don't know. I think he'd just like to see him punished for his crime."

Ah! The English and their passion for justice!

"It may be very difficult to prove. After all this time. As I say, this man is très glissant."

The French inspector pulled on his trousers and buckled his belt. Now he felt very much "the professional". A faithful servant of the Fifth Republic – even though he did not have much time for M. Mitterand. In Nice, their hero was Monsieur Le Pen. A true patriot.

He smiled at the English cocotte. She had given him much pleasure. He would return to his desk fresh and full of confidence. He would track down these criminals – with vigour. Especially Gaspard. It would be a pleasure to see him back behind bars. In Marseilles, where he belonged.

"And when will you be able to tell me?"

The sooner the better. His wife, Madame Stephanie, would be coming home on Monday night. He would be at the airport to meet her. There would be no sign of any misdeeds. All the sheets would be washed. There would be no golden hairs on the pillow. He would make sure the cocotte took everything away with her. He smiled triumphantly.

"Perhaps tomorrow? At the same time? I shall get my men to make enquiries. They will find him. You may be sure of that." His face took on a rather unpleasant leer. "And perhaps, if I do something for you, you will do something for me? Something different? Something very naughty?"

Something, Debbie thought, that his wife would never dream of doing! When she had entered the flat, she had taken note of all the family photographs. Proud Maman with all her children and grandchildren. A rather stocky woman with a large jaw – and not much humour in her eyes.

She felt sorry for the inspector but – favour or no – he would still pay. There would be no freebies with her.

"12.30pm?"

"Parfait! This afternoon, I will make full investigations into this man. It may be he has returned to Paris. The Sûreté will know."

Debbie slipped into her dress and shoes. Her next port of call was a second floor room in the Hotel Azur in fifteen minutes' time. She would have to take a taxi.

"Till tomorrow then! Au revoir, chérie!"

She was beginning to sound quite French. Richard would be proud of her.

20. *Sur L'eau*

On Thursday morning, Raynes decided that he would dispense with the services of Signor Spumante and do a little investigation on his own. He was becoming increasingly curious as to what Julius was doing in Cannes. He was beginning to wonder if the much-trumpeted monograph on Napoleon was a cover for something else. Was he really spending his time consulting ancient documents and dusty books?

The discovery that Amelie was carrying a shopping list of Leonie's treasures in her locked briefcase raised the real possibility that she was working with Gaspard, providing the inside information he needed. If she was doing this, it suggested that Julius was not as naive or as stupid as he appeared. Perhaps the planning for the attack was being done in Cannes – not Nice? Perhaps that was where Gaspard had been hiding after he had left the Rue Sébastien? Leonie had not included the shop in her itinerary; but the Inspector felt that he would be failing in his duty if he did not give it the once-over.

Raynes discussed the matter with Debbie on the Wednesday night. He arranged for her to drive him down to the station. He would have an early breakfast; but not say where he was going. He also made a point of asking Brackles exactly what time Amelie took her husband to the station. He wanted to be there before him.

So, at 9.00am, he was standing in the main concourse of the station, with a return ticket in his hand, waiting for the American to arrive. He noticed that Julius bought his ticket from one of the automatic machines. Raynes had had to join one of the long queues at the ticket office – competing with dozens of holidaymakers who had also decided to make an early start. He would remember his anxiety and frustration at guichet No. 3.

He put on a pair of dark glasses and followed Mr Foster through the subway with its green tiles and advertisements for Dubonnet. Once on the platform, he kept his distance, but when the train came in, he made sure he was in the same carriage – but as far away as possible. Julius had bought a copy of the *New York Times* at the bookstall. He read it all the way to Cannes, quite oblivious of the fact that he was being tailed.

So the Inspector sat back and enjoyed the journey along the coast, stopping at all the little stations – Cros de Cagnes, Villeneuve Loubet, Biot and Juan les Pins.

There was Vauban's massive castle at Antibes and hundreds of yachts moored in the harbour. He could see their masts. But he much preferred the pebbled beaches with the sea rolling in with great white waves crashing on the seashore.

The journey lasted forty minutes and then he was out on the platform, close on the American's heels, so that he did not lose him in the crowd.

But Julius was in no hurry. He had an easy rolling gait and his briefcase seemed extraordinarily light. Raynes wondered if it contained anything at all. He followed him up the main shopping street with all the famous designer names. Madame Yolande was not among the great and glamorous – but in a side street near a public fountain. Julius walked through the door and passed through the shop to the back regions. The shopgirl, who was rearranging the rails of dresses, did not take the slightest notice.

Raynes sat down on a stone bench beside the fountain and watched the shop for twenty minutes in case Julius came out. But nothing happened. The Inspector decided that there must be a tradesmen's entrance at the back of the shop. Perhaps he had just walked through?

Raynes took off his dark glasses and went down the street looking for some alleyway. He soon found what he was looking for – and more. A white Renault van with the back doors open and a pile of boxes containing electrical equipment being loaded into the van.

The boxes looked familiar – and so did the man who was loading them. He was the slimy little creature whom they had met in the Rue Sébastien. The man would certainly recognize him. Raynes quickly slipped back down the alleyway and positioned himself where he could see the van depart.

He waited for ten minutes. But he was pleased to note that the man who was driving was alone. Julius must still be in the shop. Raynes returned to the back door, which was open. A pile of twenty boxes still lay inside what appeared to be a kitchen with a large chest freezer, a washing machine, a stove and a double sink.

"A thieves' kitchen!" said Raynes to himself. There was also a wooden staircase. The Inspector cautiously made his way upstairs.

There were three rooms on the top landing. Two of them contained stock – but the door of the third room was shut. Raynes gave a casual knock and walked straight in.

Julius D. Foster was sitting at a large desk surrounded by photographs, reference books and many sheets of typed paper. The books were clearly those used in the antique trade and the photographs depicted some familiar objects – in particular, Leonie's gold buddha. Caught in the act!

Raynes smiled pleasantly and sat down.

"So this is where you work, Julius?"

The American looked totally shocked.

If he had ever thought about the Inspector, he would have imagined him sitting down in Leonie's dining room, enjoying a late breakfast, or swimming in the pool. But not here!

"I don't see much work being done on Napoleon. Looks more like antiques to me."

Julius grabbed the photographs nearest to the Inspector and shoved them into a drawer.

Raynes shook his head.

"Too late! I know what you're doing. In fact, I was sure this was what you were doing. That's why I came to see you."

Mr Foster did not trust himself to speak.

"You're connected with this gang who are planning to

target Leonie's house. To steal her valuables. Perhaps kill one or two of her guests. Considering all the hospitality you've received, it seems a little mean, doesn't it?"

Julius sighed.

"And there's your dear wife, working so hard to help Madame. Being given a commission of 125,000 francs. That would be enough for most people."

He looked down at the letters being written.

"I never knew you had so many friends! Have you managed to place all the goods yet? That buddha might be a bit of a problem. Apparently, it's quite well known. Bruno was telling me. . . "

Mr Foster regained his power of speech.

"Have you come here to arrest me?"

Raynes looked at him with some amusement.

"It may surprise you to know that I haven't. Thus far, no crime has been committed. Nothing has been stolen. There's nothing wrong with you photographing and itemizing Leonie's treasures – but the moment they are stolen, I shall make sure the police come straight to you. Bruno will be much relieved. . . "

Mr Foster sniffed with contempt.

"Bruno. . . a complete fool."

"I agree. This plan requires sophistication. Is that why Gaspard has been cut out of his own plan?"

"He's gone missing – as you well know!"

"Yes. Last Wednesday, wasn't it? Madame Yolande was telling me." Raynes smiled disarmingly. "I just wondered whether he might be hiding here. I didn't know the name of the shop. I might have searched in vain. But when I saw you walking into the shop this morning. . . well, it was too good to be true."

"You followed me?"

"Of course."

Mr Foster had regained some of his composure.

"If you're not going to arrest me, what are you going to do?"

Raynes smiled.

"Well, I was thinking about that whilst I was sitting beside the fountain. Our hostess has simply asked me to find Gaspard. When I find him, she will doubtless hand him over to the police. He will return to prison. There will be no raid. None of her valuables will be stolen. All your work. . . ," he gestured towards the papers and photographs, "will be in vain. I imagine you and your wife will decide to leave the Villa Rose at the earliest opportunity. You will need to find some excuse."

The Inspector looked thoughtful.

"More research needed at Les Invalides? Grim news that the Emperor was suffering from syphilis. Hence his indecision at the battle of Waterloo! I imagine you can find something less shameful. But you may rest assured I shall say nothing to Madame. I shall let you depart with dignity. But you will know. . . that I know. . . you are a complete shit, Dominic!"

He spat out the final words.

"However," he said more gently, "if you would like to regain my respect, I would be delighted if you could deliver Gaspard into Madame's hands – dead or alive – at the earliest opportunity. That way, you can atone for your sins and we can all have a happy end to our holidays. Perhaps your wife could earn a few more thousands in honest commissions for the shop? And. . . " he smiled, ". . . you can continue your research – and your naughty little affair with Madame Yolande. . . Yes?"

The look on Mr Foster's face told the Inspector that he had scored a bulls-eye. The American looked completely deflated.

Raynes enjoyed teasing him.

"Better not tell your wife. She's been telling people you're impotent. . . "

The Inspector might have spent a little longer with Mr Foster, but he suddenly heard a grinding of gears from the back of the shop. The man in the white van had returned. He must go.

Raynes leapt up from his chair and ran down the stairs.

There was the van outside the back door. The engine was switched off. Rather than meet the man, the Inspector rushed across the kitchen, pulled open the other door and found himself in the dress shop.

The assistant looked surprised.

"Monsieur?"

"Bonjour!"

He went out through the main door and rapidly made his way back to the station. He looked at the timetable. Fifteen minutes and he could catch the next train back to Nice. It had been a useful morning. After his intervention, he doubted whether the raid would go ahead. He had well and truly spiked the enemy's guns.

21. *Les Liaisons Dangereuses*

During the journey back to Nice, Raynes decided that his next objective must be Mrs Foster. "Strike whilst the iron is hot" was his motto; but this was not as easy as it sounded. He presumed that Amelie would be at La Grotte de Seraphim. Even if she had spent part of the morning with Brackles, she would turn up at the boutique some time He knew that the antique shop was near the harbour but he had not the slightest knowledge which bus would take him in that direction. He was quite incapable of explaining where he wanted to go – so he would have to walk. He had a map. It should not take too long.

He came out of the station and headed down the hill. It was extremely hot. He decided he would have a beer. He stepped into a small cafe and opened up his map. There was the harbour – le port. And there was the hill where the castle had once stood. It had been blown up in an explosion. There was the Old Town with all its narrow streets. He traced a direct line back to the station.

It didn't seem all that far. He drank his beer and felt refreshed. By keeping to the shady side of the streets, he got there in less than half an hour. Leonie's shop was a tall red building with the title La Grotte de Seraphim in large golden letters. Very distinctive.

He walked through the door. A little bell tinkled discreetly in the distance. There was a lady sitting at the desk – not Leonie.

"Monsieur?"

"I am looking for Madame Foster."

"She is having lunch with her photographer."

"Arnaud?"

There was a temptation to kill two birds with one stone, but he needed to see Amelie on her own. Fortunately, if she was with Arnaud, Julius might not have been able to contact her. He would like to get to her first.

Raynes smiled pleasantly.

"Is she expected here this afternoon?"

"She will be here by 2.00pm."

Raynes felt that perhaps a word of explanation was required.

"I am one of Madame Leonie's guests at the Villa Rose. I am the English inspector."

The lady smiled.

"I have heard about you."

"Is Madame Leonie here?"

"No, she is having lunch with her lawyer."

"Maître Duclos?"

The lady nodded.

Having established his bona fides, Raynes asked: "Has Monsieur Foster been trying to contact his wife?"

"Yes. He has phoned her several times."

"Perhaps you would be kind enough not to tell her." He smiled conspiratorially. "Not till I have gone."

"You want to wait for Madame?"

"Yes, I do. In the meantime, I shall have a look around."

There was no one else in the shop. After all, it was lunchtime. The atmosphere was one of peace and prosperity. Two or three fans revolved slowly, providing a welcome swirl of cool air. There was a strong smell of polish and a quiet conversational murmur from the clocks all ticking in their own good time and chiming in their own distinctive way. Some of the clocks were very old and beautifully constructed. Raynes looked at the price tags and was shocked. Would people really pay that much for an old clock?

Mrs Foster arrived at about ten past two.

Raynes was close enough to the door to make sure the receptionist said nothing to her about her husband phoning.

"You have a visitor, Madame."

"Ah, Inspector?"

"Have you anywhere we could speak?"

"Yes. I'm working on the second floor. We'll take the lift."

Amelie hoped she didn't look too flustered. She had spent two hours with Brackles in the flat in the Rue Sébastien. As before, the first hour had been spent in painting, the second in more passionate pursuits. She hoped it didn't show.

She had been informed that Leonie was seeing her lawyer – and lunching with him; so she knew the coast was clear. The arrival of the Inspector would provide a convenient alibi.

"Have you had lunch?"

"No. Just a beer."

"Jacqueline will get us coffee. Deux cafés, s'il vous plaît."

Amelie's room contained a series of highly polished tables, each bearing its quota of antiques and reference books. Glass ornaments, china, clocks, figurines and paintings were all being valued and priced. An expensive camera lay close at hand with several boxes of Kodak film.

"You look very busy."

"I am. We've been right through Leonie's warehouse. And now she's bought the contents of the chateau, there'll be even more coming our way."

Raynes said that he had not heard about her buying the contents of the chateau.

"That's what she's been discussing with Maître Duclos this morning. Putting in a good offer before the people change their minds."

Raynes smiled innocently.

"And how's your picture coming along?"

Mrs Foster's lips shut tight – but then relaxed.

The Inspector obviously knew about it. Brackles was his friend. He had told her about a similar picture Simon had done for Mrs May. Obviously he would have told Raynes what he was doing for her. She hoped he could keep her secret. If it came out, it would upset relations between her and Leonie.

"It's coming along beautifully."

"He's a fast worker."

Amelie knew what he was meaning.

"I hope you'll keep this to yourself."

"Of course."

The coffee arrived.

They drank their coffee silently, each of them thinking their own private thoughts.

"I went to see Julius this morning."

"Julius?"

"Yes. In Cannes. He seemed to be doing much the same as you. Consulting reference books. Analyzing photographs. Writing letters to dealers."

Mrs Foster's face turned pale.

"He never told me."

Raynes laughed.

"I must say he looked a little surprised when I walked in."

"How did you know where to find him?"

"Well, Madame Yolande told me that she had a shop in Cannes – as well as one in Paris. I thought the simplest thing to do was to follow Julius to Cannes and see where he worked. He has a very nice office."

Mrs Foster looked agitated.

"I thought I would find him busy writing his monograph. But no. Most of the stuff seemed to be about antiques. He probably helps you."

Amelie relaxed.

"He does."

Raynes nodded.

"I couldn't help noticing that most of the photographs seemed to have been taken in the Villa Rose. That little gold buddha. . . "

Mrs Foster again looked tense.

". . . Taken in conjunction with that list in your briefcase – the one with little ticks beside one hundred and sixty-seven items – I couldn't help thinking he might be pursuing a different agenda. You – working for Leonie; Julius perhaps working for the enemy?"

Mrs Foster did not move.

"I have nothing to say."

"Of course not. You wouldn't want to incriminate your husband. But Yolande seems to think the attack on the villa will be taking place this weekend. It seems very much as if Julius is arranging for the sale of Leonie's property. I did ask him; but he was too shocked to reply."

If Amelie could have run, she would have done. But, as always in such situations, the Inspector had placed himself between her and the door. It would not be easy to escape. She could throw her cup of coffee in his face which would give her a few seconds lead. But if she did run, where would she run to?

Raynes continued amiably:

"Now I am a little confused about all this. As I understood it, Bruno was supposed to be the person buying the stolen goods. He admitted this to me on Tuesday." (How long ago that seemed.) "He even paid Gaspard a substantial advance to help him in his preparations for the raid. Now it looks as if Bruno is not going to get any money. Julius will get it – plus of course a cut for yourself and Madame Yolande.

"I said to myself: 'Has there been a change of plan?' 'Is Gaspard now out of the picture?' According to that elegant lady in Cagnes, the raid was planned in her flat in Paris shortly after Gaspard came out of prison. I imagine you were there. It was Gaspard's idea. And I think that the plan was that you should provide the advance guard – to strike up a friendship with Leonie, to win her confidence and provide her with great

114

opportunities for extending her business – which you have done most effectively. Julius would of course be actively employed elsewhere.

"The plan worked very well until Gaspard appeared in Nice. He couldn't keep his mouth shut. He contacted all his old friends and told them what he wanted them to do. They would all get their cut. Very stupidly, he tried to contact Ludo – so Leonie knew what was coming. Which is why she invited me. . . " (It was a complete lie – but who cared?)

"Then, surprise. . . surprise! Gaspard went missing. For some of his gang, this was a great embarrassment. They don't know what to do. But Julius seems to be working very hard. Do I detect a rival campaign? Is Gaspard still going to make the attack – get caught – get the blame – whilst others steal the treasures? Is this to be an inside job?

"Has Gaspard been abandoned? Has Gaspard been murdered? Or is he being kept under wraps until the night of the raid when he and his troops smash into the Villa Rose to seize the loot – only to find it has gone? Bruno gets the blame? Julius gets the dosh? I would like to know."

Raynes paused.

He could see Amelie was thinking hard – trying to find a way out. He let her struggle for a few minutes; but then decided to help her.

"I told your husband that I would not say anything about this to Leonie – providing the raid does not take place. You would be able to continue your work here at the shop. . . and Julius continue his researches on Napoleon. But if there is a raid, all deals are off. The police will be told. And you will end up in jail." He looked at Amelie cautiously.

"Does that help?"

It did help – a lot.

Amelie visibly relaxed.

Unbelievably, there was a way out.

Raynes explained: "Leonie commissioned me to do one thing. To find Gaspard. That is all I am interested in doing. If you can help me find this creature, then you can breathe again.

I promise I will not reveal your secrets."

Raynes felt he could not be more generous to Amelie and her husband. They were both crooks. They deserved to be behind bars. Both of them should be booted out of the villa. But he had offered them a lifeline.

Amelie looked at him. Could he really be trusted? Would his deal stick? Was there any alternative? Nervously, she said: "It's not as straightforward as you think. We did meet Gaspard at Yolande's house in Paris after he came out of prison. He did tell us about the plan to rob Leonie. But it was not his idea. The idea came from Ludo. She had enjoyed the excitement of the life they had lived together. She wanted it to continue after he was released. She got the list of valuables from Leonie's safe. She marked them – the things that would be easy to sell. She gave the list to me.

"She told her mother that she had met me in Paris and that I had connections with an American magazine – which I do. She said I could help her. Leonie swallowed the bait and we came down here. Leonie was very kind. She put us up in her house. And everything was going according to plan.

"But as you say, Gaspard blew it. Ludo tried to control him, but he wouldn't shut up. He kept trying to see her. He sent her letters. He even went up to the house. He was a complete fool. She was infuriated. She knew he could spoil everything. In fact, she was all for calling it off.

"When she met Simon in England, she realized how much happier she could be with him. Gaspard had changed since he'd been in prison. She washed her hands of him.

"What could we do? The simplest answer was to let the raid go on – and let Gaspard take the blame. But then he suddenly vanished. Nobody knows what's happened to him. No one will say. We don't know whether he's dead or alive."

She looked at Raynes nervously.

"Julius and I decided to continue with the plan – for our own benefit; but Yolande is still hoping Gaspard will reappear."

She sighed.

"My own theory is that Ludo has killed him. But I've no proof. She's a ruthless person – just like her mother. She has no respect for the law. She does what she wants. Simon'll need to watch his step with her."

Amelie had told the Inspector all she knew. It was not a very pleasant story – but she hoped he would believe her. The very fact that she had revealed Ludo's part in the plan would discourage him from telling Leonie what he had discovered – and perhaps gain her and Julius a little more time.

She must speak to him and let him know which way the wind was blowing. If the Inspector was going to keep their secret, Julius would have to be careful what he said. Amelie also knew that if Ludo found out what she had told the Inspector, judgement would be swift and terrible. And what would happen if Gaspard still mounted his raid?

Raynes looked at Mrs Foster.

"Is that it?"

"It is."

"Tell me one thing. Where did that Braque come from? Was it really part of the junk in Leonie's warehouse?"

Amelie laughed – and was glad to be able to laugh.

"Oh, no! That was something she and Gaspard stole from an old lady in Paris. Yolande had been looking after it for them. It gave me . . . credibility."

"It certainly did – and £12,500!"

"It was worth it."

"But Leonie could find herself in the hot seat. Selling stolen property."

"I don't think the man on the yacht knew what he was buying. If it ever surfaces, I don't think he'll remember where he bought it."

"You could always blame Gaspard!"

"Everyone does!"

Raynes rose to his feet.

"Thank you for being so honest with me. Now let me be honest with you. Your husband has been phoning you all morning. You can understand why. I think you should phone

117

him back - but not from here. Walls have ears – and I think his language may be somewhat purple." He smiled. "See you at the cocktail party. Don't be late!"

22. *Un Chien Andalou*

Raynes left La Grotte de Seraphim before Leonie returned from her meeting with Maître Duclos. He left Amelie to face an agonizing phone call with her husband. His next port of call would be the photographer, Arnaud. He had already looked up his address in the local telephone directory and checked with Mrs May.

As the Inspector arrived, the latest clutch of nymphettes were being ushered out of the studio and Arnaud was in need of a cup of coffee and a strong cognac. As they ran down the stairs laughing and shouting, Raynes walked through the doorway. It was some moments before Arnaud realized he had a visitor.

"You must have a very entertaining life?"

"It's never boring."

The Inspector walked through to the office and settled himself on the large leather sofa. It felt pleasantly warm.

"Would you like a coffee?"

"Very much. And perhaps you could put up a 'Do not disturb' sign in case any more of your friends arrive."

"I'm not expecting anyone."

"Not even Mrs Foster?"

"No. She's . . ."

Arnaud stopped suddenly.

Raynes laughed.

" . . . busy having her picture painted? No, she's done that. But I think she'll be around later." He smiled at the photographer. "A good customer?"

"A very good customer."

Arnaud went off to make the coffee. As he threw back a quick glass of cognac, he wondered why the Inspector had called. Was it about his wife? Was he upset about her behaviour? Had he come to put his foot down? Or was he trying to find out where she was? He could tell him.

She was having a second session with Inspector Grimaldi. Whilst Mrs Grimaldi was away, her husband was having a whale of a time – and he was particularly enjoying this little blonde.

He came back with the tray of coffee.

"Was there something you wanted to see me about?"

"Yes," said Raynes. "Several things. First of all, I want to know who owns the flat in the Rue Sébastien?"

"I do."

"Do you live there?"

"No. I rent it out."

"Did you rent it to Gaspard?"

Arnaud hesitated.

"No. I let him have it free of charge."

"Feeling sorry for him?"

"Well, he'd just come out of prison."

"Is he an old friend of yours?"

"Not exactly a friend. But I have known him for several years. He needed somewhere to stay. The flat was empty . . ."

Arnaud shrugged his shoulders.

"What sort of person was he? Before he went to prison?"

"Noisy . . . boastful . . . A show-off. Loved doing outrageous things. He was great at a party. Drove a large car. A Mustang . . ."

"A con man?"

"He was always that."

"So you must have known his wife, Ludo?"

"Yes. She was quite a hell-raiser too." He smiled. "She's much more respectable these days."

Raynes nodded.

"But now he's vanished?"

"Yes."

"Left his suitcase in the flat?"

"Has he? I haven't been up there lately."

119

"Haven't you? You should go up some time. There's a nasty little rat storing stolen property in your front hall."

"That's Georges."

"He's also connected with Madame Yolande. I saw him at her shop in Cannes."

"He delivers things for people."

Raynes raised his eyebrows.

"Does he? Would he have been the person delivering Leonie's treasures to Monsieur Polanski?"

"Probably."

"You knew Gaspard's plans?"

"I was the person who warned Madame Leonie."

"Were you?"

No wonder Arnaud was on the side of the angels.

"Did you tell her he was living in your flat?"

"No."

"Why did you warn her?"

"Well, it seemed mean and nasty – taking all her things. I've known Ludo most of my life – and it's her home as well as her mother's. Gaspard had already stolen a few of her things – and got caught. He dragged Ludo into a life of crime. She almost ended up in jail. I thought it was better to nip his plans in the bud."

"Was Ludo one of your girlfriends?"

"Yes."

"And what did Leonie say when you told her?"

"I don't think she was surprised. She'd heard that he'd been let out of jail in December. I think she expected him to come back to Nice. I think she expected him to start pestering Ludo; but she was determined to resist him. She sent Ludo off to England to get her out of the way. I think she expected him to attack right away – but he didn't. He's given her plenty of time to prepare her defences."

"Were you part of the gang?"

"Certainly not."

"And what did Leonie ask you to do?"

"To find out where he was living. Who was working with

120

him. When they were planning their attack. And who was putting up the money."

"Monsieur Polanski."

"He never got over losing those Japanese minatures."

"And once she'd got that information, did she ask you to do anything else?"

The Inspector was treading on delicate ground. Very delicate ground. He stared fixedly at Arnaud. Would he admit it? He decided to give him a helping hand. "I know what she asked."

Although it was purely guesswork on Raynes' part, Arnaud assumed that Leonie must have told him. He relaxed.

"She asked me to find someone to kill him?"

Raynes nodded.

It was just as he had thought. Leonie had hedged her bets. She had given Arnaud the same commission she had given him.

"How long ago did she ask you?"

"About two weeks ago."

"And how much did she offer you?"

"Half a million."

And he had been offered a million. Leonie must have been getting desperate.

"Did you ask anyone?"

"No."

Raynes immediately detected a lie.

"That's not true!"

"Well, I'm not answering that! You wouldn't expect me to admit it."

"You approached Georges?"

"I didn't approach anyone to start with. It was all a bit difficult. Gaspard was occupying my flat. I knew exactly where he was. But Georges was part of the gang.

If Gaspard had known that I had told Leonie what he was up to, he might have killed me. I just kept passing the information back. But Gaspard was beginning to annoy people. He talked too much. He was always boasting what he

121

was going to do with the money. I warned Georges that Leonie knew what was happening – and that she had offered 500,000 francs to anyone who bumped him off. He didn't say anything . . . but I think he got the point."

"And Gaspard vanished last week?"

"Yes."

"And Georges uses that flat?"

"Yes."

"Do you think Georges did it?"

"I don't know. He stood to get some money out of the attack. He gets nothing if Gaspard's dead."

"So what are you doing now?"

"I'm keeping my head down."

"Are you?"

Raynes smiled one of his dangerous smiles.

"You've been doing all these photographs for Mrs Foster. Haven't you noticed that some of them are of items in Leonie's house? There are certainly things from the shop – but you must have seen the little gold buddha. Leonie isn't selling that . . ." He paused. "But perhaps Mrs Foster is?"

Arnaud seemed to have lost his powers of speech.

Raynes decided to twist the knife a little further.

"I don't think any friend of Leonie's would agree to printing pictures of her private treasures, knowing that they would be used by her enemies. Madame Yolande is no friend of Leonie. She's in this for what she can get out of it – and so is Mrs Foster. Gaspard may have set the wheels in motion, but other people have taken over. There's still going to be a heist and you've been helping the people directly involved. You can't deny that."

Arnaud looked very white.

Raynes nodded.

"You were involved – up to the hilt. I've seen all these photographs in Mr Foster's office in Cannes. Napoleon is the cover story – but Leonie's treasures are the real meat. What would Leonie say if she knew about that?"

Arnaud decided to remain silent.

This man was dangerous. He knew far too much. If anyone deserved to be bumped off, it was him. But Arnaud was too much of a coward to do it.

There was a long, unhelpful silence.

"You may like to know," said Raynes, "that Madame Leonie offered me the same commission that she offered you. She asked me to kill Gaspard. She also offered me money. But I haven't been able to find the man. I think he's already dead. Perhaps you could tell me?"

"I don't know."

"Well, that's a step in the right direction. But if he has been murdered, the police are going to be crawling all over this place in the very near future. They will find out who owns the flat in the Rue Sébastien and they'll be on your doorstep within twenty-four hours. I'm warning you, if you know where Gaspard is, you must tell me."

"I really don't know."

But he was sweating.

Raynes decided to offer Arnaud the same olive branch he had offered Amelie and her husband. Silence in exchange for his co-operation.

"I'm only interested in finding this man and preventing a raid on the Villa Rose. I will say nothing to Leonie about the photographs. I will say nothing about Mr and Mrs Foster and what they've been planning. All three of you have a chance to get out of this. But if Gaspard is not found – and the raid takes place – you will all be in the front line and will be arrested."

Raynes looked at the young man.

"It's over. Accept it. You and Leonie – and Ludo – can remain good friends. I'm sure Georges knows where Gaspard is. Offer him the money – and let's get it over and done with."

Arnaud relaxed a little.

"I can honestly tell you I don't know where Gaspard is. I don't know where Georges is living at this moment; but I could leave a message at the flat." He looked at the Inspector.

"I did wonder whether Amelie had got rid of him. She was sure he'd let them down. Since Gaspard has disappeared, everything's worked so much better."

Raynes smiled again.

"You can always say you acted in good faith. You thought that Leonie had wanted you to take the pictures of her treasures. You trusted Mrs Foster. You had no idea she was part of the opposition. You thought she was Leonie's friend. A perfect alibi?"

Arnaud cheered up.

All was not lost.

Raynes gave him a final mischievous look.

"Is Mrs Raynes still paying you your 10%?"

"She's not your wife. She told me."

The Inspector sighed.

"No, she's not. She's too damned successful in her own right. I just hope she's playing you fair?"

"It's been quite profitable so far." He looked at Raynes. "Did you know she's seeing a French policeman this afternoon?"

"I know exactly where she is. I also know that she's asking him to find out where Gaspard is. I think that by tomorrow, the French police may be joining in the search. Exciting, isn't it?"

Before Arnaud could express an opinion, there was a frantic banging on the studio door. Both men jumped.

"A desperate customer," said Raynes. "And I think I know who it is."

"Amelie?"

"Yes. She's truly desperate. But I think you'll both be safe if you take my advice."

The hammering continued.

Arnaud opened the door.

"You've no idea! That bloody policeman . . ."

She caught sight of Raynes.

He smiled.

"Just going. I'm sure you'll have a lot to talk about."

* * * *

Raynes left the studio as quickly as possible. He had had a long and eventful day. It was time to go home and see how the ungodly would react. If they took his advice, all would be well. But they might decide that he was now a more dangerous person than Gaspard. He might get a knife in his back.

He had no intention of doing any more walking. He hailed a passing taxi. It took only ten minutes to return to the Villa Rose.

As they came round the final bend, he saw a white van standing in the courtyard. It was the same white van that he had seen outside the shop in Cannes. Presumably, Georges was driving it. What was he delivering? More stolen property?

Raynes paid off the taxi driver and walked round the side of the garage. Within a few minutes, he heard the engine of the van starting up. He looked cautiously round the corner of the building. Yes, it was Georges at the wheel.

He waited till the van had gone, then he strolled casually across the courtyard and into the main hallway. Instinctively, he checked to see whether Leonie's treasures were still intact. He was glad to see the small gold buddha had not moved.

Sylvie came out of the small lounge.

"You have returned. Monsieur?"

"Yes, I've had a busy day."

"You have also visited Madame's boutique?"

It was amazing how news travelled.

"It was beautiful. I loved the clocks."

"Did you buy one?"

"No." He smiled. "I was spoilt for choice."

She didn't understand what he meant.

"There were so many. I couldn't decide which one I liked the most."

Sylvie laughed.

"I am sure Madame Raynes would like a beautiful clock for her home."

Raynes had a vision of Mrs May's tiny flat containing a gigantic Louis XIV monstrosity, richly decorated in ormolu, with gilt cherubs.

"Well, if she wants one, she can pay for it herself! She earns more than I do." He paused. "By the way, what was that van doing?"

"It is the delivery man from Cannes. Mr Foster has missed his train. The man has brought him home."

It was as good an excuse as any.

23. *Faut-il Brûler de Sade?*

The French inspector was disappointed. He had expected Gaspard to be an easy catch. But all his enquiries had drawn a blank. The Sûreté were sure he was still in Nice.

Gaspard's friends – and there were still a few of them about – they were equally certain he was still in Nice.

It was reported that he was planning a raid on a rich villa. He was said to have gathered a small team of 'experts' to do the job. But they were now becoming concerned as to his whereabouts. They had even contacted their friends in the police to see if they knew where he was.

So Gaspard was lying low. Understandable, if he was planning a big job. The inspector wondered whether their concern about his disappearance was a smokescreen to put the police off the scent. Whilst they were hunting for the missing man, the heist would be accomplished. Inspector Grimaldi was determined not to be duped.

It did not take him long to discover the object of the raid. The Villa Rose. The home of Gaspard's former mother-in-law. An obvious target. A rich woman whose house was reported to be a treasure trove of rare goods. It could of course be her shop which was being targeted; but he felt sure the house would be the stronger attraction.

And when was the raid likely to take place? His information suggested that very weekend – Saturday or Sunday. Monday at the latest.

He felt very grateful to the English cocotte for raising the matter with him. Thanks to her, he was now prepared and ready to catch the thieves. He would let them get into the villa – and then pounce. He arranged for a couple of plain-clothes men to be stationed each night in the approaches to the villa.

He assumed that the telephone lines would be cut. He assumed that they would use a van to carry the treasures away. He assumed that they would use the main drive. But, just in case, there would be other men hidden in the trees and bushes surrounding the villa from late Friday night until Tuesday morning.

It occurred to him that Gaspard might already be hiding in the villa. He might have an accomplice. Surely he must have an accomplice; someone who knew the security code for the alarm. Perhaps he would attack his mother-in-law and her staff – tie them up; lock them in a cellar – before he started clearing the house?

Inspector Grimaldi was a very fine policeman – especially in his own estimation. He attributed his success to his aristocratic background. To superior brains. He felt that with a name like Grimaldi, he could hardly fail.

His ancestors had been magnates and princes of the purest blood – blue if not slightly purple. He considered it a matter of pride that he even shared their vices.

Sadly, he recognized that he did not belong to that branch of the family which had once occupied the little castle in Cagnes. Some of his forbears must have married beneath them – as he had done himself. He had nothing against his wife – she was a good woman and had been an excellent mother to their children – but there was no doubt she was of peasant stock.

Thank heaven, she was still away!

He left the office shortly after noon – having given all the necessary instructions. He looked forward to his second afternoon with the young woman whom he knew as "Julie".

He wondered how she had come to know his name. She told him it was through a person called Arnaud. He could not think of anyone called 'Arnaud' except for that photographer who had taken his grandchildren's photographs the previous

Christmas. What could he know about his private life – his hidden desires?

Certainly, "Julie" had given him all he wanted – all he needed. And today, he could enjoy a little more forbidden fruit. She had not been in a rush. She had not been greedy. If she had lived in Nice, he would have made a point of visiting her regularly. But she had said that she was on holiday – trying to put out of her mind a tragic divorce.

He had no sooner returned to his flat than the bell rang. Punctual too!

He felt he could trust "Julie". She seemed to enjoy her work and, as he had hoped, she charged him a little less on this second visit. (He was not to know that Arnaud would not be getting his 10% commission on this one.) She appeared to enjoy all the forbidden pleasures he had been carefully planning for her. She didn't say "No" to anything. They might have had a certain novelty to him but Mrs May had done it all before – many times – and she was able to spice the experience with many little extras which had never penetrated the Inspector's aristocratic mind.

He was duly grateful and, when asked about Gaspard, he was able to give her a full account of what he had done.

Debbie was a little disappointed.

Despite all the resources of the city's police department, he had drawn a blank. Not only could he not find the wretched man, but he had also raised the alarming possibility that Gaspard might already be hiding in the Villa!

Debbie was sure that with all the servants constantly going about their duties, he could hardly avoid being seen. But suppose one of the chambermaids – Céléstine immediately came to mind – was hiding him in her room – and feeding him?

Perhaps he had formed some association with her whilst he was living in the villa and had now offered her a share of the proceeds? The French inspector clearly thought so.

And what about Ernst? He looked like a crook. He could easily be involved. Strong and silent, he would say nothing.

He could have hidden Gaspard in one of the attics or outhouses. They would be a terrifying combination. She wondered if Richard had considered this possibility? Of course he would. He was much brighter than this Gallic Mr Plod. She corrected herself. Monsieur Plod!

She wondered if she might be invited back a third time? Clearly, they had exhausted most of Grimaldi's wildest fantasies. But no doubt he would be happy to try them again. He was fairly harmless.

She looked at him.

He was still in highest heaven. It seemed a shame to bring him down to earth.

"When did you say your wife was coming back?"

The inspector was not aware that he had told her; but it seemed a fair question.

"On Monday night."

Debbie smiled.

"We could always squeeze in one more."

"On Sunday?"

"I'm not doing anything."

But perhaps he was? Perhaps by that time, he would have captured the elusive Gaspard. There would be another triumph to celebrate. Sunday seemed a good day to do it.

He smiled.

"We could open a bottle of champagne . . ."

" . . . and celebrate Madame's return?"

"Ah, non! Malheureusement, non!" The inspector laughed.

"No. I was thinking that, by Sunday, we may have found Gaspard. I am planning to search all the places where Gaspard has been. Every house, every flat, every job, every contact. We shall search the properties from top to bottom – including the Villa Rose. I have no doubt we shall find him."

* * * *

This seemed eminently sensible to Debbie. It would eliminate any threat of a raid. Even if they did not catch him, it would disrupt their plans. For if someone like Ernst – or Céléstine – was involved in the plot, they would be frightened off. In fact, such thoroughness was to be welcomed.

So Debbie did not hurry home. There were three more appointments she had arranged. Another of them was a 'repeat visit'. So Arnaud would again miss out on his cut.

Feeling somewhat 'shop-soiled', Mrs May plunged into the shower and drenched herself in expensive shower gel, generating vast quantities of white foam. Whilst sponging herself down, she told Richard her news.

He seemed very pleased.

The police were now taking the raid seriously. Their informants had confirmed that a raid was being planned. The ringleader and his associates had been identified. And the whole of the French police force were on the look-out for Gaspard. Better a full-scale search than a brutal attack which might leave someone dead. "When were they thinking of doing the search?"

"Between now and Sunday."

Raynes realized that Leonie would not be happy having gendarmes crawling through every corner of her house. In fact, she would hate it. Her wardrobes. Her boudoir. Her clothes. Everything being examined. It could be very humiliating. He must warn her.

Debbie stepped out of the shower.

"When?"

"Tonight. Before dinner."

"Well, let me get a gin and tonic before she throws me out."

Raynes looked concerned.

"I'm not going to mention your name. I shall just say that one of my contacts has informed me. A high-level contact!" He smiled.

Debbie laughed.

"Seemed pretty low-level to me!"

"She won't know."

"Well, in that case, perhaps she should reward this high-level contact for her services?"

"Perhaps? Who knows?"

"All contributions gratefully receivedl" Debbie finished towelling down her body. "The Chanel!" she said imperiously.

"Gives me confidence. Covers up the smell of corruption!"

Raynes was feeling very indulgent towards his friend. It had been her idea to quiz the French inspector – and it had worked. She had been loyally pumping him for information whilst he had been pumping Sylvie . . . He could not deny that he felt a slight scintilla of guilt. She had been totally honest with him about what she had been doing, but he would not tell her about his Norman conquest.

Of course he felt guilty!

But back to business . . .

"You'll have to be careful," he said, "when this French chap comes to search the house. He'll recognize you immediately. Even if you've got your clothes on!"

There was a twinkle in Debbie's eyes.

"I've already thought of that. I shall tell him that I am an undercover member of the Special Branch!"

"Perhaps he'll demand his money back?"

"Fat chance!"

Debbie returned to the bedroom.

"My blue dress. My silver necklace. And plenty of diamonds! That'll shut them up!"

"Whilst I break the bad news to the Grand Duchess?"

"She should be grateful. The things I do for England!"

24. *Le Petit Prince*

It was the beginning of another beautiful day.

A faint mist lay over Mount Boron but it would soon clear. The birds – like the aeroplanes – had begun to flex their wings; but not yet to fly. The trees were still. Utterly still. There was no breeze. The grass had received its full quota of dew; there was still a dampness on the stone balustrade and the patio slabs. In a couple of hours, the Villa Rose would come to life. But, this morning, Signor Spumante would not be the first in the pool.

The body lay solidly – but peacefully – in the right hand corner of the pool. It would perhaps have been more picturesque if it had floated out to the middle of the pool and stayed there. But it had gone as far as it was going; and it lay naked, pinky-grey, with a mop of dark brown hair, face down – as if exploring the watery depths and searching for the meaning of life.

The body was dead. Dead as it could be. And it floated happily on the surface. It was not waterlogged. The lungs were still full of air and the body was filled with other things which gave it a certain buoyancy. In fact, it seemed to be enjoying the beauty of a May morning as much as anyone else.

The body was male. And it had a name: Gaspard. It had a history; but not perhaps as long a history as its owner would have wished. It had first seen the light of day in August 1952. In Marseilles. His arrival had given great pleasure to his parents and all their friends. For he was their first child – and he was a boy, which is always a great cause of satisfaction.

He was called Gaspard after his grandfather who, it was hoped, would leave a substantial legacy to his family when he passed away. But Grandfather de la Nuit had lived to the ripe old age of ninety-six and by the time he reached that age, his resources – like his body – were totally exhausted.

However, in his lifetime, he had been a generous man. Especially generous to his grandson. In fact, he had completely spoilt him. Young Gaspard had grown up with plenty of spare cash and the assurance that, if he needed more, it would always be forthcoming. He was not particularly successful at school – although he tried hard. We must give him that. He was not university material but he was well-schooled in what is normally called "the university of life".

What this meant was that he had charm in great abundance, a ready wit, a sharp mind and a capacity to charm birds off any neighbouring tree. He also had an ability to get himself out of any awkward corner. In fact, he was ably equipped to become a very succssful con man. And that is what he became.

He was lucky. Yes, he was very lucky. From the moment he left school, which was in 1969, till March 1986, he never had any difficulty in obtaining money. True, his manner of acquiring it was unorthodox – criminal, one might say. But he never lacked food, shelter, a car, a woman or all the other material pleasures life could bring.

Women were one of his most satisfying discoveries.

He had been a little slow in appreciating their value but he made up for lost time. A cousin, on the rebound, had shown him the ropes – in quite amazing detail – and thus he was fully prepared for seduction – financial as well as sexual; though he usually kept the two strictly apart. The women he extracted money from were not usually the sort of women he wanted to bed; whereas those he wished to penetrate were normally cheap and cheerful.

But there comes a time in the life of every Don Juan, when he wants to settle down; to be respectable; to be the husband of one wife; to live out his days in prosperity and peace. The time for sowing one's wild oats is over; the time for being a landowner in his own right has come.

For Gaspard, that moment came in November 1984 – in Grenoble – not a place he would have expected. He was in Grenoble, engaged in some profitable scam, but he was feeling bored. He went to a party in the university, hoping to pick up some complaisant chick; but there he met the captivating Ludo – tall, elegant, sexy and – he soon discovered – immensely rich.

He persuaded her that there was more fun to be had from life than from a philosophy course at university. They could live a life of perpetual pleasure. At that time, he had a Ford Mustang (which was later recovered by the hire purchase company) and this had already proved a very compelling passport to the world of the idle rich.

Ludo had seemed like a meal ticket for life. And when he saw her mother's home – and all her treasures, his eyes almost popped out of his head. This was indeed Shangri-la – heavenly joys for evermore.

Unfortunately, at this moment, his luck deserted him. The bird who needed to be charmed off the tree refused to budge. She herself was stubborn and wilful and also highly experienced in the 'university of life'. Which meant that she could recognize a con man at more than five hundred yards and she was not convinced – not for one minute – that Gaspard was an ideal catch for her daughter. In fact, he was quite the opposite.

So she turned off the gas, put on the brakes and brought all his hopes and dreams to a grinding halt. There was no shifting her. Even running away with her daughter, marrying her and coming back to Nice as a happily married couple had not swayed her one inch. Instead, she had tightened the noose round his financial neck even more tightly. So he was obliged to return to his former way of life – which was not what he had wanted.

His heart was not in it; but Ludo had proved a very willing partner. She had enjoyed the risk. But perhaps they had been too greedy? A scam too far? Suddenly, one afternoon, they had found themselves surrounded by gendarmes bearing handcuffs. A trial had followed and jail for three ghastly years.

Ludo's mother had, of course, bailed out her daughter. She had done nothing for him. She had persuaded Ludo to divorce him whilst he was behind bars. She had never visited him – not once. When he came out of prison, he was penniless, almost friendless and thirsting for revenge. Various alternatives had suggested themselves – theft, kidnapping, murder – possibly all three. He had come to Nice prepared for action. He had laid his plans. But fate had once again intervened – how, he did not know.

So the story of Gaspard had come to a sudden, tragic end. At the age of thirty-eight, some unknown hand had struck him down, thrown him into this swimming pool and left him to be found by the people he hated most – les flics.

They would not respect his body nor cherish his memory.

He would be lifted out of the water, wrapped in a body bag, tossed on to a slab, slit open from neck to groin, have part of his skull out off, his innards pulled out and inspected.

A pathetic end for one with such high hopes. One with so many romantic dreams. How had it come to this?

Surrounded by the peaceful beauty of the Villa Rose, with its flowers, trees, lawns and gently lapping water, he awaited his fate. It would probably be another two hours before his body was discovered and, soon after, he would leave Shangrila for ever.

25. *Corps Un-diplomatique*

Camille Calvoressco donned his trunks for his daily swim. He loved getting up at this early hour and plunging into the cool waters of the pool before everyone else. It was a custom he had adopted from his earliest days at the Villa Rose. Even when it was raining, he was not deterred.

There was something cleansing about this early morning ritual It proved that he was still fit and able to cover a kilometre almost as quickly as he had when he was a student. He felt a certain pride – a superiority over those lesser mortals who were still tucked up in their beds. But he was here at 7.00am on the dot ready to do his twenty lengths. After that, he would have a hot shower, shave and dress, read the paper and drink two cups of milky coffee. That was his daily routine and he seldom departed from it.

Camille never noticed that he had company that morning. He was busy thinking about Brackles and that picture. He was sure the wretched man was going slower and slower, prolonging the job and so spending more time with Madame. He couldn't bear his being there. He couldn't bear her laughter, her pleasure at the way her painting was coming along, her compliments – and, above all, the money Brackles would receive when his commission was completed. It made him sick as a parrot. The man was a total charlatan. It was a wonder Madame had not seen through him before now.

He flung down his towel, took off his trainers and dived neatly into the water at the far end of the pool. Hell, it was cold this morning. Quite biting, in fact. Perhaps there had been a sharp frost overnight. It was not unknown. As usual, he began with a fast crawl – five lengths to get himself going. But at the end of the first length, he suddenly became conscious of the body, lying sluggishly in the water, about four feet out from the side of the pool.

He stopped swimming – and stared at it. Sadly, it was not Brackles or any of his friends. He would have greeted such a sight with pleasure; but this was a stranger. It was difficult to tell who it was when you couldn't see their face.

But the man had a tattoo on his arm. Camille felt that he would have recognized him if he had seen him before. But the man was obviously dead and the water seemed to be getting colder. Now he knew what was meant by 'the chill of death'.

He climbed out of the pool and padded into the house. It was much warmer indoors.

"Sylvie!" he called.

She was probably in the kitchen.

"Sylvie!"

Ah! There she was.

She looked at Camille in his dripping blue trunks. Not a pretty sight. He looked like a fish out of water – and a scrawny fish at that.

"Monsieur?"

"There's a body in the pool. A dead body. Madame must be told immediately."

Sylvie looked surprised.

"Madame has not yet had her breakfast."

"You must wake her up. The police must be told. Get on with it, woman!"

Sylvie raised her eyebrows. She was not used to being ordered about in that tone of voice.

Camille felt that she did not seem to be taking in the seriousness of the matter. In fact, she was wondering whether

136

Signor Spumante (even she called him that now) was indulging in fantasy.

"In the pool?"

"Oh, come and see."

So she followed him out on to the patio.

"Oh, là, là! The poor man. . . It is a man?"

"Yes, of course it's a man. Look at his buttocks!"

Sylvie looked at the buttocks, the hairy legs and the dark head of hair.

"I will go and tell Madame."

She left Camille out on the patio still staring at the corpse.

"Damned inconvenient! Dying in her pool!"

He could imagine all the disturbance that would be caused by the arrival of the police. And the Press. The questions. The photographs. The scandal. Oh, it was going to be a dreadful morning. It would be much better if he were out of it. He would have his breakfast and go.

He walked back to the other end of the pool, gave himself a rub down with his towel and put on his trainers. Then back indoors for a hot shower.

* * * *

Sylvie knocked at Madame Leonie's bedroom door.

"Entrez."

Leonie was already awake – and at her dressing table. She must be wondering why the maid had not yet brought up her breakfast.

"Madame, there is a problem. Monsieur Camille has found a body in the pool."

"A body? Is it one of our guests?"

"No, Madame." Sylvie shook her head. "It is a young man. He has no clothes on."

Leonie looked out of the window deep in thought.

"Ask Monsieur Raynes to look at the body. He will know what to do."

"Madame."

"Is Célestine not on her way with my coffee?"

"She is here, Madame."

Sylvie left the room as Célestine arrived with the coffee.

* * * *

Sylvie knocked on the door of *Les Petits Cygnes*. It seemed that the *petits cygnes* were still fast asleep. In fact, Richard was dreaming that he had been left on a deserted country road. Carlisle had gone back to his house for lunch. And yet he knew that he was desperately needed in Grasshallows. There had been an accident – and he was helpless, miles away.

He was therefore glad to be wakened from his dream.

He was equally glad to see Sylvie's large grey eyes looking down at him. He felt sudden joy – then guilt, realizing where he was and that Debbie was in bed beside him.

"Monsieur, I am sorry to trouble you and Madame, but there is a serious problem downstairs. There is a dead man in the swimming pool."

"Oh, God!" moaned Debbie and sank deeper down the bed. It was just as she had predicted.

"It's not Signor Spumante, is it?" Raynes asked hopefully.

"No." Sylvie laughed. "It was Monsieur Camille who found the body. He is much distressed."

Raynes was about to throw back the covers – but then remembered that he was naked. Debbie might wonder why he was exposing himself so willingly in front of the housekeeper.

"I will be down in two minutes."

"C'est bien."

* * * *

Raynes pulled on his shirt and shorts and strapped on his sandals. He looked at his hair in the mirror and gave it a quick brush.

"Back in a few minutes," he said reassuringly.

"Pull the other one," said a muffled voice from under the

sheets.

Raynes came down the stairs feeling quite excited. This was a busman's honeymoon. All he needed to make his holiday a complete success. Sylvie was waiting for him in the main hallway.

Céléstine was passing by.

"Make sure Monsieur Camille gets his coffee. A jug."

"Life goes on," observed Raynes. "Have the police been informed?"

"No, Monsieur. Madame wished that you should look at the body first. She said you would know what to do."

Well, obviously, the police should have been called immediately – but he could not resist the opportunity of giving the corpse a once-over.

Sylvie led the way on to the patio.

"Voilà!"

Raynes took in the immediate details at a glance.

Male, thirty to forty years old; no clothes; no visible signs of injury; a tattoo on his left arm; dark hair; probably of Mediterranean appearance if one could see his face.

He asked Sylvie: "Have you got a long pole?"

"A mop?"

"That'll do."

He would bring the body close to the edge of the pool. He could always push it out again.

Sylvie returned with a mop.

Raynes used the handle to steer the body gently towards him. He reached into the water to try and see whether he was wearing a watch. Did he have a wedding ring or any other personal jewellery?

His first impression – and it hit him immediately – was that the body was exceptionally cold. And the water round the body was also extremely cold. But he showed no reaction – and said nothing.

There was no watch – so no indication of the time of death. There were no rings of any sort – and no sign that the man had been in the habit of wearing one.

Raynes looked at the tattoo. An eagle.

He looked at Sylvie.

"Have you seen this before?"

"Yes, Monsieur."

"You know who it is?"

"I do now. It is Mademoiselle's husband."

"Yes, it is Gaspard," said Raynes. "Someone has dumped him in Madame's swimming pool. Very unfeeling of them!"

He grabbed a handful of the victim's hair and jerked the head up and out of the water.

No rigor mortis – but a slight crunching sound.

Broken bones?

As the head came up, he looked at the face of the man he had been hunting for the past three days. There was no sign of facial injury. No marks of a rope around his neck. No evidence of blood floating in the water. The most likely cause of death was drowning. And yet. . .

Raynes walked along the patio, looking to see if there was any other evidence in the pool. A wallet, coins, items of clothing. But there was nothing.

He looked over the balustrade to see if anyone had thrown the victim's clothes over the edge. Had they landed on the bushes down below? Again nothing.

Sylvie walked beside him.

"I don't suppose anyone'll be all that upset," said Raynes. "No one seemed to like him."

"Mademoiselle liked him. She will be *triste*."

"I suppose so."

They walked back to the body. Raynes used the handle of the mop to push the body further out into the pool.

"Is that how it was when you first saw it?"

"Monsieur Camille was the first to see it. He would be able to tell you."

Raynes continued to look at the water.

"Is it always as cold as this in the morning?"

"C'est encore mai."

Raynes looked uncomprehending.

140

"It is still May. Mount Boron is a mountain. And you have the hills." She pointed to the grey range of cliffs which plunge sharply down to the sea between Nice and Menton.

"Feel it. It seems extremely cold to me."

Sylvie put her hand in the water.

"I should not want to swim in that."

"Neither should I."

Raynes ran his mind over the picture which had emerged.

"Interesting," he said.

But Sylvie's mind was now on other things.

"Shall I tell Madame?"

Raynes came back to earth.

"Yes, of course. Tell her who we think it is. Then it will be for her to call the police."

"And you would like le petit déjeuner?"

"Yes, I'm ready for breakfast."

"And Monsieur would like an omelette?"

"Perfect!" said Raynes.

* * * *

"Madame, Monsieur Richard has examined the body."

"And what does he say?"

"That it is Gaspard."

Leonie sighed.

"I thought so. His enemies have killed him and brought his body up here – to put the blame on us. It is most unfair." She looked visibly distressed. "Has he been stabbed – or strangled? Is there blood?"

"There is no blood, Madame. Monsieur Richard says there are no marks on the body. It seems that he has been drowned."

"In my pool. Quel outrage!"

Leonie's face looked grim.

"Monsieur Richard thinks you should now call the police."

"Of course. And what will you be doing?"

"I shall be making Monsieur Richard's breakfast."

Leonie smiled indulgently.

"He is a good man. At least he will no longer have to search for Gaspard. The search is over." She sighed.

"But now I have one most unpleasant duty. I must tell Mademoiselle. I fear she will be much distressed."

* * * *

Raynes went back upstairs to get a pullover. He felt quite cold. As he walked into their bedroom, Debbie was stretching and yawning.

"Don't tell me!" she said. "It's Gaspard."

Raynes was surprised.

"How did you know that? You haven't seen the body."

"I've been expecting it. Even before we set off on holiday, I knew someone would bump him off. Why they have to do it whilst we are here, I don't know. But I wish they could have waited another week."

She climbed out of bed.

"Now, of course, you're in your element. The police will be around here in droves. You'll be telling them your theories. You'll be wanting to read their reports. You'll want to be in at the kill. You probably already know who the murderer is."

Raynes shook his head.

"I don't know." He paused. "He had quite a few enemies."

"Especially in this house!"

"Yes."

He looked at her. She was quite right. Gaspard's greatest enemy was the lady of the house.

There was the sound of a car door slamming and an engine revving up in the courtyard. Both of them rushed to the window to see who it was. An Alfa Romeo accelerated down the drive.

"Signor Spumante's making a quick getaway."

"I'm sure he has something to hide."

"I don't think he knew him."

Mrs May was resplendent in her nakedness. She looked at Richard.

"Do you want a quickie?"

"Sylvie's making me an omelette."

Debbie looked surprised.

He had never refused before.

"Lucky her!" she said.

* * * *

Ludo was deeply upset.

When her mother told her that Gaspard had died, she wept bitterly. Neither her mother nor Simon could comfort her. Her body heaved with sorrow – and she didn't stop crying for almost two hours. In fact, she kept weeping – on and off – for the rest of the day.

She insisted on seeing the body – which made it worse. First of all, she denied that it was him; but when she was shown the tattoo, she howled.

It didn't help for Simon to be told that Gaspard was the only man she had ever loved. She hadn't seen him for nearly four years. She had never visited him in prison. She had deserted him. If she had stayed with him, he would never have died.

Her mother was infuriated by her reaction.

"He was a complete crook! He led you into a life of crime."

"I could have changed him!"

"No, you couldn't."

"You forced me to divorce him!"

"You agreed."

Simon wisely said nothing.

Ludo declared that she could not face the police. All their questions. They would bully her, just as they had done the last time. She begged her mother not to phone the police till she and Simon had left the house.

"You'll have to face them at some point."

But she promised to give her daughter two hours. She herself was beginning to wonder what it would be like to have gendarmes everywhere – in the house, in the garden. They would probably steal some of her prize possessions.

"I shall not phone them till 10.00am," she said.

* * * *

Whilst all this high drama was taking place, Richard sat placidly eating his omelette and his two croissants. He sipped at his first black coffee of the day.

He was joined by Brackles who managed to display an Olympian detachment.

"Killed the wrong man!" he said. "They should have killed Spumante. He spends enough time in the swimming pool as it is. It'd be the ideal way for him to go."

"He's already gone."

"Gone?"

"Yes, Scarpered off in his Alfa Romeo half an hour ago."

"How very suspicious."

"I thought so."

Debbie came downstairs and had a cup of milky coffee. She also had an omelette to see if it contained any hidden aphrodisiac which might have enticed the Inspector away from her.

She looked at Sylvie with some suspicion – although she had no evidence whatsoever. It was a woman's gut instinct. Sylvie had those large appealing eyes. That cute French accent. The long dark hair. That loose black dress. She could easily imagine the temptations that Richard had to endure.

Both women were perfectly polite to each other; no one would have detected the slightest animosity between them. But each knew there was a secret battle going on for Monsieur Richard. Debbie was saying: "He's mine!" Sylvie was saying: "Well, if he's yours, why not hang on to him? Why d'you go off and leave him? Why do you need to shag every rich pervert on the Côte d'Azur?"

Richard remained in blissful ignorance of the storm which was blasting around him.

"Another café, Monsieur?"

"Thank you, Sylvie. I should love another."

Mrs May could have killed him!

26. *Les Flics*

By the time the police arrived, most of Leonie's guests had decided to leave the house. Mr Foster, quite unaware of the discovery of the body, departed for Cannes and his wife to the boutique. She had tried to persuade Brackles to join her for another session at the Rue Sébastien but, in the face of adversity, he had decided that his place was at Leonie's side – the more so since Spumante had been the first to rat.

Ludo was ordered to take Simon to see the beautiful mansion of Baroness Ephrussi de Rothschild on the Cap Ferrat. By the time they had walked round the gardens and admired the fine views over Villefranche, Leonie hoped she would have recovered her 'equilibre'. Debbie, of course, could not let murder interfere with business. She also decided that Richard would spend more time watching the police than pursuing the housekeeper. (She still thought it was pursuit.)

Ernst had also vanished. This was on Sylvie's advice. The silent, enigmatic German had a formidable police record. It would be better if his face was not seen. He would have a quiet day in Vence. If he felt any sense of penitence or remorse for his past sins, he could visit the chapel decorated by Matisse. More likely, he would drink unlimited quantities of schnapps and come home blind drunk. By that time, Sylvie hoped, the police would have done their business and the house would be returned to normal.

The first gendarmes appeared at about twenty past ten. They stood and stared at the corpse; then one of them went and phoned headquarters. Fifteen minutes later, a police photographer arrived, together with reinforcements to guard the pool until a senior officer arrived. This dignitary appeared at precisely eleven o'clock.

Debbie would have recognized him immediately. He introduced himself to Leonie.

"Inspector Grimaldi, Madame."

"I'm very glad you've arrived. Inspector. We've all been most distressed."

Monsieur Grimaldi looked at the corpse floating in the water in the bright sunlight.

"At what hour was the body discovered?"

"Oh, I don't know. About 9.00am. Perhaps a little earlier."

Sylvie, who was standing in the background, winced. It was a bad mistake to lie to the police. Once the truth was discovered, the French inspector would begin to wonder why she had lied. The rest of her evidence would then be questioned. It could only make things worse.

"And is this person one of your guests?"

"No."

"One of your staff?"

"No."

"Is he known to you?"

Leonie did not duck this one.

"One of my staff noticed the tattoo on his arm. They think he is a man called Gaspard."

"Gaspard de la Nuit?"

"That's right."

"Your son-in-law, Madame?"

"My ex-son-in-law. Are you familiar with his background?"

"I am."

Inspector Grimaldi stroked his moustache. At least the identity of the corpse had been established. But how did the man end up in the pool?

"Had Monsieur Gaspard been staying here at the Villa?"

"Certainly not!"

"He is no longer welcome at the house?"

"No."

"Why do you think he is in the pool?"

"I've no idea."

"You don't think he was exploring the house?"

"He knows the house extremely well."

"I think he once stole some of your property? The Japanese miniatures?"

The Inspector appeared to have a formidable memory. But since Debbie had spoken to him, he had read up the file on Gaspard and the facts were now fresh in his memory.

"That was four or five years ago."

"Do you think he was attempting to break in to the Villa?"

"There are no signs of a break-in. The alarms did not ring."

"Perhaps one of your staff may have found him lurking in the bushes?"

"If they had seen him, they would have told me."

"And drowned him?"

Leonie was scathing: "Do you really think that they would drown him here? In my own pool? What nonsense!"

Inspector Grimaldi pursued his point.

"You mean they'd have moved the body elsewhere?"

"Well, they certainly wouldn't have left it here! It would only cause me trouble, wouldn't it?"

The Inspector took a very dim view of her reply.

"Moving a body is a criminal offence, Madame."

"I'm perfectly aware of that."

Raynes did not know what was being said; but he was becoming increasingly impatient. He felt like shouting: "Why don't you go and look at the body before you start questioning the witnesses? See what the body tells you!"

Almost as if he had detected the Inspector's unspoken thoughts, Grimaldi gave Leonie a gracious bow.

"Thank you, Madame. I shall speak to you again later."

* * * *

The Inspector joined his men.

The body had been photographed in situ. It was now brought ashore for closer examination.

"The body is extremely cold."

147

Grimaldi touched the skin. It was solid. Frozen. He poked the body with his fingers. There was a slight movement in the outer surface, but underneath it was rock hard like a supermarket turkey.

And it was floating. If the man had drowned, his lungs would have filled with water. He would have sunk to the bottom. There must have been air in his lungs. Perhaps gas from the putrefaction of his body?

But there was no sign of the greenish discolouration which goes with putrefaction. The body was not swollen. The tissues were not grossly inflated.

Like Raynes, Grimaldi was surprised. He had thought it was a simple drowning – but it was not. The body had been frozen solid and then dumped in the pool. It would take at least forty-eight hours to defrost the body before the surgeon could perform the autopsy.

He looked at the tattoo on the stiff, unyielding arms. Yes, it was Gaspard all right. That was one of his distinguishing features.

The photographer continued his work. Grimaldi rose to his feet. "Inform the pathologist. We shall need his help."

He left his men whilst he walked the length of the pool Then, like Raynes, he looked over the balustrade to see if there was any sign of the man's clothes.

* * * *

Raynes could imagine the thoughts running through his mind. He was standing at the dining room window along with Leonie, Sylvie and Brackles. He turned to his hostess:

"I don't think Gaspard will be troubling you any more, Madame."

Leonie smiled.

"You have done extremely well, Monsieur Richard. You have committed the perfect crime. Just as I wished."

Sylvie chuckled.

"Are you putting the blame on me?"

"Why not? Do you not want to earn the million francs?"

Raynes looked at Brackles to see if he was taking it as a joke. Brackles laughed.

"It's the best offer you'll get! I'd take it, old boy!"

The Inspector looked at his hostess.

"I'm sorry to disappoint you, Madame, but seeing his body in the pool was as much a surprise to me as it was to Inspector Grimaldi."

"But you have been stirring up the scorpion's nest. All his evil comrades, they have been frightened for their skins. They have seen that their plot is discovered. That their attack will end in disaster. They do not want to face several months in prison. So they have killed him and put the blame on us. Casting his body into my pool! Quel outrage!"

Richard did not like to say that Gaspard's friends had not seen him for over a week. His disappearance had occurred long before he had ever set foot on French soil.

But it would certainly make his investigations that much easier. He was no longer dealing with a missing person. Now it was a straightforward murder inquiry. And thanks to his visits with Signor Spumante, he already had a clear list of suspects. Bruno, Pierre, Madame Yolande and her husband, the man in the flat in the Rue Sébastien. But he must not rule out the people nearer home: Mr and Mrs Foster, Arnaud, and even Ludo – daughter of the house. For all her tears, she could not be ruled out. She might be the chief beneficiary of Gaspard's death.

He was interrupted in his thoughts by the lady of the house.

"Sylvie, I shall have lunch in my room. Monsieur Brackles will continue his work on my painting. If the Inspector wishes to see me, I shall be there. If he prefers to speak to Monsieur Richard, I shall be content."

She beckoned to Brackles.

"Monsieur, we have work to do!"

She turned to Sylvie.

"The staff will bring the apéritifs."

27. *Boule de Suif*

Later that morning, Raynes was introduced to Grimaldi. It was amusing to think that he knew more about the French inspector than the man did about him. Debbie had described him most accurately and waxed poetic about all his vices. Fortunately, the man spoke English, so there was no problem in communication.

"I understand that you were the first to inspect the body?"

"Yes. But not the first to see him."

"And who was that?"

"A man called Camille Calvoressco . . ."

(Raynes was sure Leonie would have told him this.)

". . . He was taking his early morning swim."

"And what time was that?"

"He normally goes for a swim at 7.00am. He swims twenty lengths a day."

"A very active man?"

"Indeed. He is a friend of Madame Leonie."

"So I believe."

The Inspector stroked his moustache. It was one of his most irritating habits. Raynes noted that he had very white, delicate hands. It was intriguing to think of them being handcuffed to a brass bedstead.

"When this man had seen the body, what did he do?"

"He reported it to Sylvie – the housekeeper. She informed Madame and I was asked to go and look at the body."

"The police should have been informed immediately."

"I know. But Madame is very much mistress of her house."

"She is not above the law."

Raynes agreed.

"And what have you seen?"

"The same as you. The body floating in the water. . ."

He hoped Sylvie had said nothing about moving the corpse nearer to the edge of the pool.

"And what was your first impression?"

"That it was not a drowning. The body was icy cold to the touch."

"You touched it?"

"I'm afraid so."

Grimaldi's eyes narrowed.

"This is not your jurisdiction. You had no right to interfere. If I was to do this to a case of yours in England, you would not approve."

Raynes had been hoping that he could speak man-to-man with Grimaldi and perhaps help him in his investigation; but this man had no intention of sharing the limelight. To him, Raynes was not a colleague – but a suspect.

"Have you told anyone. . . ?"

". . . about the coldness of the body? No."

"That it was not a drowning?"

"I have kept my opinions to myself."

"I would be glad if you would continue to do so." He paused and stroked his moustache again. "Madame Leonie tells me that she had asked you to find this man. You have made enquiries in the city?"

Raynes had a sudden panic that Leonie might have mentioned the million francs reward. If she had done that, he would be regarded as the prime suspect. Things could turn nasty.

"She asked Signor Calvoressco and me to visit a number of places where Gaspard was known. Because I do not speak French, all the translating was done by Signor Camille."

"So I understand. And he is the man who found the body?"

"Yes."

"A very active man. Capable of carrying a body?"

"I think it would have taken at least two people to have carried the body in its present condition." He decided to slip in the knife. "Signor Camille is a sexual athlete; not a weight-lifter!"

"Ah, so?"

The inspector's eyes lit up.

"You have witnessed this?"

"No. But he has a reputation for being a ladies' man."

("Just like you!" thought Raynes.)

It was nice to think this wretched man was generously increasing Mrs May's bank account. Perhaps he would be able to follow the course of the inspector's investigations through the same intermediary?

"And where is this Camille?"

"I believe he left after breakfast."

"He did not say where he was going?"

"No."

Things were looking black for Spumante.

"And how many people did the two of you visit?"

"Three on Tuesday and two on Wednesday."

"Their names?"

"I saw a lady in the Cafe Austerlitz on Tuesday. A girl in a hairdressing salon. She was called Danielle. And a rather unpleasant fence called Bruno Polanski who sells pianos. . . "

(He wasn't going to mention the flat in the Rue Sébastien. If the inspector went there, he would see Mrs Foster's picture. That would incriminate Brackles.)

"I know Bruno."

"On Wednesday, we saw someone called Pierre – and Bruno again. Later in the morning, we went out to Cagnes to see a Madame Yolande who has a fashion boutique in Cannes."

(He would not tell him the name of the shop. Let him find out the hard way.)

Inspector Grimaldi looked at Raynes.

"Do you know a girl called Julie?"

"No."

(Raynes had no knowledge on Debbie's nom de guerre; so his reply was honest and completely spontaneous.)

"She is also looking for Gaspard."

"I'm sure there must be quite a lot of people looking for him."

"She is English."

"No, I don't know her."

(But then the thought crossed his mind that the Inspector might be referring to Debbie.) But Grimaldi had moved on.

"Madame Leonie was expecting an attack on this house?"

"Yes. That was why I was sent out to look for him."

"He was going to steal items from this house?"

"Yes. I believe the list had already been drawn up. Mr Bruno had been consulted. . . "

"Had he?"

"I also have reason to believe the raid was planned for this weekend."

Grimaldi wondered where Monsieur Raynes had gained his information.

"From Madame Yolande."

"Really?"

"Her husband was coming down from Paris to join them."

(The more he centred the inspector's attention on Pierre and his friends the better. It would leave the field clear for his own investigations.)

"What is Madame Yolande's husband called?"

"I've no idea."

"Do you think the raid would have taken place?"

"No."

"Why not?"

"Because they had lost their leader. Gaspard has been missing since last Wednesday. I think they were depending on him to give them inside information about the house – its alarms and where the goodies were to be found."

"And you think that only he could supply this information?"

The question was an open invitation to name more names but Raynes had no intention of mentioning Mrs Foster or the daughter of the house. He would help the inspector as little as possible.

"There are any number of people who visit this house. Even Maître Duclos – a lawyer."

"Yes, I know him. He is a crook. . . " Seeing the surprise on

Raynes' face, he added: "He works for crooks. Defends them in court. Tries to prevent them being sent to prison. Madame Leonie has not chosen well. . . "

Inspector Grimaldi returned to Gaspard.

"So he has been missing for a week – they say. Mm. . . " He stroked his moustache. "And I think we both know where he has been."

"Yes," said Raynes. "I think I can guess."

"And when did you come to Nice?"

"On Monday."

"And when are you leaving?"

"A week on Monday."

Inspector Grimaldi looked straight into Raynes' eyes. Cold, hard, piercing – like diamonds. Raynes almost felt the look.

"I would be very glad, Monsieur Raynes, if you would cease all your investigations into this case. Even if the lady of the house should ask you, you must do nothing. I am in charge of this case and if there is any further interference by you, I shall formally charge you – and report the matter to your Government. Is that understood?"

"Perfectly."

* * * *

The interview was at an end. It had not been a pleasant experience. Raynes felt no desire to help Inspector Grimaldi. In fact, he had been repulsed and intimidated. That was not the best way to get facts out of a witness.

It was very different to his own technique which normally paid enormous dividends. His first object was to put the interviewee at his or her ease. To encourage them to speak freely. So freely that they would tell him far more than they had intended. It was in those moments that he often picked up some vital clue.

Grimaldi would not find it easy to pin down Gaspard's killers. (Raynes presumed that there would be more than one.) If they were subject to threats, they would stonewall. Their co-operation would be nil.

The interview had made him feel highly antagonistic towards the Frenchman. He hoped Mrs May would beat him senseless. . . castrate him accidentally. . . scar him for life. He was surprised at his anger. He suspected it was born of frustration; at not being in charge of the case – of not being able to speak the language.

But first, he had to find out whether he had put himself at risk in his replies. Had Sylvie told the inspector that he had moved the corpse whilst it was in the pool?

"Mais non," she said. "I have been très discrète."

And then she added: "Comme toujours."

She had said that the body had been closer to the edge of the pool when it had first been seen. Perhaps the waves – the ripples – set off by Monsieur Camille had caused it to move? Who knows? Monsieur Richard had been most careful. He had not touched anything.

Raynes thanked her for her help.

When he next saw Brackles, he asked him how the interview had gone with Leonie.

"Quite well. He spent about fifteen minutes talking about his connections with the Grimaldi family. Leonie was quite bored. He kept looking at my picture. 'A real aristocrat!' I said."

"He wouldn't like that."

"No, he didn't. He ignored me for the rest of the interview."

"Did Leonie mention that she had offered me a million francs to kill Gaspard?"

Brackles laughed.

"Got you worried, did it? I'm not surprised. No, she did nothing but praise you. A great English detective! One who had solved so many murders. To hear her speak, you would have thought you were Sherlock Holmes reincarnated. She was trying to make him jealous."

Raynes sighed.

"She succeeded – all too well. He is jealous. Very jealous. He's even warned me off the turf! If I put a foot wrong, I shall

155

be reported to the British Government!"

"You're not going to listen to him?"

"Of course not!"

"Do you hope to make an arrest in the near future?"

"No," said Raynes. "I'm not even sure I want to. Why should I let him have all the glory? Gaspard's dead – and so far as I'm concerned, everyone should rejoice – including Ludo."

"It'll pass. Leonie says that her daughter's always had guilt feelings about how she'd treated him. But there's no chance of her going back to him. Not now, anyway. No competition!" he laughed. "Not unless you're into ghosts. Mark you, with Simon, one does wonder sometimes!"

* * * *

With the body gone – and Inspector Grimaldi departed for a late lunch, the Villa Rose became quite peaceful. Brackles was still upstairs – painting, it was said, though the Inspector had his doubts.

He himself was served with quail with fresh figs followed by mangoes in a curaçao sauce – washed down by a splendid Pouilly-Fuisse 1986. It left him feeling pleasantly mellow.

He asked Sylvie: "Is there any chance of spending a little time together this afternoon?"

"I think it would be most unwise. Monsieur."

"Unwise?"

"The Inspector is planning to return this afternoon to search the house. He is bringing many gendarmes with him. They will search every corner." Her eyes twinkled mischievously. "We do not want him to catch us *sans culottes*!"

28. *L'enfer c'est les autres*

By the time of the evening cocktail party, the worst was over. The police had searched the house and outbuildings and found no evidence that Gaspard had been inside the Villa Rose. Raynes had hidden the passport in the hiding place behind the mirror and the police had not discovered it.

Now he was thinking about the suitcase of clothes in the flat in the Rue Sébastien. It might be a good thing to remove them before the police got there. Not to mention the picture which might provoke awkward questions about the connection between Mrs Foster and the dead man.

He shared his anxieties with Brackles. He asked him whether he could approach Amelie and obtain the key.

"Why don't you just break in? If you don't, the police will. Might give them something to think about."

"We could go after dinner. Do you think we could borrow Leonie's car?"

"Ernst's got it. He's gone off to Vence. Leonie didn't want the police to see him. Apparently, he has an international reputation."

"That doesn't surprise me."

"Why don't you take your hired car."

"I don't think I could stand Debbie's driving."

"She must know the city quite well by now."

"Do you really want her to see that picture?"

"No, of course not. I'll drive her car."

Raynes looked across the room.

"Simon used to be quite good at lock-breaking."

"I think he's got his hands quite full at the moment."

Simon was standing miserably next to Ludo, who was in a long black dress. But her widow's weeds were richly enhanced by a dramatic neckline slashed to the waist. However, the dress did not match her mood which was excessively sombre.

Leonie came across the room with Monsieur Duclos who once again had been invited to dinner. In her eyes was the light of triumph.

"Monsieur Duclos has good news for us. He has bought the chateau and all its contents. He has a client for the chateau and we shall take the furnishings. You did excellent work in Grasse. I am so proud of you."

Leonie did not say that negotiations for the chateau had been proceeding for the past eleven weeks. She herself had been over to the chateau five times and inspected all its treasures. The two visits by Ludo and Simon were simply designed to keep them out of Nice.

Monsieur Duclos bowed.

"You both have excellent taste. The pictures alone will make Madame a rich woman. And, of course, you, too, Mademoiselle. You are truly your mother's daughter."

The compliments did not help. Ludo remained staring into middle distance. Tears ran down her cheeks. She twisted her glass round and round in her hands. She was drinking neat vodka – something she always did when she was depressed.

Suddenly, she lifted her glass and swallowed the rest of the vodka. Then she smashed the glass on the parquet floor and ran out of the room weeping.

Her mother, clad in white and gold, shrugged her shoulders "La pauvre petite. She suffers so much."

Leaving Simon, Leonie and her lawyer set off to find more cheerful company.

Richard went over to his friend.

"Have you had a good day?"

Simon looked despairing. "Frankly, no. I feel like going home tomorrow."

"Oh, you can't do that," said Raynes. "You've got to help me find who killed Gaspard."

"Who cares who killed that bastard? I never want to hear his name again. She's been weeping for him all day. Apparently, she loved him – and him only."

"These Russians can be very temperamental. They revel in

tragedy. Think of Tchaikovsky!"

"Don't mention him! I'm being thrown out of the honeymoon suite. All my clothes have been moved to the *1812*."

"Bit noisy?"

"Oh, don't you start! Brackles said exactly the same!"

"Look," said Raynes, trying to bring a little sense to proceedings, "I think you've got it all wrong. I have it on excellent authority that although she may have loved him before he went to prison – and may have thought she loved him when he came out of prison, she discovered a few weeks ago that his character had completely changed. No longer the dashing playboy but an out-and-out thug. He is no longer the man she loved.

"What she is feeling is guilt. That she neglected him. That she divorced him. She is feeling that if she had handled things differently, he might still be alive. Once she's got over the shock, she'll come back to you. She really loves you."

"Well, she'd better make up her mind quickly. I'm not putting up with all this misery."

"If you really love her, you should stand by her in her hour of need."

"Monsieur Richard is right."

Sylvie was supervising the sweeping up of the broken glass. She turned to the two maids.

"That will do. You will go to the kitchen and attend to the serving of the meal. In precisely ten minutes." She looked at her watch, before turning to Simon.

"I know she loves you. Monsieur. She has told me. Her love for you is deeper than her sorrow."

She gave Richard a despairing look as she followed the maids back to the kitchen.

Simon was still angry.

"You don't have to live with her. You're having a marvellous time. All three of you. But all I get is tears."

Raynes was as gentle as he could be.

"I think you should go after her. Suggest a holiday. A

cruise. Her mother would bless you. And remember! You need the money! She can earn more in a day than you can in a year."

Simon drained the last of his Winter Sunshine.

"She's not the only one!"

"I beg your pardon."

Simon pointed over to the other side of the room where Monsieur Duclos and Debbie were deeply involved in a private conversation. Nobody could hear what they were saying, but Richard could guess.

Debbie was clutching her glass of Blue Bols and the lawyer was saying: "I shall be free by twelve."

It seemed that Debbie had successfully bagged another rich bird.

29. *Night Fishing at Antibes*

"Have you got the jemmy?"

"Yes, it's in the boot. Sylvie was sure Ernst had one somewhere. She found it in his wardrobe."

"Useful chap."

"It's a wonder the gendarmes didn't find it. It was hidden inside the sleeve of a winter coat."

"Let's hope we don't get caught with it."

Brackles drove the car direct to the Rue Sébastien.

"Only been twice, but I kept my eyes on the road in case I had to walk home."

They parked some distance from No 112 and walked back.

"Seems funny coming here without my paints."

They reached the main door.

"We'd better ring first."

"Why give them any warning?"

In the event, the outer door was open.

"Do you think it's a trap?"

"Well, there's two of us."

The darkness made the steps more hazardous than usual;

but Raynes had brought a small torch.

"We're certainly not going to be able to run downstairs."

They reached the third floor – and Flat H. Raynes rang the bell twice. No reply.

"I hope the police aren't waiting for us," whispered Brackles.

"Well, we did ring."

Raynes hammered at the door. Still no reply.

Out with the jemmy. He got a good purchase on the door and pulled hard. There was a sharp snap and a sound of splintering wood. But the door would not open.

"I think there must be another lock."

"Are you wearing gloves?"

"Of course I'm wearing gloves. Sylvie gave me a pair of yellow kitchen ones."

In went the jemmy again. More sounds of splintering wood before the door opened up.

"Success," breathed Raynes. "But we'll just wait to see if we've attracted any attention."

"What do we say?"

"Sûreté Nationale." There were at least two French words he knew!

But no one seemed to have noticed the attack.

Raynes said: "Can you find the suitcase quickly?"

"There's also some clothes in the wardrobe."

"Bring the lot. Then we'll get the canvas."

"It'll only take a few seconds."

"Well, in you go. Take my gloves. I'll stand on guard."

Brackles put the light on and walked into the flat. Raynes moved out of the light and stationed himself in a dark corner.

Brackles was remarkably quick.

"Here's the suitcase."

He rushed back in.

"Now the coats and things. . . "

He finally came out with the painting.

"Will this go into the car? Yours is a bit smaller than Mrs Foster's."

Raynes looked coldly at this piece of naked plagiarism.

"If the worst comes to the worst, I can get a taxi. Have you anything to wrap it in?"

"A sheet?"

"How very appropriate!"

To the unprofessional eye, the painting seemed to be already finished; but Brackles would doubtless spin out the final touches for another few sessions.

The picture was wrapped up.

"Now give me those gloves. I'm going in."

Richard went into the flat and examined every room. There was certainly no one there. He opened the freezer in the kitchen. Empty. He picked up the phone to see if there were any messages – not that he would be able to understand them. There were none. He flipped through a couple of books – one of which was a gift "from your loving wife, Ludo". He recognized the words "femme" and "amoureuse". Better remove that. Behind the clock, he discovered the rest of Gaspard's papers, including his driver's licence.

He smiled.

"Always check!"

Then out on to the landing. Lights out. Door closed as far as it would go. He felt rather like the gentleman burglar, Raffles. The jemmy was stuffed into his belt in such a way that it would not catch the back of his knee. Raynes picked up the coats and lit the torch. Brackles carried the suitcase and the painting downstairs.

It was a slow and dangerous descent. The steps were narrow and there was so much rubbish.

When they reached the ground floor, Raynes took the suitcase.

"You go first with the picture. Go about thirty yards. If the coast is clear – whistle."

He soon heard Brackles give the "all clear".

He breathed a sigh of relief.

He plodded down the street, following Brackles to the car. As he had said, the painting was a tight fit. The suitcase was shoved into Raynes' arms and the coats used to protect the painting.

Brackles got behind the wheel.

"You're still wearing your yellow gloves!"

Raynes shook his head.

"Even professionals make mistakes." But then he had second thoughts. "Better to keep them on. No fingerprints on the suitcase."

"Have you got plans for it?"

"Perhaps."

When they returned to the Villa Rose, Brackles reversed into the garage.

"What now?"

"We need Sylvie."

"Where are we going to put everything?"

"I thought the safest place was the wine cellar. No one goes down there except Sylvie and Ernst. They won't say anything."

Brackles came round the car and removed the suitcase and clothes. Raynes climbed out of the car and stretched himself.

"Messieurs . . ."

Sylvie was already in the garage. She was in her sheepskin jacket and boots. The keys to the wine cellar were in her hand.

"The door is open."

The woman was telepathic.

In a few minutes everything was stored in a corner of the cellar near the door. Sylvie looked at the package.

"A painting of Madame Foster?"

"How did you know?"

"I have seen a few specks of paint on Madame's lingerie." She smiled. "And I have seen you, Monsieur Brackles, smuggling your box of paints into the car."

"Would you like to see the picture?"

Sylvie nodded.

Brackles unwrapped his second masterpiece.

"Oh, là, là. C'est énorme."

Everyone looked at the picture. No one noticed that they

163

had been joined by another figure who was outraged at what she saw.

"Bloody treachery!"

Both men jumped.

Debbie was standing in the doorway, her face white with anger.

"Bloody treachery! You've copied my picture." She looked at Richard. "And you never told me! I thought you were going to get Gaspard's clothes. I never realized that you were going to bring that picture here. You should have smashed it to pieces. Fancy wasting it on her!"

Every word stung.

It was highly embarrassing. Four people, standing in an underground cellar, surrounded by thousands of bottles of wines and spirits. Two men full of shame. One woman incandescent with rage; the other cool and calm, although she could understand the feelings of Madame Raynes. Debbie had told her about the marvellous picture Simon had painted. She had even shown her a little photograph of the painting she carried with her. Monsieur Brackles had grievously erred

"We had to move it." Brackles tried to explain. "If the police had seen it, they would have connected Gaspard with Mrs Foster. It could have been very embarrassing for Madame Leonie."

Debbie's fury was unabated.

"I think you should be utterly ashamed of yourself. If I tell Simon, he'll be furious. You've stolen his artistic property. He will never speak to you again. And neither shall I!"

Brackles grovelled.

"Please don't say anything to Simon. It'll only make things worse. He's as miserable as sin already. Talking about going home tomorrow. This would be the last straw."

Brackles was almost on his knees. "I'll give it to Amelie and you'll never see it again!"

But Mrs May was more angry than Richard had ever seen her.

"Why should she have a masterpiece? What has she ever

done for you? She and her husband are both crooks. You must promise me to destroy that picture."

Richard could see that Brackles was torn two ways. He could not bear to destroy one of his best paintings. Equally, he realized how hurt Debbie was – and Simon would be. Something had to go. . . but what?

"Perhaps tomorrow," said Sylvie, "after we have slept, we think again?"

Debbie shook her head.

"It goes now."

She looked around her.

"There's a blowlamp. Burn it!"

Caught between the frying pan and the fire, Brackles hesitated. But Debbie was determined. The painting must go.

Raynes intervened. "I think you'll have to do it. Tell Amelie that the police have seized it. You can always do another picture of her – with a different pose," he added diplomatically.

There was some trouble getting the blowlamp primed and lit. But eventually, it was blazing away. Brackles picked it up and with a sinking heart, he pointed it at the painting. The canvas caught fire immediately – and shrivelled up, leaving only the four stretchers. Brackles switched off the lamp.

He looked shell-shocked.

"Thank you," said Debbie. "Now we can be friends again."

"And you won't say anything to Simon?"

"My lips are sealed."

The tension diminished perceptibly in the wine cellar. Sylvie tried to think how this unhappy scene could be resolved peaceably.

"Monsieur Brackles, would a very good bottle of Courvoisier make you feel better? And Madame Raynes, a bottle of champagne?"

Brackles nodded glumly.

"In the circumstances. . . . thank you."

But there was a glint of triumph in Debbie's eyes.

"Make it a Roederer," she said, "and we'll call it quits."

Sylvie winced. It was a high price to pay for domestic harmony. But Madame Raynes had been justified in her fury. "Quelle passion!" she said to herself.

There was an awkward silence whilst Sylvie went off to get the bottles. Richard stared at the floor. Everyone felt better when she returned with the two bottles encrusted with the dust of ages.

"I hope you will all sleep peacefully," she said. "I will send Céléstine up with the bottles and glasses – when the bottles have been cleaned."

"Not Ernst?" said Raynes. "I noticed that Madame's car had returned."

Sylvie looked at the Inspector.

"He has returned the car safely – but he is very drunk. I will put the jemmy back in his coat whilst he is asleep."

Debbie turned on her heel and walked out of the cellar and up the ramp to the garage. She was still very annoyed; but at least the picture had been destroyed. And a couple of glasses of that lovely champagne would ensure perfect bliss.

As Sylvie put out the lights, locked the doors and reset the security alarm, Raynes thought of the last time they had been cuddled together between the two doors.

Perhaps she was remembering it as well?

"There is one bit of good news, Messieurs."

"Thank heaven for that!" said Brackles. "Has Spumante been murdered?"

"No. Not yet. But Simon has been re-admitted to the honeymoon suite. I do not think he will be going home tomorrow!"

30. *Les Nourritures Terrestres*

Raynes sat out on the patio in the morning sunshine. He had a newspaper in his hand and a large cup of sweet black coffee on the wooden table beside him. The newspaper was the *Nice-Matin*. There was a picture of Gaspard and a headline: "Voleur trouvé mort dans la piscine" which Sylvie had translated: "Thief found dead in swimming pool". She had also translated the rest of the article for him.

Earlier that morning, the swimming pool had been drained; now it was being refilled. Signor Spumante had again been deprived of his early morning swim. In fact, he had looked very uncomfortable. Raynes reckoned that he had received a roasting from the Grand Duchess for deserting her in her hour of need.

Just before the cocktail party, he heard her saying: "And where have you been, Monsieur?"

Rather shakily, Spumante had replied; "Menton."

"Menton? What is there in Menton to occupy you, Monsieur? You might have done better to have crossed the border and returned to your own country!"

The only person who had spoken to him at dinner was Mr Foster. The American had been conscious that he too was skating on thin ice. Every time he looked in Raynes' direction, the Inspector had been watching him. The Emperor was the only subject he dared to talk about – but even that was risky. Signor Spumante had corrected him on several points. The boat which conveyed him to Elba was *H.M.S. Undaunted* – not the *Bellepheron*; and Elba belonged to France – not Spain. It had been acquired from Spain in 1802.

Mrs Foster had talked about her American childhood. When she mentioned Maryland cookies for about the eighth time, Raynes turned the conversation to antique clocks.

Brackles told a funny story about one of his models hiding inside a grandfather clock when her husband came to look for her. Debbie denied that anyone could hide inside a grandfather clock – not even a skinny model with anorexia!

Brackles claimed that it was true, but Simon said that he had heard the story before and that Brackles had later admitted it was a lie.

Ludo had rejoined the company in time for the main course and consumed a large portion of roast venison. She still looked utterly tragic but she had stopped crying.

Raynes had noticed that Leonie was keeping a watchful eye on her daughter during the meal and Monsieur Duclos had been exceedingly gallant in talking to her – even though he had received very few replies.

This morning, she had actually smiled – and hugged Simon in public. They had held hands during breakfast and were once again reunited in their romantic cocoon.

Monsieur Duclos had again been closeted with the lady of the house. Doubtless, he would have been thinking about his assignation with Mrs May. Having drunk two and a half glasses of the Roederer, she had revealed to Richard that she would be seeing him at 12 noon. They would be lunching on langoustines and asparagus au gratin.

"He is a very rich man!" she said, "with many important contacts in the business world. He says that I could make much more money here than in Grasshallows. What was it that he called me? *A poule de luxe*? Sounds très chic, don't you think?"

Raynes didn't think it sounded at all chic. But, suitably mellowed by the champagne, he did not feel like spoiling her enthusiasm.

"And he's got a wonderful bed. It was once owned by the Empress Eugénie."

"You'd better check the springs!"

Now she had gone to see her rich lover and he was once again on his own. Brackles was hard at work on some essential – but probably quite trivial – alterations to Leonie's picture. Raynes hoped that her springs were in good condition!

To tell the truth, the Inspector was feeling sorry for himself. But he had the comforting knowledge that Sylvie was looking after him – and every now and again, he would hear her charming English accent asking him if there was anything he wanted. Of course, there was! He knew it. She knew it. But there was le déjeuner to be prepared; Ernst to be coaxed back to sobriety; Célestine to be prevented from entering Madame's bedroom. Monsieur Richard would have to wait.

So Raynes had begun to think about Gaspard. He had been thinking about the wretched man all week – but now he had to decide who could have murdered him. The police would not yet have any clues. It would be Sunday or Monday before the body thawed out and they could perform an autopsy. After that, it would be interesting to hear what they found. Perhaps Debbie could be persuaded to pay a third visit to the unpleasant Inspector Grimaldi? But perhaps he could identify the murderer before the police surgeon even lifted his knife?

Raynes sipped at his coffee and, in the margin of his folded newspaper, he started to list all the possible suspects. He put Georges at the top of the list; closely followed by Bruno Polanski; Pierre, he thought – not. He put him further down the margin. Danielle, the hairdresser? No.

He hesitated whether to put Amelie next on the list. Or Ernst? Instead, he put Leonie; followed by Amelie, Ludo and Ernst. He would be the ideal person to do the murder.

But the body had not been physically attacked. He was fairly sure about that. There were no signs of violence. Perhaps that ruled out Madame Yolande? But what about Mr Foster? Was he the sort of man to kill a rival? At first sight, he had thought him a complete fool; but he had been wrong.

Arnaud?

His pen hovered over the page. Despite his claims of ignorance, he too had been offered money to kill Gaspard. He would have to be included. As would Signor Spumante. He couldn't be left out.

Why had he run away so quickly yesterday morning? Had he really gone to Menton? Raynes squeezed in his name after

Bruno Polanski. And put Arnaud after Ernst. How many had he got? Twelve.

Georges, Bruno, Spumante, Leonie, Amelie, Ludo, Ernst, Arnaud, Mr Foster, Madame Yolande, Pierre, Danielle.

No, he really couldn't include Danielle. That made it eleven. Was there anyone he had missed?

"You would like more coffee, Monsieur?"

That lovely sing-song voice.

"Yes, that would be lovely, Sylvie."

Those big grey eyes.

She looked at the writing down the edge of the newspaper. "What are you doing?"

"I'm putting down a list of all the people who might have wanted to kill Gaspard."

"It will be a long list."

"I've got eleven so far."

He read out the names to her. She seemed quite amused.

"Georges? I do not know him. Bruno? That is possible. And Monsieur Camille? You really do not like him!"

Her eyes opened wider.

"Madame? She would not like to see her name on that list!"

"No. But she hates him."

"She does. But she would not kill him."

"Maître Duclos? Perhaps I should have included him?"

"He knows many bad people."

"Amelie and her husband?"

"Perhaps. It is difficult to imagine..."

"Ludo?"

"Oh, là, là! Simon would not like to think he is making love to a *meurtrière*!"

"Perhaps Simon and Ludo?"

"That is better."

"Madame Yolande? Pierre?"

"C'est possible. " She laughed. "But you have forgotten the most important suspect!"

"Have I?"

"Monsieur Richard himself! I have heard what Madame

said yesterday. She thinks you have committed the perfect crime."

"But I only arrived in Nice on Monday. And Gaspard went missing last Wednesday." He looked at Sylvie. "And what were you doing last Wednesday?"

"I was making love to Ernst. 1 was so desperate, waiting for my Englishman!" She chuckled to herself. "I will get you the café. Monsieur, whilst you add your name to the list."

Raynes smiled to himself – and added Brackles, Simon, Sylvie, Celestine – and even Debbie to the list. And not forgetting Monsieur Duclos! Including himself, that made a grand total of eighteen known suspects. Let alone the unknowns.

Now to the manner of Gaspard's death. This was much easier. Ice; He had been frozen to death. That suggested a freezer of some sort. Having seen the film, *Coma*, a butcher's shop was an obvious possibility. But a good-sized freezer would easily accomodate a body. He thought immediately of the freezer at the back of the shop in Cannes. Georges was a regular visitor to the shop. He had a delivery van. He had brought Mr Foster home on the Thursday night. Perhaps he had delivered the body at the same time? Thinking of Georges reminded him of the freezer in the flat in the Rue Sébastien. He had seen it again the previous night; but he had never thought to look inside.

On their first visit, Georges had been very unwilling to let them into the flat. The Inspector had assumed this was because of the electrical equipment stacked in the hallway. But perhaps there had also been a body in the freezer?

Sylvie returned with his coffee.

"How many freezers are there in the Villa Rose?"

Sylvie counted.

"Five – but they are all filled with food. You may inspect them before lunch."

"I'm just checking. Pierre had a freezer in his cafe. Monsieur Bruno . . .?"

"I am sure he will have one. Most people have one in the

171

south of France. In summer, it is so hot."

Raynes nodded.

"The man must have been put in a freezer some time last week. He would have been there for a week. Then the murderer must have been alarmed. Perhaps by our visits? He is frightened of getting caught..."

". . . and he brings it up to the Villa and puts into Madame's swimming pool. Tiens! At least the man has a sense of humour!" She laughed. "Perhaps Monsieur Brackles has been hiding it in his grandfather clock!"

"Perhaps Signer Spumante has a secret flat in Menton?"

"But why bring the body here?"

Raynes tapped his pen against his chin.

"Why not put him in the sea? Why not leave him out on the hills? Why not put him in a skip and cover him with bricks?"

Sylvie became more serious.

"It must be someone who hates Madame. Who wishes to cause her *l'embarras*. To bring the police to her house – not theirs."

"But to transport a frozen body... it would need at least two people to carry it. Two men.... perhaps a man and a woman?"

Sylvie laughed.

"I've told you already, Monsieur Richard. Ernst and I were making love. Ze passion was so hot, the body would have melted in our hands!"

Raynes looked at her reproachfully.

"I think you have a better taste in men."

"It is true. I prefer the English man. Perhaps, after lunch, I shall not be so busy. It is Saturday. Everybody is out. We shall not be disturbed."

Raynes cheered up. There would be a happy afternoon in that little room beneath the eaves. All was not lost. Debbie was sampling the delights of Monsieur Duclos' imperial bed, whilst he would be enjoying himself on a bed which he already knew was well-sprung!

He carefully tore the list of suspects off the newspaper. He would keep it for his future investigations. He wondered whether Inspector Grimaldi had a similar list.

He drank his coffee whilst he trimmed down the list to manageable proportions. But he still included Leonie, Ludo, Mr and Mrs Foster, Bruno, Georges, Ernst and Spumante. Perhaps Pierre? Perhaps Arnaud? Ten in all.

The sun got hotter. The Inspector fell asleep. The little slip of paper blew away. Sylvie took away his cup and moved the sunshade to protect him. She looked at him with an indulgent smile.

"My lover – the great detective!"

Twenty minutes later, she returned with a large Dubonnet with ice on a silver salver.

"Monsieur Richard! Votre apéritif! You will need all your strength for this afternoon!"

31. *La Prisonnière*

Debbie enjoyed her lunch with Maître Duclos. He was a large, thick-set man with a bald head – but his tastes were impeccable. He was dressed in an old-fashioned morning coat with pin-striped trousers. His cuffs were of dazzling whiteness and there were two diamonds in each cuff link. Round his neck, there was a ribbon bearing a Papal cross.

He entertained her in a small private dining room in his villa on Cap Ferrat. She didn't know precisely where she was. A car had been sent for her and the drive through Villefranche and Beaulieu had been tortuous and confusing. All she knew was that it was on a tree-covered hillside overlooking the Mediterranean. The house was dark inside with highly polished parquet floors. There was a large window with white muslin curtains fluttering delicately in the breeze.

The table cloth was cream-starched linen. Knives, forks and spoons all silver. Gold-edged plates and fluted glasses. Champagne was served immediately by an elderly retainer wearing white gloves. He brought in the dishes, served the meal and removed the plates. The champagne was not the

Roederer '29 but a very acceptable Moet et Chandon.

As agreed the previous night, they lunched on Canadian lobster and asparagus au gratin. The dessert was crêpes suzette followed by coffee and Bénédictine.

Monsieur Duclos was a gracious host. He had a very soft, caressing voice. He took every care to see that his guest was happy and well-served. He spoke perfect English. He knew instinctively how to put Debbie at ease.

After the lunch, he asked her if she would like a few moments to refresh herself. Debbie was grateful for his solicitude. She was frightened that she might be too inebriated to give of her best. But he was an elderly man; perhaps he would not be too demanding. She performed her toilette, touched up her make-up and put on a little more lipstick.

He escorted her to his bedroom – another dark room with the walls covered in tapestries. There was the large bed belonging to the Empress Eugénie with its white canopy and curtains and the imperial crest embroidered in gold. It stood upon a platform. A much larger bed than the one in the Villa Rose. But. . . slightly spooky.

The shutters were closed, but daylight came in through the slats. There was a small chandelier in the high ceiling which gave off a faint yellow light. It was not exactly a welcoming room.

Monsieur Duclos handed her a white envelope. Presumably, the money. He smiled at her – and bowed slightly.

"Madame, I believe you are used to such things."

Debbie nodded.

One would do most things for ten thousand francs.

"I would be glad if you would take off your clothes for me."

So it was humiliation. He wanted to look at her. He wanted her to be weak and vulnerable. But she did as he asked. She took off her clothes and laid them on the leather chest at the foot of the bed. She turned to face him with a nervous smile.

"Monsieur."

"Madame," he said, " I have here a remarkable chair which once belonged to the Medici family – in which I would like you to sit. In fact, I have bought this chair from Madame Leonie. It is carved and may be a little uncomfortable since you have no clothes on. I would like you be as comfortable as possible."

The chair sat in the middle of the parquet floor, facing the bed. It was like a small throne with a high back and a box-like seat. She sat down on it.

He smiled.

"You are comfortable, Madame?"

She wasn't – but he obviously wanted her to say she was. So she said: "Yes."

From his pocket he produced two lengths of yellow ribbon.

"Would you mind putting your arms on the arms of the chair, Madame?"

So it was to be bondage of some sort. Her rather than him. She hoped it would not be too painful.

He placed the ribbons round her wrists and tied them with a neat bow. He then produced two more ribbons from his other pocket and tied her ankles to the chair. Whilst he was bending down, she tested the strength of the ribbons. She could always use her teeth to tear off the bows.

But he had already thought of that. A dark red ribbon was looped around her neck and tied to the back of the chair. It was not tight or uncomfortable but it restricted her movements in an emergency.

"You are comfortable, Madame?"

"Do you want me to be comfortable?"

"I want you to be very comfortable."

He smiled – and again bowed.

"You are Mrs Debbie May. You are divorced – twice, I believe. You are not the wife of Monsieur Raynes. In fact, you are a common prostitute, normally working in England?"

"Yes."

Debbie was not sure she liked the description: 'common' but if it made him feel superior – so be it.

"And you have come to Nice at the invitation of Madame Leonie – as her guest?"

Debbie realized that he was speaking to her as if she were in a court of law.

She nodded.

"Please do not nod. Please answer correctly."

So that was it – a mock trial.

"We have very much enjoyed our holiday with her."

"Yes, she is an excellent hostess." He paused. "But you have not been a very good guest. You have interfered in her affairs."

"I have not."

"You have spoken to Inspector Grimaldi – twice, I believe. You have discussed with him the whereabouts of Monsieur Gaspard."

"We were trying to find out where he was. Nobody knew."

"It was no business of yours."

His voice was now cold and angry.

Debbie retaliated forcibly.

"Madame Leonie asked my friend, Richard, to find this man. She even offered him money. She sent him out to meet the man's friends. And he has done this."

"But who asked you to involve the police?"

Debbie paused.

"I decided. . . "

"Precisely! You decided!"

"In my country, when you have a missing person, you go to the police. . . "

"In your country, Madame. . . " He sneered. "But this is not your country. This is a private matter involving Madame and her former son-in-law. It is not a matter for the police."

Debbie was puzzled.

"I didn't think I had done anything wrong."

"You have interfered in a private matter. You have brought the police into Madame's house. You have encouraged them to search her property. To destroy her privacy. To put the lives of her loved ones at risk."

Was he referring to Ludo?

Debbie shook her head.

"I haven't put anyone at risk. The police didn't search the house till after the body was found."

Monsieur Duclos waved an imperious finger at her.

"But, even before the body was found, they were planning to search the house."

"They were planning to search all the places where Gaspard had been. That was the idea."

"Your idea!"

"No. It was Inspector Grimaldi who decided where his men should go. Not me."

Monsieur Duclos leaned closer.

"Perhaps it was your friend asking all his questions which provoked the murderers to dispose of the body in Madame's pool?"

"Perhaps."

Debbie began to wonder whether Maître Duclos was mad. Most sadists and masochists were mentally ill but you could normally humour them. But, if it was a game – and Debbie had her doubts – she must act her part, whatever was said and done. "Think of the ten thousand francs!" she said to herself.

"There is no 'perhaps' about it."

"I don't think Madame has anything to be frightened of. I'm sure she hasn't done anything wrong."

"Of course she has done nothing wrong. She is a good woman. But why should she have to suffer the failures of others? Traitors living under her roof. Eating her food; drinking her drink; stabbing her in the back?"

"I haven't stabbed anyone in the back. I was only trying to help her find the man who was about to attack her house. What was wrong with that?"

"You didn't think of the consequences! Suppose the murderer was one of her guests? One of her staff? Her daughter? Your actions could have led to their arrest! No one was going to bother about Gaspard. . . " He flicked his fingers with contempt. "Whether he lived or died doesn't matter. He was a worthless individual. But Madame has a place in society. If there was one whiff of scandal, her position might be destroyed. You did not think of these things."

Debbie was in no mood to give way.

"If she was in any way guilty of Gaspard's death, then she should face the consequences."

"Does Inspector Grimaldi suspect Madame? Is this what you have been discussing together?"

"He never mentioned it."

"That is what you say now! But perhaps you have been plotting to get her arrested; then you will steal her treasures and escape back to England." He laughed. "I know women. I can read them like a book. All of them are treacherous! All of them can be bought! You think about nothing but money! If you have a chance, you would seize as much as Gaspard. Perhaps more!"

This accusation made Debbie very angry. Whatever her occupation, she had always been very scrupulous never to take a penny more from her clients than had been agreed. Even when she had felt they had got the better bargain, she would never have dreamt of stealing their property or pinching their money.

Debbie's voice was icy cold.

"I have never stolen anything in my life!"

"Why should I believe you? You take every penny you can. From me. And I suppose from Inspector Grimaldi? He too enjoys being tied up." He laughed sarcastically. "You make a fine pair!"

He paced around her chair like a tiger inspecting his prey.

"But to return to Madame . . . You have abused her hospitality. Never has she had a guest who has so abused her hospitality. At the Villa Rose, you have free food, free drink, a free bed. And yet, every day, you go to a whole string of men to make more money. Have you never considered Madame's reputation? Your behaviour is shameless! You have offered no apology! You have used her. . . Why should I believe a word you say?"

Debbie was silent.

"I say that you are trying to bring her down. You have contempt for her. . . For everyone!"

Debbie had originally thought all this was mere play-acting; but Monsieur Duclos was now treating her as a hostile witness in court. His language was getting sharper and more vicious. His contempt for her was obvious. The way he looked at her body did not display lust – but sheer disgust.

He returned to the attack.

"Just suppose that Madame was involved – or one of her friends. And the police discovered evidence linking them to this man's murder. She would go on trial. She might go to jail . . ."

"I'm sure you'd be able to get her off. You did it for her daughter, didn't you?"

"I most certainly did – but it was a hard battle. This time, it may be more difficult. Because you have brought the police to her door. It is your doing, Madame. And I shall make sure you suffer for it. You will not escape!"

"Well, get on with it!"

If he was going to beat her – or whip her – let him do it. Get the game over. Let her get a taxi home.

But Maître Duclos had merely fired the opening rounds of his cross-examination. He wanted to know precisely what she had said to Inspector Grimaldi. He wanted to know where Richard had been; whom he had spoken to; whether he had obeyed Leonie's orders or whether he was pursuing his own lines of enquiry. The questions rained down endlessly. For over two hours he ranted and raved at her. He repeated himself continuously trying to find any inconsistency in her story.

Debbie hoped that sheer exhaustion would make him give up. But his strength seemed undiminished.

"I want to go to the toilet," she said eventually.

"You will sit in your own filth!" he replied. "You will not leave this room – this chair – until you have signed a confession."

A confession?

"Of what?"

Monsieur Duclos smiled. This was the breaking point. He paused to savour the moment.

"A confession that you and your partner are responsible for Gaspard's death."

"I'm not signing anything!"

"You will stay here till you do. All night, if necessary."

"If I'm not back in time for cocktails, everyone will notice. They'll ask questions. They'll come and look for me."

Monsieur Duclos laughed.

"I think Madame Leonie knows my passion – for justice. She will explain. Nobody will worry about you!"

Forgetting all about the ten thousand francs, Debbie said: "You're mad! Stark, staring bonkers! Inspector Grimaldi said you were a crook! He was right!"

"A crook? Who is he to judge? He is just an ignorant peasant. Because his grandmother had an affair, he thinks he is one of the aristocracy. He is nothing. I will show him!"

He looked down at Debbie.

"But you will sign. And, if I choose. . . if you do not do what I wish, I will show it to your Inspector Grimaldi. He will be most interested."

Debbie wondered if he was trying to break her psychologically. Perhaps aggression was not the best policy? A few tears might do the trick. Perhaps he wanted her to submit?

"It's no use crying," he said coldly.

"Well, what else can I do?"

She tried to wrench her arms off the chair.

"You will sign the confession. I have it here."

He took a folded sheet of paper out of the inner pocket of his morning coat – and read it to her.

Debbie was going to say: "No" – but she realized that this might be the quickest way to escape.

"You'll have to release my hand."

How quickly could she tear the ribbon off her other wrist?

"Certainly not, Madame. You have sufficient freedom of movement to sign your name. And I shall require your correct

180

signature."

He walked over to her heap of clothes and opened her handbag. He took out her passport. He opened it and looked at her photograph and her signature. He walked back to her chair.

"You have one chance to sign."

He placed the white sheet of paper on a clipboard and took a slim gold pen out of his top pocket.

"Madame."

She shook her head.

"You wish to wait? We have the whole night before us." He took her passport into the next room; and there was a sound of a drawer opening and shutting. A key turning in a lock.

This was getting serious.

Debbie could see the light fading through the slats in the shutters. Time was passing. When would this misery cease?

He returned to the room and sat down on the chest at the foot of the bed – watching her.

Another quarter of an hour passed.

"All right," she said. "I'll sign. But I'm signing under duress."

"It doesn't matter. So long as you sign, it will stand up in a court of law."

She signed.

It was a bitter moment. Her 'confession' incriminated both herself and Richard. He would never understand what she had had to go through. He would blame her for giving way. She looked at Maître Duclos. There was a light of triumph in his eyes. He was mad. Completely mad. And dangerous. Did he really think she would forgive him for the misery he had inflicted on her this afternoon?

"Thank you, Madame."

He repeated the ritual of going through into the next room. But this time, there was no sound of a drawer being opened. This time, she heard the metal clang of a safe being shut. Her "confession" was indeed in safe keeping. He returned.

"Can I go?"

He looked at her with something approaching lust.

"I shall beat you," he said. "Then I shall give you back your passport. If you resist me – or try to cheat me – I shall burn it."

She did not doubt that he was capable of doing it.

It was better to submit.

The last ordeal took another twenty minutes. It was slow and painful.

He handed her her passport. (It had not been hidden in the drawer but in his inside pocket.)

"Madame, you are free to go."

Debbie was shaking as she put on her dress and her shoes. Shaking and sore. She kept saying to herself: "I can't believe this is happening to me." Never in her life had she been so totally humiliated. He had broken her – but she would not let him know it. She wouldn't give him the pleasure.

"Please remember, Madame, that I have your confession. If you say a word to anyone about this, it will be sent to the police."

Debbie snatched up the white envelope. She looked inside to see if he had cheated her as well – but the money was all there – and a few thousand more.

She looked at him.

Maître Duclos smiled – and bowed slightly.

"It will pay for your defence!" he said.

32. *La Nausée*

A car was provided for the return journey.

In the back of the car, Debbie wept.

She was so worried that Richard would see her in this condition that she stopped the car at the entrance to the villa.

"I shall go on foot," she said to the driver.

"Be careful, Madame. There are some very dangerous people about."

She looked at him – with disbelief.

As she walked through the growing darkness, she tried to compose herself. She stopped crying and anger took over. Even if he had paid her, she should not have been subject to such inhuman treatment. He had taken advantage of her in every possible way. She hoped he had not marked her body. If he had, Richard would probably kill him.

Despite her anger at being upstaged by Sylvie on Friday morning and the row over Brackles' picture, Debbie felt a surge of warmth for Richard. She recognized his innate goodness and kindness towards her. He would never beat her or humiliate her. She knew he loved her; but she couldn't burden him with this. It was a result of her own greed.

She managed to slip into the house without anyone noticing. She ran upstairs and into their room. Fortunately, it was empty. Into the bathroom. She pulled off her dress and looked at her back in the mirror. Her skin was fiery red but there were no open wounds.

She went into the shower but the hot water stung. She leapt out quickly and turned down the heat to luke warm. She towelled herself gently and rubbed cream all over her back and buttocks.

She was already dressed when Richard appeared.

"Gin time," he said. "I'm needing it."

"What have you been doing all day?"

(Rule number one: Deflect attention!)

"Sitting beside the pool thinking. . . "

(That at least was partially true.)

". . . And Simon and I have been having a talk."

He looked at her brushing her hair. Tonight she was wearing a black dress with a white collar – and pearls.

"Are we in mourning?"

She looked at him with tears in her eyes.

(If only he knew.)

"I wouldn't weep for him. He's caused enough misery in his short life. Even Ludo was in tears again."

She put in her diamond earrings. They boosted her confidence. Richard started stripping down and had his usual problems with his white shirt and his cuff links. She helped him.

"Was Maître Duclos all right?"

"He was very generous" was all she would say.

At the cocktail party, before dinner, Debbie stayed close to Richard – for protection. She felt safe only with him. But Brackles made her laugh.

After about ten minutes, it was difficult to believe that the scene in the villa on Cap Ferrat had actually happened.

As they were going into the dining room, Leonie spoke to her: "Did you have a pleasant afternoon with Maître Duclos?"

Was she mocking her?

No. There was sympathy in her eyes.

"I think you can guess, Madame."

"He loves playing his little games with people. Sometimes he goes too far."

Debbie's lips were sealed; but her eyes showed her feelings. Only a woman could understand what she felt.

33. *Farcis Niçoises*

Leonie looked at the Inspector for several minutes before she spoke.

"Well, Monsieur Raynes, what do we do now?"

It was Sunday morning and Richard had been summoned into the presence of the Grand Duchess. This morning, there was no shop to be opened; no business to be done. Leonie was free to concentrate on the problems facing her own household.

The Inspector smiled.

"Gaspard is dead. That is what you wanted. There will be no raid on the house. Your valuables are safe. And you will no longer need to carry a pistol in your handbag."

Leonie looked surprised that he should have mentioned the pistol. Raynes wondered if it had been a lie. After all, Gaspard must have died several days before he and Debbie arrived in Nice. Even at their first meeting, on Tuesday, Leonie would have been in little danger. Had she known that he was dead? And if she had, why had she sent him and Signor Spumante on such a wild goose chase? On this occasion, he would be a little more cautious in accepting his hostess' views.

"But we still have the police."

"I think the worst is over, Madame. They have searched the house and the grounds very thoroughly. I don't think they have discovered anything suspicious."

"But they will return to question everybody. Inspector Grimaldi has spoken to you. And you have not yet told me what he has said."

The Inspector smiled more broadly.

"Well, he has not arrested me, Madame, even though you have accused me of committing the perfect crime!"

"I must know what he has said."

"Well, first of all, he said that we should have reported the body when we first saw it. He said there had been deliberate delay. I said that you were very much the lady of the house and that you had phoned immediately you had ascertained the facts of the case. He said that you should not regard yourself as being above the law.

"Secondly, he was not pleased that Monsieur Camille had disappeared. He was the person who had found the body. He was the prime witness and yet, no one could tell him where he had gone. He found this very suspicious. Thirdly, he accused me of interfering in the case. I should not have pursued my investigations into Gaspard's plans or his disappearance. I should not have examined the body in the pool.

"And finally, he demanded that I should not interfere any further in this case – even if you asked me. If I was foolish enough to disobey, he would take action against me and report me to the British government."

Leonie looked at the Inspector.

"And will you obey him?"

"Certainly not."

"You will continue to investigate this case?"

"I will."

"I am very grateful. This man is an arrogant fool. Maître Duclos has told me all about him. He is disliked by all the police in Nice."

"I think he has a sharp professional mind. I think he could be quite a thorn in your flesh."

"Maître Duclos will deal with him."

She looked at Richard's face to see if there was any reaction? No. None. Obviously his friend had not spoken to him about her afternoon with the lawyer.

Leonie did not know what had happened. She did not want to know. But her tormentor had obviously gone too far. She admired the young woman for her discretion.

"So what do you think happened to Gaspard?"

Raynes tried to be as objective as possible.

"He was not drowned."

"Not drowned?"

"No. If he had been drowned, his lungs would have been full of water. He would have sunk to the bottom of the pool.

There was air in his lungs."

Leonie looked thoughtful.

"He was not drowned. He was not physically assaulted. He may have been poisoned. He may have been given an injection. He may have been drugged. . . or drunk. There are quite a number of possibilities. One way or another, he was incapacitated. And in that helpless condition, he was placed in a freezer – where he died remarkably quickly."

"When do you think this was?"

"His friends say that they have not seen him since Wednesday the 16th. So I imagine it was then that he died."

"And where has his body been since then?"

Raynes smiled grimly.

"Everywhere I go, there are freezers. In the flat in Rue Sébastien. In Madame Yolande's shop in Cannes. I am sure she will have one in her house. Pierre has one for his ice cream. And I am told there are no less than five in the Villa Rose."

"But they are all in the kitchen. You would not be able to hide a body there."

"Certainly not."

"So they have brought the body up to my house and put it in my pool?"

"It looks like it."

Rather than voice his deeper suspicions, Raynes added: "The man who lives in the Rue Sébastien has a white Renault van. He delivers stolen goods. He works for Madame Yolande. His van was seen in the grounds of the Villa Rose on Thursday night. It is possible that he brought the body to the house that night."

"I thought that the flat in Rue Sébastien was where Gaspard was living?"

"The flat is owned by Arnaud, Madame."

"Is it?"

Madame Leonie looked genuinely surprised.

Raynes decided to give her more food for thought.

"When you asked Arnaud to find Gaspard – when you put

out your first contract – for 500,000 francs," he added maliciously, "Arnaud knew precisely where Gaspard was living. He had given him the use of the flat, free of charge."

"And he did not tell me?"

"Not till after he disappeared. When he was no longer in the flat."

"Why did he not tell me?"

Leonie's eyes suggested that Arnaud had already been marked down for retribution. He had known – but he had done nothing. His behaviour was unpardonable.

But Raynes put in a good word for Arnaud.

"He had known him for several years before he went into jail. He had never liked him; but he felt sorry for him."

Raynes looked speculatively at the Grand Duchess.

"And I am also told that Arnaud was a friend of your daughter?"

"We do not talk about that."

"He told me that he had a great affection for your family." (Better not mention the photographs.) "And that was why he warned you of the danger of the house being burgled."

"One cannot trust anyone!"

"I agree. But Arnaud did speak to Georges – and tell him there was a price on Gaspard's head. It was shortly after that that Gaspard went missing."

"Who is Georges?"

"The man who is living in the Rue Sébastien. The man who drove the white van up to your house on Thursday night."

"No one has asked me for any money."

"A request may still come. I think that the gang panicked after we started asking questions. I think that by that time they had killed him. And once I started talking about the police searching all their premises, they decided to get rid of Gaspard's body."

"So you think that Georges. . . ?"

"It is one possibility." The Inspector looked at Leonie hesitantly. "The other possibility, Madame, is that the body was hidden in this house. Perhaps you did not know about it.

188

Ernst may have discovered Gaspard hiding in the grounds –
and killed him. And then hidden his body."

"Where?"

"I don't know."

"The police have not discovered any other freezer. I do not
know of any other freezer except those in the kitchen."

Raynes smiled.

"Perhaps Georges took the body away in his white van?"

Leonie welcomed his suggestion.

"You must investigate this, Monsieur Raynes."

"Even though Inspector Grimaldi has forbidden me to
interfere in his juridiction?"

Leonie's face lit up with admiration.

"But you are a much greater detective than he will ever be.
You will run circles round him and he will never know. You
will find the killer before he has even started his
investigations!"

"You have enormous faith in me, Madame."

The Grand Duchess nodded.

"I have told Grimaldi that you are England's greatest
detective since Sherlock Holmes. Monsieur Brackles has
given me the full story of your achievements whilst he was
painting my picture. I have no doubt about your abilities."

Raynes smiled happily.

It was nice to receive such flattery; but he needed to keep
his feet firmly on the ground. He still felt that the answer to
most questions lay within the Villa Rose. But it was important
to retain Leonie's trust. Without that, he could achieve
nothing.

"Madame," he said, "Sherlock Holmes was a fictional
character. All his successes were created in the mind of Conan
Doyle. I have to work in the real world."

Leonie seemed to have made up her mind.

"You and Camille must go and search these places for the
chest freezer in which Gaspard died. Then we can tell the
police. You must see Georges and find out what he has done.
You may offer money. I shall speak to Arnaud."

Raynes put in a plea on the young man's behalf.

"Please don't be too hard on him, Madame. He has done a lot of good work for you – and your boutique. He has reproduced the pictures of your antiques quite brilliantly. He has been an enormous help to Mr and Mrs Foster. It would be a shame to upset him. I think he will always have your best interests at heart."

"I shall think about it."

So he was being sent on another wild goose chase with Signor Spumante. They would revisit all their previous haunts. It was quite pointless. The birds would have flown. For all he knew, Georges might also have been killed. At least he had been alive on the Thursday night.

However, the interview had bought him time. He had Leonie's blessing to continue his investigations. And that could include the people in her house – especially her daughter! That would not be easy.

He had come to the conclusion that very little happened in the Villa Rose without the Grand Duchess' approval. She was the puppet mistress who pulled the strings – but was herself invisible.

He admired her. He admired her skill. Her cunning sleight of hand. Even if he found her guilty of Gaspard's death, he would not necessarily tell Inspector Grimaldi. It would be enough simply to discover the truth. The Grand Duchess was the sort of person who enjoyed the thrill of the chase. And Raynes had already decided that Signor Spumante should be the fox!

34. *Coquillages et Crustaces*

Brackles asked Raynes much the same question as Leonie.

"What are we going to do now?"

Raynes had no doubt.

"Stick it out to the bitter end."

"You don't think anyone else'll get murdered?"

"Not so long as they're still useful."

Brackles looked thoughtful.

"I'm coming to the end of the painting. There's not much more I can do."

"If you want, I'll have a word with Spumante."

"For God's sake, don't! She loves that picture. If Spumante touched it, she'd murder him."

"So I shall have to think of something else."

"Oh, yes. The revenge?"

Raynes nodded.

"You've probably guessed what I'm thinking."

"You're going to plant Gaspard's clothes and his passport in Spumante's room – then phone the police?"

"I've also got his driving licence and the rest of his papers."

"Where were they?"

"Behind the clock. You didn't look far enough. I've also picked up a book, signed: 'From your loving wife, Ludo.' That should be pretty convincing."

"What was the book?"

Richard's face was utterly deadpan.

"How to win friends and influence people."

Both men laughed.

"So all that goes into his room. . ."

". . . or into his car."

"Then what?"

"We phone the police. Light the blue touch paper and stand clear! Even though he won't be convicted, it'll give him a nasty fright."

"When do we move his clothes?"

"As soon as you like. Get Snow White to open up the pearly gates and hide them somewhere in your room. I've hidden away the book and the documents."

"The police won't find them?"

"I think not."

"What about the murder? Any clues?"

"Plenty," said Raynes, "but they all point in opposite directions. Leonie's sending me off tomorrow to search for freezers from here to Cannes. I am to find Georges, the greasy cove who was occupying the flat in the Rue Sébastien and examine his white van to see if there's any sign of him transporting freezers or dead bodies. And – what is worse – infinitely worse – Spumante is coming with me."

"It sounds like a wild goose chase."

"That's precisely what I think. Still, I have to keep in with top brass; and that's what she wants. But whilst Spumante's out of the house, you've got a chance to stash away Gaspard's clothes. On top of a wardrobe – or under his bed. But you'd better warn Sylvie."

Brackles looked thoughtful.

"It does look as if the Grand Duchess is trying to get you out of the house. I wonder why?"

"She doesn't want me to clash with Inspector Grimaldi. He's coming to see Spumante tomorrow. And since he's already warned me off his turf, I have to obey. If I'm caught, interfering, I shall be charged – and a complaint sent to the British government."

"That's ridiculous!"

"Of course it is. But I'm determined to go on asking questions until I find the answers. And most of the answers are to be found in this house!"

"I'm sure they must have a chest freezer here."

"They have five. All in use. And all in public places."

Brackles continued to search his memory.

"I'm sure I've seen one somewhere else. Perhaps it was in the Cafe de Turin. You must try it some time. Wonderful place for seafood. Lobsters, crabs, sea urchins and oysters. Splendid aphrodisiac!"

"Do you really need it?"

Brackles laughed.

"No. I'm managing quite well on my own!"

"By the way," said Raynes, "have you told Mrs Foster about her picture?"

"Yes. She was very upset. Burst into tears. Quite inconsolable. I blamed the police."

Raynes sighed.

"Why not? Everyone does."

35. *And God Created Woman*

"Simon said you wanted to see me."

Raynes, who was leaning on the balustrade, looking over the city of Nice, turned to face Ludo. She was wearing a simple white cotton dress covered with pink splodges. Her long legs were pleasantly brown and she was wearing pink sandals.

"Yes, that's right."

"Is it about Gaspard?"

"We can't really avoid him, can we? There are so many questions still to be answered."

Ludo was silent.

"Are you feeling any better?"

"I suppose so. I'm not crying any more."

"And Simon's been re-admitted to the honeymoon suite?"

Ludo smiled – an enigmatic smile.

"It was nothing personal."

Raynes was uncertain whether to engage in private chit-chat for a few more minutes – or go straight for the jugular. He decided to compromise.

"The Braque," he said, "the picture you sold to that yachtsman. . ."

She smiled broadly. A happy memory.

". . . Madame Yolande told me that it didn't come from your mother's shop – but from her flat in Paris."

(Better to blame Yolande rather than incriminate Amelie.)

"What else did she tell you?"

"Perhaps we could settle my question first?"

""I'm sure Amelie found it in some back corner of the warehouse. Have you asked her?"

"Not yet."

Clearly the interview was going to be difficult. The Inspector tried again:

"Madame Yolande said that it was something Gaspard stole from an old lady in Paris. She looked after it whilst he was in prison. True or false?"

"False."

He knew she was lying.

"Is Madame Yolande in the habit of lying?"

"I don't think I know the woman."

Another deliberate lie.

"You surprise me. That's where Gaspard was staying when he came out of prison. She was an old friend of his. You must have met her when you were together in Paris. She has a dress shop."

"Ah, the famous dress shop!"

Raynes was silent.

Ludo planted the palms of her hands firmly on the stone balustrade and looked west.

"You want me to say something?"

"I should like you to tell me the truth. It would make things a lot easier."

"Easier for whom? The police?"

"I'm only making enquiries because your mother asked me to."

"I bet she didn't tell you to interview me!"

"No, she didn't. But you seem to hold the vital keys to solving this murder. If you have nothing to hide, you can speak to me quite openly. But if you won't tell me the truth, then the police will do it – and much more brutally."

"They won't do anything to me. I shall have my lawyer . . ."

"Like you did last time?"

"Yes."

"I don't think Inspector Grimaldi will give up quite so easily."

"You policemen all think the same. 'Once a crook, always a crook'."

Raynes decided to move into deeper waters.

"Well, that was certainly true of Gaspard; but is it true of you?"

Ludo said nothing.

Raynes continued: "I know you like living dangerously; but is it worth risking your life – sacrificing your future happiness – denying what has happened?"

"What has happened?"

Raynes spoke quietly.

"You planned this attack. It was your idea. When Gaspard came out of prison, he was quite excited about it. It was an excellent way of getting some money – and getting his revenge on your mother. He hadn't forgiven her for putting the police on his trail. That's why he came back to Nice. He didn't return to Marseilles – his home town. He came back here. Gathered all his chums. . . including Madame Yolande. . . "

"Oh, stop going on about her!"

"Well, she's part of the gang."

"She may have been his friend, but she wasn't mine."

"She didn't give you the Braque?"

"No, of course, she didn't."

Raynes paused significantly.

"So you did see Gaspard after he came to Nice. It must've been him who gave you the picture."

There was a deep, ominous silence.

Raynes said: "I know you saw him. He sent you letters. He phoned you. I'm sure you had secret meetings."

"We're divorced."

"There are such things as arranged marriages. I'm sure one could equally well arrange a divorce!"

"My mother ordered me to do it."

Raynes smiled.

"At last we can agree on something. She felt it would be the best thing for you. But you waited for Gaspard to come out of prison, so that you could resume your old life again. All the excitement. All the fun. . . "

(He hoped that Amelie had told him the truth.)

". . . But when Gaspard came out of prison, he wasn't quite the man you knew. He was no longer the smooth young playboy. He was rougher. Coarser. More talkative. Foolishly boasting about his plans to attack this house. And someone killed him."

"It wasn't me."

"Of course it wasn't you. You were with Simon at the time. You had washed your hands of Gaspard. Perhaps he was jealous of your new relationship. You just gave someone a nod and they did the dirty work for you."

"You're making all this up!"

"Some of it. But your mother gave me a very good picture of his character – and I think I can see what happened."

Ludo gave him a withering look.

"You can't see anything!"

Raynes hit back hard.

"Well, you haven't helped much either. You haven't given me a straight answer to any of my questions."

"Why should I speak to you?"

The look in her eyes – one of lofty disdain – made Raynes think (probably for the first time) that there might have been some justification for the Bolshevik Revolution if all the aristocrats were like her.

Raynes kept his temper.

"If you tell me the truth, we can stop this misery going any further. Your mother is desperately worried. . . "

"My mother!"

Her voice sizzled with contempt.

(How very revealing!)

"She is worried about you. Whether you were involved in

the plot to attack this house. Whether you were involved in Gaspard's death. Whether you are likely to be arrested. Whether you have deceived her. . . "

He ended on a quiet note.

"I don't think you need to worry about my mother, Mr Raynes. She is quite capable of looking after herself. She was quite capable of ordering my husband's death. In fact, I am quite sure she arranged it. She gives the orders round here. Other people leap to obey her. No suspicion ever attaches to her. She surrounds herself with faithful lackeys who will do her bidding. Her lawyer, bowing and scraping; Camille, grovelling at her feet; you, Sylvie, Ernst and all the staff. . . she throws money and favours at all of you. And you do what she tells you to do. Don't think that I don't know what she does. She is a cruel, ruthless woman. She always has been. And always will be."

Raynes stood up to her attack.

"I think you forgot to mention Arnaud. She offered him money as well."

"Well, there you are!"

"He didn't take it."

"Good for him."

"He was your boyfriend once!"

"He's a pimp. And you should know that better than most. He's put plenty of business in the way of your. . . friend!"

"He told your mother about the plot. He heard Gaspard boasting about what he was going to do."

"Creeping Judas!"

"Well, you have to remember that if this attack had been successful, some people might have been killed."

"No one would have been killed."

"How can you be so sure?"

"All Gaspard wanted was money. He wouldn't have hurt anyone."

Raynes nodded.

"You're quite right. All he wanted was money. Is that why you gave him the insurance papers from your mother's safe –

with the exact insurance value for every item? Is that why you ticked the best stuff?"

At long last, a shaft went home. Clearly she didn't know that he knew anything about that. He was sailing very close to the truth. What else did he know?

There was another long silence before Ludo replied. Her eyes were icy cold. Her knuckles were white and tense. He felt that she would like to attack him. To throw him over the balustrade and break his neck thirty feet below.

Eventually, she spoke:

"Mr Raynes, you know too much for your own good. I think you should take care. Things could happen to you. Nasty things. And I mean that.

"You have made some very foul allegations but I think you will find that my mother killed Gaspard. She has been longing to do that for some time. The opportunity was too good to miss. And you are part of her cover-up. It is a dangerous job – because if you don't succeed, she could turn against you. My mother has no friends. She uses people. She has used me. But we are very alike. I understand her. She hates that.

"For the past four weeks, I have been constantly in Simon's company – by day and night. If you believe that I killed my ex-husband, then you must believe that your friend was also involved in his murder. Perhaps you mistrust him as much as you mistrust me.

"Simon loves me. And I love him. He will stand by me. He would be very angry if he heard all the accusations you have made against me. He knows I am innocent."

Raynes said quietly: "But you lied. People who are innocent do not lie!"

* * * *

Although the atmosphere was less festive since the murder, the cocktail parties continued each evening. On the Sunday evening, four members of the Nice Opera were invited to dinner along with a small party of Americans who were staying at a villa in Roquebrune. They provided welcome company for Amelie and Julius. Debbie was thankful there was no sign of Maître Duclos.

During the party, Leonie reminded everyone that her birthday would be celebrated on the following Friday. She said pointedly that she hoped Brackles would have finished her portrait by then; but refused to say exactly how old she would be.

"She could be sixty," said Simon. "I think she was born in 1930. Ludo was born in March 1963."

"I think it would be diplomatic not to ask her."

"Let's see how many candles she has on her cake."

Before they went in to dinner, Leonie drew Raynes to one side. She did not look very pleased.

"I believe you have questioned my daughter?"

"Yes, Ma'am."

"I did not ask you to speak to her."

"No. But I regard her as a key witness."

"She was very angry at the allegations you made."

"I believe them to be true."

Leonie was irritated by the Inspector's tone of voice.

"You may take my word for it Monsieur Raynes, that my daughter did not kill Monsieur Gaspard."

Raynes raised his eyebrows.

"I did not accuse her, Madame. In fact, she accused you."

"I am aware of her views; but I have my alibi."

Raynes decided to be brutally honest.

"The reason why I spoke to her was because I believe she was actively involved in the plot to attack this house. The plan was arranged in Madame Yolande's flat in Paris, sometime last December when Gaspard came out of prison. I cannot prove that your daughter was there but I have no doubt they have been in regular contact since that date."

Leonie looked at Raynes with chilling eyes.

Raynes continued: "The picture which they sold to the yachtsman on Monday was stolen from an old lady in Paris. It was not in your shop – or your warehouse. Madame Foster may have found it there – but I believe it was planted there – deliberately – to allay your suspicions."

"You have evidence for this?"

Without the flicker of an eyelid, Raynes said: "Yes."

"Who told you that?"

"A friend close to Madame Yolande."

(Which was true.)

Leonie did not look convinced. But Raynes was determined to justify his questioning of her daughter. He was sure she would not have told her mother about the insurance lists.

"You might also like to know, Madame, that the list of your treasures, kept in your locked safe, has been photocopied and circulated. The items selected have been marked and photographed."

This clearly came as a surprise to his hostess.

"She did not tell me that. How could she have got the key?"

"I do not think, Madame, your security is quite as good as you think. You are employing a skilled safe-breaker who can get into anything. The preparations for the attack were extremely detailed. You fail to realize how deeply your daughter was involved in these things."

Leonie looked across the room at Ludo. Her face was white and angry.

"I shall speak to her after dinner. It will not be pleasant." She looked at the Inspector. "You are sure of your facts?"

"I have seen the marked list."

Leonie was silent.

Raynes could understand what she was feeling.

"That's why I took it upon myself to speak to her. But she would not answer any of my questions. She told me several lies and threatened me with unpleasant consequences if I continued with this case."

Leonie looked apologetic.

"I am sorry you have had to face this unpleasantness in my house. It is most regrettable. As I have said, I shall speak to her later." She looked at Raynes with an imperious gaze. "But I would be most grateful if you would continue to carry out the orders I gave you this morning."

Raynes bowed his head just a fraction.

"As you wish, Madame."

He had no intention of obeying any orders; but appearances must be maintained. He was determined to discover the truth. He was quite convinced that Leonie knew who had killed Gaspard. Ludo could have been right; she might very well have given the orders. And of course, she would have provided herself with an excellent alibi. That would presumably have been Brackles or Signor Spumante. Both men were at her beck and call.

She was an extremely clever woman. And he had no doubt she was using him as part of her cover plan. The trouble was that the more he investigated the case, the more sure he was of her involvement. Her efforts seemed self-defeating; and that was something he could not understand.

He was suddenly conscious of Sylvie standing at his side.

"Dinner is served, Madame."

36. *Homard à la Crème*

On the Monday morning, Raynes found himself once again standing beside Leonie's battered estate car, waiting for Signor Spumante. He seemed very agitated this morning.

Once again, he had trouble with the ignition.

"I hate this car," he said. "It is old. It rattles. It smells. It is a pig to drive."

Raynes himself would have preferred to travel in the Alfa Romeo; but the Grand Duchess had spoken and Spumante was not a man to disobey.

But he groaned and muttered to himself as they drove down Mount Boron. Raynes wondered if he could endure this all the way to Cannes.

"What exactly is troubling you, Monsieur?"

His respectful tone at least brought a response.

"I am not sleeping well. I am suffering from depression. I

am taking pills but they are not helping."

"Not helping what?"

Spumante cast a glance in Raynes' direction.

"I'm sure you can guess. Your friend – the painter – has taken away Madame's love for me. I can see it in her eyes. She has love only for him."

Raynes was surprised that Spumante – at his age – should feel such powerful emotions. But he tried to sound comforting.

"I'm sure it won't last. It's only a passing affair. Once the picture is finished, my friend will return home to England – and you'll never see him again. Madame may pine for some time, but I'm sure she'll come round."

But Spumante was not convinced.

"The relationship has changed. We are not the same."

Raynes reckoned that what the Italian lacked was a sense of humour. Whilst Brackles had been painting Leonie's picture, there had been sparkling conversation, many jokes, much teasing. After Brackles departed, she would feel the loss acutely.

But to make the journey more bearable, Raynes asked: "How long have you known Madame?"

"For two years. We met at an exhibition. She was hoping to buy some pictures. They were needing restoration. I introduced her to some friends of mine who did the job quite beautifully. She was very grateful for my help."

Raynes decided that it might be best if he talked to the Italian about paintings and what was involved in their restoration. It proved a wise decision. Spumante talked most of the way to Cannes – with great enthusiasm – and all the Inspector had to do was listen. The depression soon evaporated and when Spumante stepped out of the car, he seemed a much happier man.

Raynes showed him Yolande's shop. First of all, they went round to the back, but the door was locked. They returned to the main entrance and walked in.

"Is Madame Yolande here?"

"No. She has returned to Paris."

"Is Monsieur Foster here?"

"Not today."

"I wonder if we might look at your kitchen?"

"The kitchen?"

Richard nodded.

"Are you from the police?"

Hearing the word 'police', Raynes nodded and walked through the door which led to the back of the shop. The freezer was still there. The contents looked as if they had been there for some time.

"I'm going upstairs," said Raynes.

He wanted to see how Mr Foster's researches were progressing. He was not surprised to see that the desk was clear and all the drawers were empty. A complete clear-out. It did not look as if Mr Foster was intending to return. He cast his eye over the other two rooms – but they were still full of stock.

He returned to the kitchen, where the shop girl was making Camille a cup of coffee.

"Ask her if she knows Georges."

"Georges?"

"The man we met in the Rue Sébastien."

Signor Spumante asked the question – and a few more. No, the girl didn't know him. He just delivered things. She thought he came from Marseilles. At present, he lived in Nice. No, he would not have gone to Paris with Madame.

They drank their coffee and left.

"This is a bit of a wild goose chase, isn't it?" said Raynes.

"A complete waste of time."

However, at Madame Yolande's house, they found the white van. It was parked in the driveway but nobody seemed to be at home. At least, no one answered the door. To make Georges' life more difficult, Raynes lowered the pressure on all four tyres. Unless the man carried a pump, the van would be impossible to drive.

They got back into the estate car.

"I am very worried for Madame. I fear she is in very deep water. She is not telling the police the truth."

Raynes nodded.

He remembered that Leonie had told the police that the body had been found at 9.00am. Sylvie had translated her words for him. But she knew the body had been found at 7.00am and Spumante would confirm this when he spoke to the police. He had no reason to lie.

But neither had she – except to justify the delay.

Raynes said: "I wonder if she told the police that she'd put out a contract for Gaspard to be killed." Camille looked sharply at the Inspector. Raynes laughed. "I know all about it. Arnaud told me."

"You have seen Arnaud?"

"On Thursday. He told me he was offered 500,000 francs."

Spumante smiled.

"I believe you were also offered money."

"Yes, but I refused. I don't go round killing people. And neither does Arnaud. But if he were to say anything to the police, it could cause Madame a lot of trouble."

"I am worried that the inspector will find out. . . "

"Find out what?"

"Many things." He sighed. "Many things."

The Inspector said nothing. He felt that if he kept silent, Camille would say more. He was making no effort to start the car, which was a good sign.

Clearly, Spumante was torn between loyalty to his mistress and a desire to speak the truth.

Eventually, he said: "I saw Gaspard on the Wednesday afternoon."

"The day he disappeared?"

"Yes."

"Where?"

"In a taxi. He was travelling up to the Villa Rose. I don't think I was supposed to see him. I was sent on an errand, but I was late getting away."

"Do you think he had an appointment?"

"Yes."

"Why do you think she wanted to see him?"

"She was planning to bribe him. To offer him a lot of money to call off the attack. I think that was why he came up so openly in a taxi."

"Did she see him?"

"I don't know."

"Was Brackles there?"

"Yes, he was painting her picture."

"So, if Gaspard called, he might have known she had a visitor?"

"I don't think she did see him. I told her I'd seen him in the taxi but she didn't look particularly bothered. She said he'd delivered a personal letter to her daughter."

"Was she there?"

"No. She was supposed to be out with Simon."

"So who would have given him the money?"

"Sylvie, I suppose."

"And the rest of the staff would have been off that day?"

"Yes, it was Wednesday."

"But you think he may never have left the house?"

"Well, it didn't occur to me till I saw him in the pool. Up to that moment, I assumed that he was still in hiding somewhere in Nice."

"Well, perhaps he was. Why should Madame arrange for him to be found in her own pool? It doesn't make sense. Knowing the trouble it would cause, you would have expected her to have him moved elsewhere. She had over a week to arrange it."

Spumante sighed.

"She has not told me anything. All she does is talk to her lawyer."

"Maître Duclos?"

"Yes. I do not trust him. He tells Madame to treat the police with contempt. I do not think that is wise."

"Certainly not."

"He has a bad reputation, that man. He plays games with

205

his victims. Even in court he does it. He is a sadist. I fear he is playing a dangerous game with Madame. He is promising to defend her; but perhaps he will not succeed."

For the first time in a week, Raynes felt that Spumanfce was treating him as a friend. He had shared with him his deepest fears – and added one new piece to the jigsaw.

Camille turned the ignition key.

"And this afternoon, Inspector Grimaldi is coming to see me! What can I say?"

"He'll want to know why you left the villa so quickly after you found the body."

Camille shrugged his shoulders.

"It was nothing to do with me. I knew there would be much unpleasantness. I did not want to be associated with such things."

"And where did you go?"

A slight hesitation.

"To Menton."

"Why Menton?"

A much longer hesitation.

"My brother is there. . . " And then, almost shamefully, he admitted: "He is head waiter at one of the hotels there." He looked at Raynes. "You will not tell Madame this?"

"Certainly not."

There was silence in the car as they drove back into Nice. The Inspector found himself in a strange position. He was actually feeling sorry for Spumante. The shell had cracked and he had perceived a very vulnerable man within.

As they pulled up outside Monsieur Polanski's piano shop, he said to Raynes: "When we've finished seeing Bruno and Pierre – and inspecting their chest freezers, may I suggest we have lunch together?"

"Not in the Negresco!"

Camille managed to laugh.

"No. Not the Negresco. I know a very fine seafood restaurant – crabs, mussels and such things. We shall have a bottle of Muscadet – and I shall pay for everything."

Raynes accepted the offer graciously.

Having lunch with Spumante was not exactly his idea of fun; but he hoped to squeeze out more information. In vino veritas – and all that!

The Inspector ordered Canadian lobster which appeared to be the most expensive item on the menu. The Italian ordered a dozen oysters. (Raynes reckoned that he probably needed them at his age!)

Having approved of the Muscadet, Camille leant confidentially over the table.

"There was a terrible row last night between Madame and her daughter. I have heard nothing like it. Both of them were so angry. Madame was accusing her daughter of being – how do you say it – hand in glove with the enemy. She had been at meetings with them, telling them what to steal. She had even stolen lists from her mother's safe!"

Raynes was pleased to note that Leonie had been using his ammunition against her daughter.

"She was also saying that the picture she sold to the man in Monte Carlo had been stolen from a woman in Paris. Gaspard had stolen it and Mademoiselle had planted it in Madame's shop. She could be found guilty of handling stolen property."

Raynes nodded in agreement.

"Mademoiselle accused her mother of killing Monsieur Gaspard. She said she had always wanted to kill him. Madame said that, on the contrary, Mademoiselle had become disillusioned with her ex-husband. His attack on the house would have been bungled and she would have been arrested.

"So Mademoiselle had turned against him. She had made a new plan to seize the valuables herself – and blame it on Gaspard so that he would take the rap. When he discovered that she had double-crossed him, he was extremely angry. He had come to Madame to tell her what her daughter was doing. But her daughter had killed him. Deliberately – and spitefully – she had put the body in the pool so that the finger of suspicion would fall on her mother.

"Madame said that her wickedness had been unforgivable.

She had done everything she could to protect her and save her – but she had deceived her and turned against her. She had betrayed her utterly. It was a terrible row, Monsieur. I was distressed beyond measure."

Tears came to Spumante's eyes.

"Which one of them did you believe?"

"Oh, Madame - of course. She has always acted honourably - and with generosity. She may be a ruthless businesswoman, but in personal matters, she is *sans reproche*."

"Ludo thinks she is very similar to her mother."

"Perhaps in looks; but she has those cold, hard eyes. They frighten me."

Raynes nodded his agreement.

"I know what you mean. She warned me yesterday that if I continued my investigations, something nasty could happen to me. I told Madame what she had said."

"She would have been most distressed."

"She was. I think that it was perhaps what I said that provoked the quarrel."

"It was terrible to hear the hatred in her daughter's voice. Monsieur, I think she is capable of anything."

The lobster and the oysters arrived at the table.

Spumante poured each of them a second glass of wine.

"Another bottle?" suggested Raynes mischeviously.

"Why not?"

Raynes decided that Spumante was now beyond caring. Once the extra wine had been ordered, he asked: "What are you going to say to Grimaldi?"

Camille sighed.

"Of course, I shall protect Madame. I shall not say anything against her. But I have no respect for Mademoiselle. She is not a person I like or trust. I believe she has been - utterly disloyal to her mother. I think she should take responsibility for her actions. If she is arrested, *tant pis*." He shrugged his shoulders dismissively. It did not look as if it would be a very good afternoon for Ludo.

37. *La Fin de Chéri*

"'Julie'" paid her third and final visit to Inspector Grimaldi at lunchtime on Monday – just six hours before the expected return of his wife.

Realizing that this might be his last chance of being alone with this remarkable young woman, he sought to extract every ounce of pleasure he could. Debbie understood his feelings and, remembering her own ordeal on the Saturday afternoon, was extraordinarily kind to him.

He was almost tearful in his gratitude – and full of apologies for missing their date on Sunday. He had had important work to do. The results of an autopsy had come through.

Grimaldi remembered that it was "Julie" who had asked about Gaspard on her first visit.

He stroked his moustache thoughtfully.

"We have found the man your English friend was looking for."

"I saw it in the paper. He drowned in a swimming pool."

"No! No! That is not correct. He was not drowned in the swimming pool. That is what we were meant to think. No, he died elsewhere."

"Julie" said nothing. A little knowledge was a dangerous thing. If she opened her mouth, she might put her foot in it. She continued to stroke the inspector's manly chest.

"He died in a freezer."

"In a freezer?"

"Yes. He was full of ice." He laughed. "He was so full of ice that we could not even begin the autopsy till yesterday."

He looked at 'Julie'. She looked suitably surprised.

"Chérie, you do not understand these things." He proceeded to explain. "A body is full of water. 76% of our bodies are water. When the body freezes, you find ice in the thick muscles of the thighs, the buttocks. There is ice in the

209

heart, the liver and the kidneys.

"But we did not have to wait to find this out. When we found the body in the pool, it was really solid. Perhaps it had melted a little – but the arms were stiff. He was like a frozen turkey."

Debbie laughed.

"Yes, it is amusing. But not for poor Gaspard! We have to wait for him to. . . how do you say it in English?"

"To defrost."

"Just so." The inspector stroked his moustache. This was a good story and he was enjoying it. "Often I have seen climbers who have died on the mountains. They bring down their bodies in a helicopter. We have to wait for them too."

"But he hadn't been up a mountain?"

"No. He had been in a freezer. I decided that immediately. The position of his arms and legs. In his lungs, there was still the air. Carbon dioxide! That was why he floats. But because he has no oxygen, he dies. It is *l'asphyxie*."

"The what?"

"*L'asphyxie*. I am sure you have the same word in English. It is a technical term."

"So who put him in the freezer?"

"That is what we shall now find out. As I said to you before, he has many enemies. He has only just come out of prison. It may be a gangland killing. Or. . . " he paused. ". . . perhaps it is *plus sophistiqué*?

"I think I have said to you that he was planning an attack on a villa. Well, that was the house where he was found! Perhaps he was preparing for his attack? He was caught – and they have put him in their freezer."

He looked at "Julie".

"They have five freezers in that house. I have inspected all of them. They are in the kitchen – full of meat and vegetables and things. It would be difficult to hide a body in those freezers. The staff open and shut them many times every day."

"Perhaps they have another freezer?"

"No. I have searched all the outhouses, the wine cellars, the garages! Only five freezers. . . So I begin to wonder if they have hidden him elsewhere. In the house of a friend."

"But if they killed him – '*l'asphyxie*'. . . ?" She looked at him to see if she had got the word right. He nodded. ". . . why would they put him in their own pool? Why not throw him into the sea?" She laughed. "Why not take him up a mountain?"

"That is what I have been wondering. It would be very stupid to put him into their own pool. Perhaps they make *la plaisanterie*? Or perhaps his enemies have put him in the pool to confuse us? But we know who these people are. We shall soon make them confess."

Grimaldi sounded extremely confident – as indeed he was. This was such an outrageous murder, someone would soon croak. You couldn't keep a thing like this secret. Never! 'Julie' pressed herself closer.

"You have been very clever, Inspecteur."

It was nice to receive compliments. Very few people ever congratulated him. He was always so arrogant and sure of himself. People resented his success.

"Alas, chérie, your Englishman will never see his savings. They are gone." He laughed. "But at least he has the justice. The English justice."

Mention of the Englishman reminded him of that English policeman up at the Villa Rose. He had asked him whether he knew "Julie" – and he had said "no". But perhaps he should ask his bedmate the same question?

"D'you know an Englishman called Raynes?"

This was dangerous.

Debbie looked thoughtful.

"There is a famous English detective called Raynes. I have read about him in the papers."

Grimaldi dismissed him immediately.

"He is not famous. I have never heard of him."

"Julie" did not say any more.

"He is at the villa."

She feigned surprise.

"Where the body was found?"

"Yes. I think he is trying to protect these French people from my investigations. He will not succeed. I have all the facts at my fingertips. He knows nothing!"

Debbie thought to herself: By the time I report back, he will know as much and more. She was glad Richard had encouraged her to keep phoning Grimaldi. At least he would know what the opposition was up to.

The Inspector turned to look at her.

"You are very quiet, chérie?"

"I am thinking you have only another five hours before you go to the airport."

Her words brought Grimaldi down from the very heights of self-adulation – to distinctly hard earth. All his freedom – all his joys – were about to come to an end.

Feeling desperate, he put his arms round "Julie" and hugged her tightly as if frightened of letting her go.

Although Debbie's back no longer bore any signs of her recent beating, it was still very tender. She could not help wincing when the inspector pulled her towards him. He was full of concern.

"What is wrong, chérie?"

"My back is a bit painful at the moment."

He looked at her full of concern.

"A man has beaten me very hard – on Saturday."

"Your husband?" He corrected himself quickly. "No, no! You are divorced."

He had an excellent memory.

He made her lie face down on the bed and examined her carefully.

"I can see signs of bruising." He touched her. "There!"

"Oh!"

"It must have been very bad. At least he has not damaged your skin." He ran his fingers gently down her back. "Your lovely skin." He shook his head. "Why has he done this to you?"

Debbie sighed.

"For money."

"You let him do this to you for money? That is terrible." He laughed. "It is all right you beating me for money. I am a strong man. I can take it. It excites me. But to do this to a woman, it is cruel."

"I thought so too. But I couldn't escape. He had taken my passport. He said that if I didn't submit, he would burn it."

She turned to look at the French inspector. There was such tenderness in his voice – but there was real anger in his eyes.

"I will deal with this man. He must be punished."

What should she say?

Debbie realized that if she mentioned Maître Duclos by name, he would immediately connect her with the Villa Rose. Bang would go her cover! He would realize she had been pumping him for information. Perhaps he would turn against her? And if he did, what was to stop Maître Duclos from producing her signed confession – declaring that she and Richard had killed Gaspard de la Nuit?

She had already said too much.

But she felt so bitter towards her assailant that she wanted him to suffer. And if the inspector could do that, then so much the better.

So she looked puzzled.

"I don't know what his name is – but I think he is a lawyer."

"Ah, a lawyer! They are always the worst!"

"He lives in a house – an old house with tapestries – somewhere beyond Villefranche. It has shutters."

"Most houses in the south of France have shutters."

"He has a large bed which belonged to someone called Eugénie. An Empress."

"Yes, yes. She was the wife of the Emperor, Napoleon III."

"He has lots of old furniture. He tied me to a chair which belonged to the Medici. I was naked. He kept me in that chair for over four hours."

The picture conveyed to the inspector aroused him – even though he had the same naked body lying beside him. He begged her pardon. And he asked her to describe *ce sadiste inhumain.* (It sounded worse in French.)

"He had a completely bald head. A very thick neck. But he had very delicate hands. And cuff links with diamonds."

"Diamants? Yes, I know this man of whom you speak. He is a man with a very bad reputation where women are concerned. Normally, they do not speak about it. He bribes them to keep silent."

He looked tenderly at "Julie".

"He did pay you?"

"Yes, he paid well; but if I'd known what he was going to do, I would never have gone there. There are easier ways of making a few hundred francs!"

Inspector Grimaldi got off the bed and stretched himself.

"I will tell you. Mademoiselle, I have recently been in contact with this man. He has offered me money to drop one of my criminal cases."

"Is that legal?"

"No, chérie, it is not. In France, we do not accept the bribes." He pulled on his bright red briefs. "The law must take its course. But he has – privately – asked me to drop this case. Can you guess which one?"

Debbie shook her head.

"It is the case of the man found dead in the swimming pool. He is trying to protect his friends. He is a criminals' lawyer. Always he fights to prevent them being sent to jail. But I will not take his *sale monnaie*. His friends will be found guilty. I shall make sure of that."

He pulled on the rest of his clothes and Debbie put on her dress and shoes. She looked at Inspector Grimaldi – perhaps for the last time.

"Time is short," she said. "I will help you put on clean sheets and pillowcases – so that Madame Grimaldi will find the bedroom perfect when she comes home."

"Chérie, tu es une ange!"

He was so sorry for her that he increased his offering by one hundred per cent. Debbie accepted it gratefully. But she did wonder – if they met again – whether he would still think she was an angel? When he discovered that she was the mistress of the much-despised Monsieur Raynes; and had imparted all that privileged information to him? It was likely that he would then see her in a very different light.

38. *Huis Clos*

Raynes was in the bath when Debbie returned home. He was covered in thick white foam – and every now and then, he turned on the hot tap, which seemed to make things marginally worse.

"How much shampoo did you put in the bath?"

"Just a little."

"I hope it wasn't my expensive stuff?"

Raynes changed the subject.

(It was the expensive stuff.)

"Did you have any success with Grimaldi?"

"Of course." Debbie sat down on the lavatory seat and put her handbag on the floor. "He says you are not a famous detective."

Raynes raised his eyebrows.

"He has never heard of you! He thinks you know nothing. He has all the facts at his fingertips. Soon he will make an arrest." She smiled. "He is very arrogant – but he can be quite sweet."

"I couldn't agree. I think he's insufferable."

"He is very upset about his wife coming home. I helped him tidy up the flat. She won't know that I have been there. He has put his handcuffs back in the car."

Raynes waited patiently, hoping she would not recount all the gory details.

"So what did he say about Gaspard?"

"Lass – fixy. . . "

"Asphyxia? Lack of oxygen? That sounds right."

"He thinks he has been in a freezer. Hence the ice."

Debbie struggled to remember the details of their conversation.

215

"His muscles would have been thick with the stuff. Especially his thighs – and his bum. Does that sound right?"

Raynes nodded.

"His heart, his lungs and his liver. . . "

"Not his lungs!"

"No. They were filled with carbon dioxide. It poisoned him." She paused. "The human body is 76% water. So, lots of ice."

"Has he done the autopsy?"

"Yesterday. They had to wait for him to thaw out. He says that he has seen many frozen people. Usually on the mountains. They bring them down in helicopters. I don't think he's seen a person in a freezer before."

Raynes poured in a little more hot water.

"I had one once. A butcher's assistant in south London. It was amazing how quickly he died. But that was quite a large commercial freezer. You could walk around in it."

He turned off the tap.

"Well, he had a look in all the freezers downstairs. They've got five. He didn't think they'd been used. Too public. When you were getting out the mangetout, you might notice a body lying there!

"I did suggest there might be another freezer elsewhere; but he said that he had searched all the outhouses, garages – even the wine cellar. He didn't see one."

"Spumante probably took it to Menton with him."

"He wouldn't get it in an Alfa Romeo."

"No," said Raynes, "but you could get it in a white van."

Debbie shrugged her shoulders.

"Anyway, he's not convinced. He can't see why Leonie would dump the corpse in her own pool. Not unless it was a double bluff. He thinks it might have been."

Raynes sighed.

"I don't know. I'm beginning to think it was sheer panic. 'The police are coming. Where can we put it?'"

"So you think the body was here?" She looked at Richard with a mischievous smile. "Perhaps it was in Sylvie's

216

bedroom?"

Richard's face was innocence itself.

"I wouldn't know."

"You liar! I bet you've been with her. Her room's *The Little Russian*. Brackles told me."

"Has he been there?"

Was there a slight touch of jealousy?

"No. But he says that Sylvie is deeply smitten. 'Oh, Monsieur Richard'," she mimicked Sylvie's accent. "'Would you like annuza café au lait – or a morceau of omelette. . . ?' She hates me."

"I don't think she does."

"She thinks I treat you very badly. She doesn't realize that I am conducting private investigations on your behalf. Three visits to Monsieur Grimaldi. Such hard work!" She laughed. "Such poor pay!"

Raynes smiled.

"You should give him a frequent user discount!"

"Actually, he paid me double this afternoon. He was so grateful. He dreads his wife coming home." She laughed again. "Do you know he wears red briefs? Very smart!"

Richard thought a compliment was due.

"You've done an excellent piece of investigation."

"There was one thing I didn't understand. This lass-fixy. . ."

"It means that you die from lack of oxygen. The freezer is airtight. When the lid goes down, there's only a limited amount of oxygen left in the freezer. You breathe in oxygen; you breathe out carbon dioxide. Your lungs struggle to take in more oxygen – but there's only carbon dioxide. Your lungs get full of the wrong stuff."

"So he wouldn't have died of hypothermia?"

"No."

"It's rather nasty, isn't it?"

"It's quick. It would only take a matter of minutes."

"Why couldn't he climb out?"

"Drugged. . . drunk. . . Did he say anything about the contents of his stomach?"

"No."

"He wouldn't have gone into the freezer willingly! He'd have needed a little help."

There was a thoughtful silence in the bathroom.

"So it was definitely murder?"

Raynes nodded.

"Whoever shut the lid – killed him."

"And you know who it was?"

"Actually, no. I'm still trying to think which one of them it was. There's a ruthlessness about this murder. A cold Russian ruthlessness. Leonie. . . Ludo. . . "

"I still think it was Ernst."

"You may be right. His father may have been a Russian soldier. He has the look of a Cossack about him."

Debbie was reminded of a final piece of information she had to give Richard:

"There's one more thing. The inspector told me that Maître Duclos (she almost shuddered as she mentioned his name). . . Maître Duclos has been trying to bribe him to give up the case."

"The French police wouldn't accept bribes."

"That's what he said. He doesn't have a very high opinion of Monsieur Duclos. He says he's a 'criminals' lawyer'."

"That's what he said to me. He's a very nasty piece of work."

Debbie looked at Richard with pitying eyes. If only he knew. . .

39. *La Belle Dame Sans Merci*

Following his interview with Camille Calvoressco, Inspector Grimaldi went straight to the airport to meet his wife. The plane was only five minutes late and Madame Grimaldi emerged from the baggage collection zone with an immense amount of luggage – presents for all her children and grandchildren. It took some time to pack it all in the car.

Then they went off to one of their daughters for a family gathering which seemed to last for hours. Having drunk an unusually large amount of alcohol, Madame Stephanie found herself in a highly romantic mood and when they returned home, she claimed her matrimonial rights. Having indulged himself so shamelessly during her absence, her husband could hardly refuse.

On the Tuesday morning, Mrs Grimaldi set about cleaning their flat, whilst the Inspector escaped to the office and dictated what he could remember of his interview with Camille.

His evidence seemed to be heavily weighted against Madame Leonie's daughter. The words: 'deceit' and 'betrayal' had been used quite frequently. It appeared that there had been a violent argument between the two women on Sunday night, in which serious allegations had been made on both sides.

What had emerged was that Gaspard had visited the house on the Wednesday afternoon – the last time he had been seen – and been entertained by his ex-wife. Perhaps 'entertained' was the wrong word. He had been given some drugs; plied with champagne and cast into a freezer. Whose freezer it was, was still uncertain. Monsieur Camille had spent part of Monday looking for it.

Madame Leonie apparently had a cast-iron alibi. She was being painted by one of her English guests. So it was undoubtedly the daughter who had met Gaspard. At that moment, it would have been quite possible to move the body out of the Villa Rose. And perhaps it had been moved? Once the English policeman had arrived, it might have been more difficult since his bedroom window overlooked the courtyard. Even he might have noticed a body being moved!

The Italian had overheard the argument. Inspector Grimaldi suspected that he had probably had his ear to the keyhole. But what he had heard was extremely interesting.

It appeared that Madame Leonie kept a list of all her property – for insurance purposes – in her safe. This had been removed and photocopied; then given to Monsieur Polanski and his friends. The most desirable items had been indicated.

But then, it seemed, the daughter had had second thoughts. She had decided to kill her ex-husband and prevent the attack from taking place.

Inspector Grimaldi sent for Ludo's file and details of the court case in Paris where both she and Gaspard had been found guilty. The more he looked at her record, the more certain he became that there had been a miscarriage of justice. She was a dangerous woman and should have been jailed along with her husband. It was only the skilled defence of Maître Duclos that had saved her.

How he hated that man! Doubtless, he would once again be mobilized to protect Ludo from the full force of the law. Inspector Grimaldi decided that the time had come to make an arrest. Even if it was not the right person, it would certainly concentrate minds – and perhaps provoke a few more revelations.

So, shortly before the noontide cannon was fired, he arrived at the Villa Rose.

* * * *

Sylvie brought the grim news.

"Madame, Inspector Grimaldi has returned."

"Who does he want to see this time?"

"He won't say."

"Show him to my study."

It had been a difficult morning. She had not gone to the shop – even though two important customers had promised to call. In her place, she sent Madame Foster, who was not quite sure which pieces Leonie was referring to. The menu for dinner had been changed twice. She had hoped for a quiet morning with Brackles – starting a second portrait – a more intimate portrait reminiscent of the Rokeby Venus, but they had not been able to get started. Camille had been his usual interfering self, constantly coming into her room. How she wished she had sent him off for another morning in town with

Monsieur Raynes.

So, very little had been accomplished. Now it was the police! She descended to the small walnut-panelled room beside the front door.

"Monsieur Grimaldi. . . "

"Madame."

He inclined his head.

"I believe you have come to ask more questions?"

"Not you, Madame. Rather, your daughter."

"She's out. Shopping with her English fiancé."

Grimaldi stroked his moustache.

"And when will she return?"

Leonie was about to say: "In time for lunch" but, as she looked out of the window, she saw Ludo's white Citroen pulling into the courtyard.

"She is here now."

"Excellent."

Grimaldi managed a smile.

"Was there anything specific you wanted to ask her?"

"We feel she may be able to help us in our inquiries into the death of her ex-husband. You will remember that she was out of the house on Friday when I called."

"You may use this room. Inspector."

"Thank you, Madame, but it will not be necessary. We shall speak to her at police headquarters."

"Are you arresting her?"

"I am."

Leonie was white-faced.

"On what grounds?"

"We believe that she has been responsible for the death of Monsieur Gaspard, her husband."

Leonie reached for the phone.

"I must contact her lawyer, Maître Duclos."

"I'm afraid he will have to see her at the police station." He paused ominously. "When I have finished speaking to her."

Leonie sat slumped in her chair, her face white and drawn. She was so used to getting her own way, that this came as a shock.

"With your permission, Madame. . . "

Inspector Grimaldi walked out into the entrance hall and bowed graciously to Ludo and Simon.

"Madame de la Nuit, I am arresting you in connection with the murder of your late husband. I would be very pleased if you could accompany me to the police station. My car is at the door."

The Inspector may have expected high drama – screams – perhaps even a contrived faint – but Ludo was completely self- controlled. Of course, it had happened before. The police always took you completely by surprise.

Her face coloured; her blood pressure rose; but her eyes were as cold and imperious as those of her mother. They demonstrated her utter contempt for this lackey of the Fifth Republic who had dared to accuse her.

Simon was more agitated.

"What are you saying? Have you got a warrant? You just can't walk in here and arrest people! This is a democratic country!"

Inspector Grimaldi ignored him.

He continued to look at Ludo. All he said was: "Your friend may come as well – if he wishes."

Grimaldi gestured towards the door. Ludo put down several carrier bags. She looked at her mother who was standing in the doorway of the study. For once, there were tears in her eyes.

"Is this your doing?" she asked.

"Certainly not. I was only told five minutes ago."

Ludo looked slightly relieved.

"Kindly phone my lawyer. He will deal with this."

"I've already tried to phone him; but he's out. I will speak to him as soon as I can."

Ludo turned on her heel and walked out into the bright sunshine. What a miserable end to a beautiful day!

* * * *

Raynes was not even aware that the Inspector had called. He was sitting beside the pool under a large orange sunshade sipping his apéritif.

It was Brackles who enlightened him.

He sat down heavily in an adjoining seat.

"Grimaldi's arrested Ludo."

"When?"

"Just now – in the front hall. Leonie's weeping her heart out. I've done my best to comfort her, but she's very hurt and very angry."

"Where's Simon?"

"He's not been arrested, but he's gone along with her. Moral support, I suppose. Or immoral. Depending which way you look at it."

"Has she phoned her lawyer?"

"That's what's upsetting Madame. He's out. Probably still at the law courts or having lunch with some client. She feels quite helpless. We'll have to do our best to cheer her up at lunchtime – give her some hope."

"What about Spumante?"

"He's gone too. He's been annoying her all morning. Coming and going. Constant interruptions. We couldn't get anything done. Eventually, she gave him a round of the guns – and he fled."

"How very convenient!"

Brackles looked thoughtful.

"Do you think he could be the cause of all this?"

"Could be."

"I think he knows more than he lets on. He's always listening at keyholes. He may have said something to Grimaldi when he was being interviewed yesterday afternoon."

"I think he probably did. He said a lot to me yesterday – mostly against Ludo. If he repeated all that to Grimaldi, it's no wonder he came and arrested her." He looked at Brackles with a broad smile. "As you prophesied, 'the truffles have finally hit the crème brulée'!"

Brackles looked apologetic.

"I did suggest to the Grand Duchess that our Italian friend might have spilled the beans."

Raynes smiled happily.

"I feel the moment of revenge is drawing closer."

"Much closer," Brackles agreed.

"If we drop a word to the police that they can find Gaspard's clothes and his passport in Spumante's room, that should take the pressure off Ludo."

"I'm sure Leonie would be most grateful."

Raynes sipped a little more of his apéritif.

"I think that we might also suggest that the pills which put Gaspard out of action are to be found in Spumante's room."

"I'm sure they are."

"So am I."

Brackles looked at Raynes with a certain quiet pride.

"By the way," he said casually, "I've remembered where I saw that other freezer!"

Raynes smiled broadly.

"So have I. And did you receive the same inducements to oblivion?"

Brackles laughed.

"That's one way of putting it!"

"It was the blowlamp that made me start thinking. You know. . . when we destroyed that picture. . . "

"Don't remind me!"

"I mean, what was a blowlamp doing in a wine cellar? Warming up the Beaujolais?"

"They must have used it to defrost the body. It must've been stuck to the sides. Unnerving in an emergency?"

"Very. But once they'd got him out, their chief aim was to get rid of that freezer. They forgot about the blowlamp. It must have given Sylvie quite a jolt to see it still sitting there – and us using it."

Brackles looked over his shoulder to see if they were alone.

"I did speak to Sylvie – yesterday. I said to her that I was sure I had seen a freezer in the cellar on my first visit."

"And what did she say?"

"'You are quite mistaken, Monsieur.'" He mimicked Sylvie's English accent. "But I didn't believe her. I can see it now. It had a lot of junk stacked on it. It's amazing they didn't get rid of it right away."

Raynes stared at the ripples on the surface of the pool, his mind miles away.

"You can always rely on murderers to make some fatal mistake – to leave some vital clue. It's just a question of recognizing it when you see it." He paused. "Everything round here works to a command structure. Orders were given to kill Gaspard – but not to move him. Better the element of mystery. 'Where is Gaspard?' So everyone goes hunting round Nice, rather than looking too closely at the Villa Rose. I can see the logic of that. But once Debbie spoke to Grimaldi and he decided to search all properties connected with the missing man – that pushed the panic button."

"Ernst put the body in the pool?"

"I should think so. I also think he moved the freezer. You will remember both he and Madame's car were missing on the Friday morning."

"Sylvie must have been involved."

"She has the keys."

Both men were silent.

"And the Grand Duchess. . . "

"What was she doing that Wednesday afternoon?"

"Getting her picture painted. No hanky-panky that afternoon. Spumante was sent off on some fool's errand and we got down to it. We worked hard till about 5.00pm."

"So you were her alibi?"

"Most certainly. I can vouch for her every movement." He smiled. "Not that she did move very much. She's a very good sitter. Looking back, I think she was a little anxious; but I assumed she was worried about the picture."

"Shall we be seeing it soon?"

"It's being unveiled on Friday. Her birthday."

Raynes saw Sylvie approaching.

"Messieurs, lunch will be served in ten minutes." She looked down at the table, "Tiens! Monsieur, you have nothing to drink!"

"I wouldn't say 'no' to a strong brandy."

"A large, strong brandy?"

"Parfait, Mademoiselle."

As Sylvie headed back to the house, he said: "Funny to think of her as a murderer."

Richard was thinking of the two passionate afternoons he had spent in the *Little Russian* room under the eaves. He asked himself a question, he had asked so many times before: "How could women be so treacherous?"

To Brackles, he said. "I hope not. She said she wants to marry me."

"If I were you, I'd stick to the one you've got. She's one in a million."

Raynes laughed.

"But she'll be the one with the million! Not me."

40. *Les Confessions*

Debbie was worried that Maître Duclos might seek to get Ludo released by producing her own signed confession. If he did, then Grimaldi might suddenly turn up at the house and arrest both of them. Richard would know nothing about it and, because they would probably be put in separate cells, she would be unable to tell him what had happened.

There was never going to be a 'right time' to break the news. Better get it over as quickly as possible.

She had just put on her elegant dark blue dress. It went nicely with the diamond earrings. She put a silver bangle on her wrist.

She said: "I think there's something you should know."

The serious tone of her voice made Richard turn and look at her. What was coming? Her face was white and strained. She gave a final glance at herself in the mirror and took a deep breath.

"I have signed a confession admitting that we murdered Gaspard and put his body in the swimming pool."

Raynes looked at her with total disbelief.

"*We?*"

"Yes. I didn't tell you at the time – but I was forced to sign it."

Raynes was about to say; "How could you have been so stupid!" But he realized that Debbie was far too worldly-wise to sign any incriminating document. (Not even a tax return!) It must have been a very compelling reason that made her do such a thing.

"Who forced you to sign it?"

"Maître Duclos."

"On Saturday?"

"Yes. He wouldn't let me out of the house till I'd signed it. He threatened to burn my passport."

"Why didn't you just walk out?"

"Because I was tied to a chair. I couldn't move. I was there for four hours!"

Tears came into her eyes. She couldn't control herself. She began to sob bitterly.

Richard immediately took her into his arms and held her whilst her body heaved with emotion. He had never seen her quite so upset. On Friday night, with Brackles' picture, it had been anger. Now it was something worse. He felt himself at a loss to cope.

He had always found Debbie incredibly strong-minded, resilient, capable of dealing with most of life's tragedies with a laugh or a wry smile. But not tonight.

Even before he knew the full story, he decided to get his revenge on the lawyer.

He said quietly: "It didn't turn out as you expected?"

"No."

"No imperial bed?"

"The bed was there but he never used it."

"But he tied you to a chair?"

Fingers digging into his shoulders told him how she felt. Perhaps she didn't want to talk about it?

"It wasn't a normal sort of chair. It was a sort of wooden throne. He tied my hands to the arms, my feet to the legs and my neck to the back. So I couldn't move. I couldn't escape."

"Did he get pleasure from that?"

She shrugged her shoulders.

"He may have done. I was naked. But the room was very dark. He kept walking around asking me questions as if I was in a court of law."

Raynes tried to imagine the scene.

"What was he questioning you about?"

"About bringing the police into this house. He said that I had put Leonie and her daughter at risk. I had interfered in her private affairs by asking Grimaldi to find Gaspard. I was destroying her privacy. Bringing down a great woman, he said. She might be jailed. Her staff might be jailed. . .

"It was a complete cross-examination. He kept asking the same questions over and over again. It was quite frightening. I answered him back. I thought that was what he wanted. But when I cried – that made him worse. He just lashed me with words. After that I went silent – but that didn't do any good. He just sat and waited till I agreed to confess. He seemed prepared to sit there all night.

"So I decided to give way. I didn't think it would matter. I mean, I know you didn't kill Gaspard – and neither did I.

"I felt it was just a cruel game he was playing. But I know now that he would use that confession – if it suited him. And if Leonie wants Ludo released, I can see him using it – to help her; and landing us both in the shit."

Raynes could also see the danger quite clearly. And it worried him.

Debbie continued: "I didn't tell you because I knew you'd be angry." She looked at Richard. "Not with me – but with him. In fact, I thought you might attack him."

(She was right.)

"Did you tell Grimaldi?"

"I didn't tell him about the confession. . . "

"What did you tell him?"

Debbie sighed.

"I told him about the beating. . . "

Raynes raised his eyebrows.

"He beat me horribly. My back was terribly sore. And he shoved things into me – knives. . . I was terrified he would cut me. . . I was shaking so much."

She didn't really like telling Richard all this. She normally kept quiet about her work. She was afraid he might persuade her to give up her job and settle down. But she had never suffered quite so much from one of her customers. Even now, she couldn't tell Richard the whole story. It was so disgusting. At least he would realize that she hadn't confessed lightly.

"I didn't notice that he'd beaten you."

"I didn't want you to notice."

Raynes thought quickly.

"That was the night you were wearing your black dress? You were crying. . . I thought it was because of Gaspard."

Debbie shook her head.

"No, I was crying for myself."

Raynes was inwardly furious.

"That bastard! I shall deal with him. . . " He caught Debbie's eye. "Well, if I get the opportunity, I shall deal with him."

"Be careful. . . He's evil. He's complete ruthless."

"Does anybody else know what happened?"

"I think Leonie knows. I didn't say anything to her – but she asked me how the afternoon had gone. I think she expected it to be unpleasant."

"Is she on his side?"

"I don't think so. She looked very sympathetic. I think she must know what he's like." Anger burned deeply inside her. "He's mad. He's living out a fantasy. Cross-examination, punishment, torture. Then he throws you out like a piece of rotten meat. That's what it felt like."

"Did he pay you?"

"Yes."

229

"You said he was generous."

"He was. But I wouldn't go through that again for any amount of money. I normally enjoy my work; but that was sickening. He told me I could use the money for my defence."

"What did Grimaldi say?"

"He was livid. He said he would deal with him. He knows him – professionally. I'm sure if he did see the confession, he'd know how it was obtained."

"Is your back all right now?"

Debbie nodded.

"He didn't mark me – but I was bruised. My back felt red hot. I put lots of creams on it. After about two days, it went. But, at the time, it really stung."

"I don't like that thing about the knives. He could really have hurt you."

Debbie picked up two more silver bracelets and put them on her wrists.

"It was hellish. If I could carve him up, I would. And that's the truth."

Raynes wondered how he should handle this information. What if Duclos appeared at another cocktail party or dinner? Would he be able to prevent Debbie attacking him? Would it be better – more dignified – just to walk out? Should they pack their bags and go to a hotel? He was upset to think that Debbie had suffered so much; and he had been completely unaware of it.

Still – now he knew.

He looked at Debbie who was once again looking at her face in the mirror – trying to do something about her pink eyes.

"I think we should keep this information to ourselves. But if we get the opportunity, we must hit back hard."

"I don't want anyone else to know. It was so humiliating. It really broke me." She looked at Richard. "You may not believe it, but something inside me just snapped."

"I believe every word."

"I'm so sorry."

Richard put his arms round her and held her tight.

There was nothing more he could say.

41. *Les Chimères*

Camille was not present at dinner that night – and neither was Leonie. Rumour had it that more strong words had passed between them. It was even suggested that Signor Spumante had been told to pack his bags and go. Simon, who arrived back in the Villa Rose just in time for dinner, was the chief source of information.

He reported that Leonie had been to the police station, accompanied by her lawyer, but had not been accorded the respect she deserved. A five minute meeting in the presence of police officers had ended in a slanging match.

Simon had not been allowed to see Ludo. He had come home with Leonie, who was sizzling with rage against Inspector Grimaldi. She was also deeply dissatisfied with Maître Duclos who had been unable to obtain bail for his wealthy client.

It appeared that Ludo was being charged with the theft of a picture, stolen in Paris. Simon couldn't believe it was the Braque. The picture had been found in Leonie's shop. He had been involved in identifying it.

Raynes noticed that Amelie Foster, who was busy sipping her bouillabaisse, did not look up from her plate.

Simon reported that Inspector Grimaldi had accused Ludo of killing her ex-husband and hiding his body somewhere in the Villa Rose. She had also stolen secret documents from her mother's safe and given them to Gaspard's friends to help them in their raid on the house.

"Who could have told Grimaldi such things?" Simon demanded angrily.

This time, Mrs Foster did look up from her plate. She stared accusingly at Richard.

The Inspector instantly defended himself.

"That was what Camille was saying yesterday when we had lunch together. He was wondering how much he should tell the police. I think he claimed to have overheard some conversation."

Mrs Foster continued to look at Richard.

What a liar he was!

Raynes shook his head.

"1 haven't said a word to Grimaldi. He told me to keep my nose out of this case."

"Well," said Simon, "Madame thinks it's him. In the car coming back, she said she was going to deal with him once and for all."

Brackles breathed a sigh of relief.

"Thank God for that! Now we can get on with the picture."

Simon looked at him with some surprise.

"I thought you'd finished it?"

"We've started a new one."

"Another commission? Lucky you! What have you got in it this time? More circus animals?"

"No. A classic pose."

Amelie now turned her wrath on Brackles. She could not forgive him for abandoning her painting in the Rue Sébastien. She had been up at the flat on Monday morning with Arnaud, looking for it. They had found the front door smashed open. The flat looked relatively intact but the picture had gone. She wished she had taken a photograph of it; but she had never expected it to be stolen.

Simon turned to Sylvie who was supervising the clearing of the dishes.

"Is Monsieur Camille having his meal upstairs?"

Sylvie nodded.

"Is it true he's been asked to pack his bags?"

Sylvie was the soul of discretion.

"I do not know what Madame has decided."

Ernst was pouring out the wine for the next course. Raynes fancied there was a slight smile on his face – but perhaps it was just his imagination. He turned his attention to the wine –

a Bikaver from Eger – with a black label and a rather menacing bull's face.

Brackles asked a few questions about the wine. What part of Hungary did it come from? Lake Balaton? Sylvie was not sure. She thought it was from further north. Anyway, it was the traditional Bull's Blood. A fairly recent vintage.

During the next course, there was general speculation as to whether Leonie would ask Signor Spumante to leave. He seemed to have few friends around the table. Even Julius Foster thought Madame would be better off without him.

"He's far too old for her. She needs a younger man."

Brackles nodded his head vigorously.

"Well, I can tell you," Simon said forcefully, "when Ludo comes home, she will insist that he goes. We can't have a traitor living under the same roof."

Mrs Foster quickly changed the subject.

"Do you think she'll be released tomorrow?"

Simon was not entirely sure.

"Mr Duclos thought it might take a couple of days. He intends to see Monsieur le Maire tomorrow and bring political pressure to bear on the police. He's going to do everything he can to get Ludo released."

Debbie looked at Richard.

He sighed.

Ludo's release might lead directly to their arrest. Who could predict what Grimaldi might do? Everyone did their best to comfort and support Simon but, several times, he was reduced to tears.

"I just can't bear to think of her spending a night in some cold cell – and here we are, dining in luxury. It seems so unfair. I just wanted to talk to her; but they wouldn't let me. I shall be there tomorrow. . . whatever happens!"

No one felt inclined to linger over the meal – even though it was a good one. As they rose from the table, Richard came round to Brackles and said: "I hope you removed those clothes from Spumante's room?"

Brackles nodded.

"Did it after lunch."

"And where are they now?"

"In Simon's room. I didn't think he'd notice. He's got bigger things on his mind."

Raynes felt like saying: "Haven't we all?"

* * * *

When Raynes descended to the dining room, thirteen hours later, he found Brackles busy writing at the table.

He helped himself to a bowl of fresh raspberries and poured over them a generous helping of cream.

"You'll be glad to hear he's gone," said Brackles.

"Who?" asked Raynes.

"Spumante."

"And not even a word of farewell?" He put his bowl down on the table. "Did he leave a forwarding address?"

"I believe not."

"When did this happen?"

"Early this morning. I think it came as a surprise even to her ladyship."

"Well, she did tell him to go."

"Not quite in this way."

Raynes looked sharply at Brackles.

"Was it suicide?"

"Looks like it. Overdose of pills. A deep sleep. A quick trip to the hospital. A rapid transfer to the mortuary. And that's it!"

"I should get up earlier in the morning. I'm missing all the fun. Have the police been yet?"

"They're expected shortly. That's why I'm doing this."

Raynes took his first mouthful of raspberries. What a delicious way to start the day! But perhaps they needed a little sugar to enhance the taste. He sprinkled on two spoonfuls. Yes, that improved things.

He looked back at Brackles.

"So what are you doing?"

"Forging Spumante's signature. Madame has been typing

his farewell note on her typewriter and I'm hoping to add a little verisimilitude to the document."

Raynes thought this could be quite dangerous – but Brackles shook his head.

"We've got quite a few samples to go on. They vary – depending on his mood. I'm trying to give the impression of hopeless despair." He held up two pieces of paper.

"What do you think?"

"Plausible. But if you're using Spumante's pen, remember to remove the fingerprints and don't touch the final document. Wear plastic gloves. And burn all those." He indicated Brackles' early efforts. "And the originals. Don't bin them! Burn them. Destroy all evidence."

Brackles laughed.

"You sound like a professional! But you forget, I'm old in sin."

"Just one mistake and they'll get you."

"They took all his pills with him – so they'll be covered with his fingerprints."

"Who discovered him?"

"Ernst. Took in his coffee – and there he was."

"I'm surprised Madame didn't call me."

"I don't think there was any problem with this one. Straightforward overdose. It's just a question of exploiting the opportunity."

Raynes raised his eyebrows.

"I see."

He returned to his raspberries and cream. But food was no longer uppermost in his mind.

"So what's going into this farewell note?"

"A full confession. A tale of unrequited love. Frustration. Despair. A desire to save Madame from her enemies. To thwart the dreaded Gaspard. Spumante dipping into his fortune and offering the young man a handsome bribe to go away and sin no more. A contemptuous refusal. The young man drugged and despatched to the freezer. The fear of a police search. Sudden panic. The body cast into the pool. . .

235

Remorse. . . "

Raynes shook his head.

"It begs a lot of questions. I don't think Spumante had any fortune. He lived by his wits. Even if he had had any money, I don't think he'd have given a penny to Gaspard. If anyone was offering money, it was Leonie. Neither can I see Spumante carrying the body down to the cellar. He'd have needed help both ways. And, anyway, who moved the freezer? I'm sure it was Ernst. It couldn't have been Spumante. It just couldn't."

The Inspector looked more pointedly at Brackles.

"Can you even be sure it was suicide? It looks too well timed. Madame needs a scapegoat to take the heat off her daughter. She knows Spumante shopped her to the police. This could be revenge. I presume the pills he took were the same ones that were used to silence Gaspard. I can see the motive writ large and clear; and so will Grimaldi. He'll think this is a put-up job."

There was silence whilst Céléstine brought in fresh coffee and a wicker basket of hot croissants for the Inspector.

"And where is Sylvie this morning?"

"She is with Madame."

Raynes nodded. He was beginning to get the picture. The first and second gravediggers. "Alas poor Yorick. I knew him well. . . " He must be careful what he said – especially in front of the servants.

He buttered one of his croissants.

"And whose idea was this confession?"

"Her lawyer's."

Of course. He should have guessed. Maître Duclos was making feverish attempts to blame anyone he could for Gaspard's murder. Anything to get Madame off the hook. This latest confession would take the pressure off Ludo – it could also help him and Debbie. For that at least, he should be grateful.

The Inspector continued to feel sorry for Signor Spumante. He had fallen like Lucifer from heaven and become the universal scapegoat. He could understand Brackles joining in the campaign to do him down. But it could easily be something more sinister. Brackles had been with Leonie on the Wednesday afternoon when Gaspard disappeared. He was her alibi. Was he also involved in Spumante's death?

As Raynes had already noted, when you had served your purpose at the Villa Rose, you could be quickly disposed of. Even Maître Duclos would be ditched if he failed to deliver the goods. He must realize how ruthless his client could be. No wonder he was behind this ridiculous confession. He must be grasping at straws. Raynes smiled to himself. At least Ludo could not be accused of murdering Spumante! She had a perfect alibi. But what about Simon?

Brackles continued to perfect his signature.

"And where is this letter supposed to have been found?"

"In his jacket pocket."

"Waiting for Grimaldi to find it?"

"No. Once I've signed it, Ernst is taking it down to Monsieur Duclos."

Sylvie walked into the dining room with a sheet of cream paper in a plastic file.

"Bonjour, Monsieur."

She laid the paper in front of Brackles.

He picked up the pen and added the signature with a confident flourish.

Sylvie looked at Richard.

"You have heard the news, Monsieur?"

"Yes. But I can't imagine anyone is weeping for him."

"Madame is *triste*. She feels that perhaps she has been too hard on him."

Raynes disagreed.

"I think he is very lucky to have been tolerated for so long. His jealousy and rudeness must have been very difficult to bear."

Brackles laughed.

"You can say that again! He was a public nuisance. How we never came to blows, I shall never know. Madame showed amazing self-control, putting up with all his tantrums. I'd have put him out long ago."

Sylvie put the letter back into its plastic folder. She looked at Brackles with an indulgent smile.

"Madame would like to speak to you. Perhaps you could take the letter with you?"

"I'm sure Richard would like to hear it first."

Raynes nodded.

Of course he would like to hear it, even if it was a tissue of lies.

"It's in French – not English, so I shall have to translate. Fortunately, it is not in Italian – but Madame has put in a few of his bons mots!" He coughed discreetly. "Ma chère Madame. . . "

The letter contained much of what Brackles had already said. It was written more in sorrow than in anger. It was full of apologies for having embarrassed his hostess. He blamed his actions on *trop de zele*. He had been trying to protect her. Her home. Her treasures. He accepted all the blame for killing Gaspard and hiding his body. No one else had been involved – just him. He said that he now felt very guilty for what he had done. It had greatly troubled his conscience. As a man of honour. . . Brackles almost choked as he uttered the words. As a man of honour, he thought he should do the decent thing. . . accept full responsibility . . . and bow out gratefully from her presence.

There were a number of wistful references to the happiness of their time together. There was no mention of his rival. Brackles was neatly airbrushed out of the picture.

It was so beautifully written that tears came to Sylvie's eyes. "C'est tres émouvante," she said.

"Yes," said Brackles, "Madame has created a beautiful epitaph – more gracious than he deserved. He'd never have written anything like that himself."

"I would imagine not," said Raynes, to whom the whole thing sounded completely phoney. Grimaldi would demolish it line by line. In fact, it was a very dangerous document; for once he started investigating the provenance of the confession, the finger of suspicion would point directly at Leonie. She would have been much better advised to say nothing – to write nothing. This bogus confession could do untold damage. Raynes began to wonder whether perhaps Maître Duclos was trying to destroy Leonie. Was this another of his sadistic games?

Brackles stood up.

"I shall deliver this letter to the Grand Duchess. And perhaps give her a few words of comfort whilst I am there."

Sylvie smiled.

"I shall make sure you are not disturbed. Monsieur."

42. *J'accuse*

Sylvie started clearing up the breakfast table.

"It was a wonderful letter," she said.

"If you happen to believe it," said Raynes.

She stopped.

"You do not believe it, Monsieur?"

"No. And neither do you. Madame created that letter. She said what she wanted to believe; what she hoped others might believe. But it is pure fiction. Fantasy. Monsieur Camille could not have carried the body. He could not have moved the freezer. And when the Inspector sees the letter, he will not believe it either. It could be very dangerous for Madame."

"So you do not think it was Monsieur Camille?"

"No."

Raynes smiled one of his dangerous smiles.

"But I have a very good idea of who it was. I think it was you!"

"Moi? Mais non, Monsieur!"

The grey eyes grew larger in mock horror.

"Mais oui, Madame. I think you have played a very clever part in all this. Others may have been deceived – but I think I know what happened." He looked at Sylvie in a kindly fashion. "Would you like to sit down and have a coffee with me? There is plenty of coffee. . . "

At any other time, Sylvie would have been delighted to sit down and chat with Richard; but it was difficult to accept that a friend – and, even more, a lover – should accuse her of such a terrible crime. With the utmost reluctance, she sat down and poured herself a café noir.

At that moment, Céléstine came in to collect the dishes.

"Céléstine, do not disturb us. And do not disturb Madame. She is with Monsieur Brackles. And. . . " as she turned to go, ". . . . please shut the door."

Sylvie returned to Richard, who was watching her like a hawk. But his voice was very soft and beguiling.

"When I first visited your room – for that very happy afternoon we spent together, I asked you if you knew where Gaspard was. You said you did not know – but you lied to me. You knew precisely where he was. He was in the freezer in the wine cellar. He had been there for the past week.

"When the body was discovered in the pool – frozen, everyone immediately started talking about freezers. You told me that there were five freezers in the Villa Rose – all in public places. Five freezers should be enough for any establishment – and, sure enough, when the police started searching the house, only five freezers were found.

"Brackles and I both felt we had seen another one; but we couldn't remember where. It was, of course, in the wine cellar to which you have the keys. Brackles and I had both seen it; but it did not entirely register in our minds. Quite frankly, we were more interested in the booze; and when we came out of the cellar, you made both of us so welcome that we tended to forget what we had seen.

"Now, when we went into the cellar on Friday night, to destroy Mrs Foster's picture, there was no freezer. But there was a blowlamp! Very convenient for destroying the picture, but also very useful for defrosting a body which was sticking to the walls of the freezer."

Raynes smiled grimly.

"Now I have no doubt the body was there. I think Madame also accepts that it was there. But when Brackles asked you about it on Monday, you denied it." He paused. "But how did Gaspard end up in that chest freezer?

"I am told that he came to the Villa Rose on the Wednesday afternoon. Camille saw him coming up the drive in a taxi. This was not an undercover operation; it was open and above board. The visit had been arranged. A suggestion had been made that Madame might offer him a substantial amount of money to call off the attack. But so far as we know, no money changed hands.

"Leonie was told that a letter was handed over for Ludo, but you reported that the letter had been destroyed. I am sure there was no letter. This was a business meeting.

"That afternoon, Madame was having her portrait painted by Monsieur Brackles. She had left instructions that she was not to be disturbed. The staff were having their afternoon off. So who would Monsieur Gaspard be seeing when he came to the villa? You. I am sure you gave him a warm welcome. A cup of coffee perhaps? A glass of wine? Madame was delayed – she would be down soon. Perhaps Monsieur would like to visit the wine cellar and choose a nice bottle of champagne to celebrate the deal?

"None of this was done on the spur of the moment. It was all carefully planned. The freezer had been switched on several hours before. Monsieur Camille's pills had been carefully ground down and added to the coffee. They would take a little time to work; but the impact of wine or spirits would soon make Gaspard feel groggy."

Raynes smiled more confidently.

"I think we could say that you have brought your guided tours of the wine cellar to a fine art. A long trip round the dusty bottles and a brief opportunity to be warmed up in the passage outside. Time to sample the vintage charms of Madame Sylvie herself?"

She shook her head.

Raynes didn't believe her.

"Probably, whilst he was with you in the wine cellar, Gaspard began to feel faint. He wanted to lie down. He felt drained – as one does on such occasions. So Gaspard collapsed just a few yards from the chest freezer.

"I would imagine that you needed some help at this point. Ernst perhaps? Someone who could help you load him into the freezer. Before putting him in, you would have removed his clothes and his shoes. It would have been more difficult later.

"So Gaspard entered the freezer; the lid was shut; heavy items were placed on top to prevent any escape. And within five minutes, Gaspard would be dead of asphyxia. Lack of oxygen.

"Now I would imagine that it was your intention to leave Gaspard there till the hue and cry died down. There would be no attack on the house and there would be confusion amongst his friends. You needed a quiet moment to move the body elsewhere.

"Unfortunately, Madame Leonie had many guests – including a police inspector – roaming round the house, questioning Gaspard's friends, stirring up a 'scorpion's nest', as Madame calls it. On his very first morning, the police inspector asked to see the wine cellar. He was only a few feet away from Gaspard's body. This was very dangerous.

"It became even more dangerous when the inspector's mistress discovered that the police were about to search the Villa Rose!. The body would be found! Panic! There was very little time to get the body away. But what about a double bluff? Who would think that Leonie would put his body into her swimming pool? It must be the enemy. They had killed their ringleader. All of them have access to freezers and a white van!

"Quite an effort was required to get the body out of the freezer. He was well and truly frozen. And even when the body was placed in the pool, the freezer still had to be moved up the ramp and into Leonie's car. Ernst must have worked extremely hard that night!

"'No freezer – no proof!' It must have seemed like the

perfect crime; but people ask questions. They search their memories. They calculate how long it takes a body to thaw. They speculate endlessly on where the freezer might be. Both Inspector Grimaldi and I have been asking ourselves the same questions. But Signor Spumante has got the blame. It seems unfair – but he is now in no position to complain."

Raynes smiled.

"At all costs, Madame must be protected. No whiff of scandal must touch her. She has given the orders and her orders must be obeyed. But you are the one who killed Gaspard. Wouldn't you agree, Madame?"

Sylvie's eyes were as hard as nails.

He had never seen them like that before.

"I am not saying anything, Monsieur."

"I wouldn't expect you to say anything," said Raynes, "because – sadly – I know it is true. Like you, I want to protect Madame from any accusations; and I would be very unhappy if you were sent to jail. But I cannot protect Madame if she sends that letter. It is false – and the police will discover that very quickly. They will ask who wrote the letter; who has signed the signature? It is extremely dangerous. I do not think Monsieur Duclos is giving Madame good advice."

There was a long silence.

Eventually, Sylvie rose from her chair. Her hands were shaking and her face was white.

"I must speak to Madame."

"Madame is not to be disturbed."

Sylvie hesitated – then sat down again. Raynes poured her a second cup of coffee. This kindly gesture seemed to relax her.

"Monsieur Richard, you are right in much of what you say; but I did not kill Monsieur Gaspard. You must believe me."

"I will only believe you if you tell me the truth."

"I cannot say more – not until I have spoken to Madame."

"Shall we see her together?"

There was another long silence – interrupted by a ring at the doorbell.

"I think," said Raynes, "that is probably the police."

"Quelle merde!" exclaimed Sylvie.

Raynes laughed.

"I couldn't put it better myself."

43. *The Man in the Iron Mask*

It was indeed the police – but fortunately not Inspector Grimaldi. Two officers had come to search Camille's room and to interview the staff. Their arrival mercifully prevented Leonie's letter being sent off to Maître Duclos. It also gave Raynes time to rethink the case he had made against Sylvie. Had he gone too far?

She obviously knew what had happened. But if she had not administered the drugs or committed the murder, she must be involved in a cover-up – just as he had been.

Orders were orders in the Villa Rose and not a fly moved on the wall without Leonie's divine decree. It seemed unlikely that Leonie herself would have negotiated with Gaspard – such was her hatred of the man. Therefore, there had to be a go-between.

Raynes felt a need for fresh air to help him think more clearly. He went out on to the patio and leant on the stone balustrade. He reconsidered the basic facts.

Gaspard's death had been carefully planned. The pills were ready. The freezer had been switched on. Leonie had her alibi – and so did Ludo. The meeting was arranged for Wednesday afternoon when most of the staff were out of the house. There would be no witnesses.

Spumante too had been sent away, but he had seen the young man arriving. He had guessed that some sort of deal was in the making – and was deeply unhappy about it. He knew – before anyone else – that Leonie was getting into deep water. He was very worried about her being involved. It was not just Brackles that concerned him. There was another factor in the equation. What was it?

Raynes leant more heavily on the balustrade. Whose idea was it to do a deal with Gaspard? Of course there was no intention of doing a deal – that was merely the bait! But it must have been such an attractive bait that Gaspard was willing to bite. Leonie must have offered a very large sum of money. She wouldn't have risked the money unless she could be sure Gaspard would die. The deal was – that there was no deal!

Whom would she trust to handle such a deal? The answer was so blindingly obvious that the Inspector was surprised he had not thought of it before.

Maître Duclos was the puppet master behind all this. He was Leonie's chief adviser – and not only in legal matters. She referred to him at every turn. Following his supremely successful defence of Ludo in the Paris trial, he could do no wrong. Leonie would be eternally grateful to him for preventing her daughter being sent to prison. He would regard himself as her defender. Her guardian angel. And, because he had a sublime confidence in his own ability, she would listen to him.

When Gaspard appeared on the scene, it would have been Duclos who would have said: "We must get rid of him. Ludo will not be safe till we do get rid of him." It must have been Duclos who thought of putting Gaspard into the freezer. No marks on the skin. No signs of violence. A quick, almost painless death. The body must be kept securely under lock and key until it could be safely moved. Then, when things had calmed down, he could be buried deep inland or dropped overboard into the Mediterranean. Perhaps the sharks would get to him before the police?

Debbie had discovered that Maître Duclos was a cruel sadist who would not hesitate to torture and break people who got in his way. Debbie had been punished not because she had put Leonie at risk – by involving the police. She had also put Monsieur Duclos at risk. She had upset his plans – which in his eyes was quite unforgivable.

So he would have been the person waiting for Gaspard that

Wednesday afternoon. He would no doubt have put on a great display of bonhomie – as he had done for Debbie. The perfect gentleman. There would have been a coffee to accompany the negotiations. The pills would have been thoroughly dissolved in the cream or the milk. Sylvie would know Gaspard's taste in coffee.

Then would come the cheque or the package of notes. Gaspard would have to sign a document saying that he had received the cash and that he would abide by the conditions – never to see Ludo again; never to attack Madame's house or property. Probably, that too was now in the lawyer's safe – along with Debbie's confession.

After that, there would have been a glass of champagne or a liqueur to toast the deal and conclude the business. Gaspard would be thinking what a brilliant deal he had pulled off. But as he rose to his feet, there would have been a sudden, sinking feeling as life drained out of him. A helplessness. He would have seen the smile on Maître Duclos' lips. He would know that he had been deceived. Ernst and Maître Duclos would have carried him across to the wine cellar and put him into the freezer. There would have been no mercy – no hesitation. Gaspard would have been stripped and placed in the icy chamber. The lid would have been slammed down. The keys would be handed back to Sylvie. The cheque torn up or the money returned to the bank. The clothes dumped in a waste bin. Leonie would not be disturbed. Her lawyer had seen to everything.

But when it was announced that a police search was imminent, Monsieur Duclos had begun to make mistakes. The body should have been taken far away – not dumped in the pool. Wherever the body had been placed, it should have had time to thaw – so that the question of freezers did not arise. The lawyer should not have tried to bribe the police. He should not have beaten and humiliated Mrs May.

Leonie had been only too aware of what Duclos could do to women; but she couldn't say anything.

He saw it clearly now.

Leonie was afraid of her lawyer. He had her in his grip – just as he had had Debbie in his grip. Leonie was open to blackmail. She dared not speak. When it came to the crunch, Duclos needed scapegoats. Debbie had been his first choice, but Camille Calvoressco seemed even better. Debbie had not been in the country at the time of Gaspard's disappearance – but Spumante had been a rival for Leonie's hand. Perhaps Duclos had also wanted to marry her? Perhaps he had demanded marriage as the price of silence? Perhaps he was after her money like everyone else?

And she could say nothing. She was like putty in his hands. It must be a very difficult position for a proud woman who was used to having her own way. Sylvie was sworn to secrecy. Of course she could not tell Raynes the truth. But he had got there at last.

He was suddenly conscious that Sylvie was standing beside him.

"Monsieur, the police have gone."

"Good."

There was an unhappy silence.

"Monsieur Richard, I am sorry that I was unable to tell you the truth."

Her voice was full of apology.

"I have spoken to Madame."

"It doesn't matter. I've worked it all out. It was Maître Duclos, wasn't it? He's the one who killed Gaspard."

Sylvie's mouth fell open in amazement.

"You know?"

He smiled at her.

"I should have thought of him before. Madame trusts Maître Duclos with all her business matters. She consults him regularly. He is a frequent visitor to the house. When she had a problem with Gaspard, he offered to deal with it. She gave him a free hand. Gaspard would come to the house, agree to a deal and then be struck down. Maître Duclos and Ernst would put him in the freezer. You and I – and the rest of the poor suckers – would be involved in the cover-up."

Raynes looked at the housekeeper.

He could sense her relief.

"Is that how it was?"

She nodded.

"And has Madame given you permission to speak?"

"She has. She has been very troubled. Monsieur Duclos has taken charge of all her affairs and she is obliged to do what he tells her. She was not happy about the letter from Monsieur Camille. . ."

"Has she sent it?"

"No, she has torn it up."

"Thank heaven for that!"

"She is grateful for your help. . ."

Raynes stared out across the Bay of Nice with unseeing eyes.

". . . And she is very sorry for what Monsieur Duclos has done to Madame Raynes."

"She knows about that?"

"He told her. It upset her very much."

"The man is mad."

"She would agree."

"Does he want to marry her? Get all her money?"

"She thinks so. He's been putting pressure on her for several months. He calls it 'his reward'."

"He is a very dangerous man."

There was another long silence – but a happier one. Now that he knew she was not the murderess, Raynes' affection for her had returned. He hoped she would forgive him for accusing her so forcefully.

"I'm sorry I was so unpleasant to you."

"It doesn't matter. It was difficult for both of us."

"At least I know the truth. That's something."

"And what are you going to do now?"

Raynes laughed bitterly.

"What am I going to do now? I'm going to do something very nasty to Maître Duclos. I'm going to smash him into little pieces. I just hope Madame Leonie will approve."

Sylvie gave him a complacent smile.

"I'm sure Madame will be most grateful."

44. *Justice Poetique*

"It was the lawyer!" said Raynes.

"I still think it was that Norman bitch!" said Debbie. "She's riddled with deceit. She can wrap men round her little finger. You'll believe anything she says."

"Well, I accused her to her face this morning. All I can say is she looked pretty shell-shocked."

"But she denied it?"

"Of course she denied it. But it gave me time to have second thoughts. It was then that I realized it must have been Duclos. I thought you might be pleased. I think the police'll have enough to put him away for several years."

"Do they still have the guillotine round here?"

"No. I think it was abolished some years ago."

"Pity!"

They were discussing the events in the Villa Rose that morning. Debbie had left the house early – even though she had no appointments till 11.00am. She had been frightened that Inspector Grimaldi might come and arrest her. She was surprised to hear about Signor Spumante. No one had mentioned it at breakfast. Everything had appeared perfectly normal.

"So what did you do next?"

"I went to see Madame. Brackles had been painting all morning. You should see the picture. It's quite amazing."

"I thought he'd finished it?"

"This is the new one. It's tremendously erotic. No wonder Spumante committed suicide. He just couldn't compete."

Raynes shook his head.

"Anyway, I told her what I'd discovered. She confirmed that it was true. She admitted that there had been a deliberate cover-up to give the impression that Gaspard was still alive.

Duclos had convinced her that Gaspard was better dead – I don't think she took much convincing. The lawyer took full responsibility for getting rid of him. He promised to dispose of the body – but he didn't.

"His excuse was that visitors were coming to the house. It was safer to leave the body where it was till they went. The body was under lock and key – and Sylvie held the keys. The lawyer said not to worry. The 'English policeman' would never find it. But the knowledge that it was still there seems to have unnerved her. At least, that's what she said.

"When you revealed that the French police were about to search the house, Monsieur Duclos panicked. He told Ernst to put the body in the pool. Leonie didn't know anything about it. She told me that Ernst is one of the lawyer's protégés. Interpol have been looking for him but Maître Duclos obtained false papers and hid him away in Madame's household. All she could tell him to do was to get rid of the freezer. And that's what he did. Apparently, he sold it to someone in Vence and got drunk on the proceeds. It all begins to fall into place.

"She says she's very sorry for what happened to you. She knows what happened because Duclos told her. He actually boasted about what he'd done to you. She's terribly sorry that such a thing could happen to one of her guests; but she admires you for suffering in silence. Now, at least, you should be able to get your revenge.

"Leonie's been too frightened to do – or say anything – because of what Duclos might do to her. She says he's quite unhinged. She did everything she could to protect Ludo but now she's been arrested and her lawyer can't even get her out on bail. She's worried he might turn the blame on to her. It may surprise you to know that he wants to marry her. . . "

Debbie was amazed.

"God help her!" she said. "I wonder how she'd enjoy being tied to a chair, naked, for several hours!"

"I'm sure he only wants to marry her for her money. He's as greedy as the rest of them. But it's not going to happen.

Duclos seized upon Spumante's death as a way of passing the blame on to someone else. He got Leonie to write a confession and Brackles to forge the signature – but I told her it was madness. The police would see through it immediately. It would inevitably lead to her arrest. So she's torn it up and we're writing another confession – this time incriminating Duclos!"

"About time too!"

"Simon came back to the house at lunchtime. He was full of despair. He was allowed about ten minutes with his beloved, but they said there was no chance of her being released. He was in tears – several times."

Richard's voice increased in confidence.

"Anyway, I've planned it all out. Later this afternoon, Maître Duclos is coming to the house for a business meeting with Madame. He is going to have a nice cup of coffee, served by your Norman chum. The pills will be a little more powerful than those administered to Gaspard.

"Once he is incapacitated, we shall take his keys and go down to his house. Brackles and Simon will carry his body out to the car – his own car – and they will follow us down to his villa on Cap Ferrat.

"I am assured that Monsieur Duclos has a chest freezer. We are going to put his body into that freezer – but not shut the lid. Madame wanted me to kill him, but as I told her before, I have no intention of killing anyone."

"I would happily shut the lid," said Debbie. "It wouldn't worry me."

"I think he's more value to us alive," said Raynes cautiously. "We're going to leave Gaspard's clothes and suitcase near the freezer. We're going to put his passport and driving licence into the safe. And whilst we are there, we shall remove your confession."

Debbie breathed a sigh of relief.

"On his desk, we are going to leave another signed confession. I have drafted it out and Madame is translating it into magisterial French. Brackles is doing the signature. He says it is much easier than Spumante's.

"The suggestion is going to be that Maître Duclos is suffering remorse for what he did to Gaspard. He has decided to confess and then commit suicide in the same way that he killed our French friend. A few extra pills will be left lying on the desk. His fingerprints will be on the confession. He will – naturally – climb into the freezer but forget to shut the lid. So he will not die.

"The moment he is placed in the freezer, we shall phone the police and say that Monsieur Duclos has attempted suicide and we have seen his body in the freezer. With a bit of luck, they will be at the villa within fifteen minutes. Gaspard's belongings will be found. Brackles is adding a luggage label to the suitcase to make quite sure they understand the connection. We're also throwing in Ludo's book which should convince them.

"Duclos will take some time to wake up. When he does, he will be in police custody. He will not understand what has happened, but the confession should soon enlighten him. The suggestion will be that Gaspard's body lay in the same freezer. In a moment of complete madness, he decided to put the corpse into Leonie's pool. The fact that he tried to bribe the police to give up the case will make things look even worse. He was not seeking to protect his client; he was trying to save his own skin.

"Madame will be spared any further embarrassment. Duclos will have the legal fight of his life. Let him talk his way out of this one! You will be avenged. Ludo will be released. His arrest should greatly increase the sum of human happiness."

It seemed a good idea to Mrs May. Only two things bothered her. "What if Ernst sees you moving the body?"

"We've thought of that. Miraculously, it's Wednesday afternoon. All the staff are having their afternoon off – including Ernst. They're not due back till 6.00pm. By then, it'll all be over."

"And when is Monsieur Duclos calling?"

Raynes looked at his watch.

"In about fifteen minutes. That's why I wanted you back. I thought you might like to be in at the kill."

Debbie was silent. She had given up a lucrative appointment to come back to the house; but she could always see the man tomorrow. The reason why Richard had been able to contact her was because she had phoned once or twice to see if the coast was clear. Richard had asked her to come back immediately.

The only other thing which troubled her was that Richard kept saying: "us" and "we". Did he really expect her to go back to Monsieur Duclos' villa? She couldn't face it.

"I don't think I dare go into that house again. I'd completely break down."

"Is there anything you'd like me to do?"

"Burn it! The house. The bed. There's plenty of wood and old draperies. It'd go up like a bomb."

Raynes smiled indulgently.

"It might destroy all the evidence we've carefully prepared."

Debbie cheered up.

"Well, if I stay here," she said, "I could keep tabs on that Norman bitch. Make sure she didn't double-cross you. . . phone the police. . . so that they catch you redhanded. If she lifts the phone, I'll clobber her!"

"That's a good idea."

"Is everything ready?"

"Yes, we're just waiting."

There was the sound of a car turning into the courtyard. Debbie looked out of the bedroom window.

"I think he's arrived early."

* * * *

Raynes' plan worked very smoothly.

Leonie welcomed her lawyer; Sylvie served the coffee. Within five minutes, Maître Duclos was deeply sedated.

Raynes searched his pockets and took charge of his keys.

Simon and Brackles picked up the lawyer and carried him out to his car. Both men were wearing rubber gloves. Sylvie and Debbie stood at the front door and watched him go. Madame Leonie got into her estate car with Raynes. Simon sat in the back of Monsieur Duclos' car, guarding the body, whilst Brackles drove.

At the villa on Cap Ferrat, the Inspector and Leonie let themselves into the house and made sure there was no one else in the building. Wearing plastic gloves, they tackled the safe and withdrew Debbie's confession. In its place, they deposited Gaspard's passport and driving licence. The fresh confession was laid neatly on Monsieur Duclos' desk, together with the pills.

Then they hunted for the freezer which was found in la cave – the basement under the house. It was in full use and the contents had to be removed. Raynes insisted that it should all be bagged and carried out to the car so that no wet patches should appear on the floor. Brackles did most of the disposal. There was plenty of room in Leonie's car.

The suitcase with Gaspard's clothes – and the book – were placed on the floor near the freezer – to ensure it caught the police's attention.

Then came the final act of the drama. Monsieur Duclos was carried into the house and down to la cave. A couple of towels were laid on the bottom of the freezer and Maître Duclos was laid on top of them. Brackles rather unkindly pinched his body several times to see if he was really out cold. But the lawyer continued to breathe heavily.

Raynes made sure that Brackles did not lower the lid of the freezer in a final act of spite. He also made sure they wore their gloves until they left the building. They also put Monsieur Duclos' keys back into his pocket and he and Leonie examined the lawyer's appointments diary to see if there was any reference to his movements on May 14th – or on that day. Fortunately, it seemed that Duclos recorded only his professional appointments.

Once he was sure that everything was as it should be, the Inspector let Leonie phone the police. She had a range of different accents and the one she used for the police seemed suitably confusing. He didn't understand it – but the police did.

It was reported that an unknown female had called to see Monsieur Duclos. The front door was open. She had gone inside. All the lights were on. She had searched the house and seen a body in the freezer. She didn't say whether it was dead or alive. Once she had delivered the message, the phone was put down.

With a final look at the desk and the safe, they left the house and got into the estate car. They went out through the main gate and parked near the junction which the police would use on their way to the villa. It took the gendarmes seventeen minutes to get there. Whether Inspector Grimaldi was one of them, they did not know.

Justice had not just been done – but also seen to be done. So with a light heart and the sense of a job well done, they returned to the Villa Rose for a well-deserved glass of champagne.

* * * *

The celebrations were even more ecstatic when, later that evening, Ludo returned to the Villa Rose. She looked pale and puzzled. She couldn't understand why she had been released so suddenly. She suspected a trap. Of course, no one could tell her the truth. All Leonie could do was to suggest that fresh information must have been given to the police.

Simon devoted himself to relaxing the tension and easing Ludo back into normal life. He urged her to have a hot bath and put on one of her most eye-catching dresses. He blamed the arrest on Signor Spumante supplying false information to the police. But Spumante was now dead.

Ludo wondered if her mother had killed Camille – just as she was sure she had killed Gaspard. She decided that the less said, the better. There was still the possibility of charges being preferred against her – particularly over the picture; but providing she continued to deny that she had ever seen it – let alone sold it – it would be difficult to make the charges stick. Whilst having her long, hot bath, she impressed on Simon the importance of saying nothing about the picture.

The cocktail party and dinner were delayed for forty-five minutes. Raynes and Brackles used this time to have a private chat about Signor Spumante.

"I find it very difficult to believe that a man of his age – and experience – would die of a broken heart. It doesn't ring true. The person Spumante loved most was himself. I find it almost unbelievable that even wounded pride would cause him to destroy the one person he really loved."

"You think Duclos arranged that one too?"

"I don't know. But Spumante was – how shall we put it – expendable. He had grossly offended Leonie by shopping her daughter to the police. It could have been revenge. After all, they used the same bottle of pills."

"But Spumante didn't end up in the freezer!"

"No. But I think they needed him as a scapegoat – hence the confession."

"D'you think it was Madame's idea?"

Raynes shrugged his shoulders.

"Who knows? But there is a certain ruthlessness behind these deaths. Leonie would not leave anything to chance."

He looked at Brackles with a faint smile. "You better be careful if you're offered a café au lait."

Brackles laughed.

"I'll stick to the brandy. It's safer!"

"It is round here."

"I don't think the laws of France extend to the Villa Rose. It's more like Muscovy in the time of Peter the Great." He looked anxiously at Richard. "You're not going to report her, are you?"

"Good heavens, no. But I just don't like loose ends. I shall presume that Spumante was murdered until proved otherwise."

The heavy gong sounded down in the entrance hall. Brackles' eyes lit up. "Ah, drinks at last!"

"Yes, I'm feeling a bit parched myself. That champagne

didn't go very far."

"It never does. You're better sticking to spirits."

Richard put his arm round the artist's shoulders as they went downstairs.

"Just remember to keep an eye on Ernst. See if he shows any signs of knowing about Duclos. See if he behaves any differently. Tears in the eyes. Forced laughs. Signs of nervousness. Dropping knives on the floor. That sort of thing. I'd like to lull him into a false sense of security."

"And what about the Queen of Spades? Does she still have her uses?"

That was a good question. Raynes had not forgotten Debbie's suspicions about Sylvie. He laughed sadly at the thought of what he might be missing. But it was better to be safe than sorry.

"There's one thing I never forget," he said. "That the female of the species is more deadly than the male."

45. *Le Bal Russe*

On Friday morning, Leonie celebrated her birthday. Although there had been much speculation, no one could say with any certainty which birthday it was. Being a Russian, she was naturally secretive; but this year, she was determined to celebrate it in style. All her professional friends had been invited, civic leaders and members of the Russian community.

Opera singers and ballet dancers added a dash of culture; and the inclusion of a Jewish rabbi, a Catholic bishop and an Orthodox patriarch demonstrated the breadth of her ecumenical tastes. Over one hundred people filled her large salon It would be an understatement to say that the champagne flowed freely. It was poured out in generous abundance.

Only the best champagne was served – not a rare vintage, but the best Rheims could currently offer. The drinks would be followed by a buffet lunch served in the small salon.

Speeches were expected from admirers – and Leonie would

doubtless say a few words herself. And then, of course, there was the picture – discreetly hidden under a blue silk cloth – waiting to be unveiled. A large gold frame had been delivered the day before. No one had yet seen the painting but it was expected to be a very flattering picture of the lady of the house.

Debbie had forsaken business for the day. She had already passed her target figure and there were still two more days to go. She felt somewhat overwhelmed by the large number of guests who had invaded the house and filled it with a babel of foreign tongues. They all seemed to be at home in the Villa Rose – laughing and joking – whilst the English contingent felt distinctly beleaguered.

In such circumstances, Brackles' company was always good value. He took such a cynical view of mankind; held such a healthy contempt for those in authority and showed scant respect for the rich and famous.

Debbie asked him: "Have you bought her a present?"

"No. Have you?"

"You're a bit closer to her than we are."

"I consider that my painting is the best gift she could receive."

"But you're being paid for it!"

"That makes it the ideal birthday present!"

Brackles' eyes twinkled happily.

"Do you know what Simon's giving her?"

"I know what she'd like from him. A good, solid engagement that would take Ludo off her hands. I did hear on the grapevine that she was thinking of buying that chateau in Grasse for them. That's what she was supposed to be discussing with Maître Duclos on Wednesday afternoon. But, of course, it could have been a complete blind."

"Is there any sign of an engagement?"

"It could be announced this afternoon."

"It'll never last."

Brackles agreed with Debbie.

"I give them six months at the most. I can't see Simon

living in a chateau."

There was a thoughtful pause. No one could imagine Simon living in a chateau.

Richard asked: "Are you going to make a speech?"

"My French is execrable."

"We shall never know."

"But they will. I shall need to drink more to give myself Dutch courage. I shall then smile a lot. Say: 'Messieurs. . . Mesdames. . . Quel plaisir. . . ' I don't think they'll pay much attention once they see the painting. They'll be totally gobsmacked." He looked round the assembled company. "If the drink doesn't get to them first!"

The same thought had occurred to Leonie. Now that everyone was suitably lubricated, she called for silence. This was her moment of triumph. The past few weeks had been full of anxiety and fear. The possibility of an attack on the house. The theft of all her treasures. The death of Gaspard. The body hidden in the wine cellar. Maître Duclos demanding marriage as the price of silence. The body dumped in the pool. The arrival of the police. The arrest of Ludo. The death of Camille. It had been one tragedy after another.

But she had escaped from the nightmare. She could not deny that her survival was due in large measure to Monsieur Richard who had laid bare not just one plot – but two. He had discovered the truth about Gaspard's death and then neatly turned the case against Monsieur Duclos without involving her at all. (Well, of course she had been involved – but the lawyer would never know.)

So she was riding high. She had a roomful of guests. She was rich, powerful, free. She felt like a young woman still in her prime. She radiated confidence and joie de vivre.

Surrounded by friends, Romanovs and countrymen, she spread out her arms in a gesture which embraced them all.

"Mes amis . . . "

None of the English-speaking contingent could understand what she was saying – but it was a tribute to the Russian community in Nice which had contributed so richly to the

259

history and prosperity of the city. She looked back to the regular visits of the nobility – and even the Emperor himself. The generosity of the Empress which led to the building of the impressive Cathedral of St Nicholas – an architectural gem at the heart of the city. The beautiful artefacts which had been donated before and during the revolution.

Ninety years had now passed since the Cathedral had been commissioned; and sixty years since her grandfather had founded La Grotte de Seraphim. It too was part of the imperial heritage. Precious gifts had been bought and passed on to successive generations. Countless icons and Fabergé eggs had passed through her hands. Leonie made it sound like an act of piety rather than what it was – naked salesmanship.

To complete her apotheosis, she called upon the patriarch to unveil her picture. A bearded man with a bejewelled pastoral cross stepped forward and thanked the lady of the house not only for her generosity to the Russian church and the Russian community but also for the honour of being asked to perform her coronation.

He delicately pulled off the blue silk cloth to reveal a majestic picture, clearly modelled on the portrait of Maria Fyodorovna, the wife of Alexander III. Leonie was portrayed in official court dress – silver brocade with a train of imperial purple velvet. Over her left shoulder, she wore the pale blue sash of the Order of St Andrew with the blue and silver badge, embellished with diamonds.

On her head, she wore a tiara and round her neck collettes of diamonds and rubies. An ermine cape was cast over a tapestry chair with golden arms and legs.

This was Leonie in her full glory – omnipotent, victorious. Her face was proud, courageous, implacable. If she had been a Russian Empress, there would have been no revolution. Tchaikovsky would have written a symphony in her honour.

The audience let out a gasp of surprise. They didn't know whether to clap or go down on their knees. It was difficult to clap when you were holding a glass of champagne.

So when the assembled company got over the shock, there

were cries of "Magnifique!" and "Bravo!" The Russians shouted: "Hura!" and "Ziveo Madame Leonie!" Not knowing the original painting by Vladimir Makovsky, even Simon had to concede that Brackles had produced a masterpiece.

The patriarch was perhaps the first to recover. "Mes félicitations, Madame. C'est vraiment magnifique!" Sylvie was at hand to offer him a pontifical glass of Pol Roger.

He lifted his glass.

"A Madame, en toute sa gloire!"

The toast was enthusiastically echoed throughout the salon. "A Madame, la gloire!"

Brackles was delighted by the reaction to his painting. He glowed happily. Sylvie offered him a glass of brandy which he accepted graciously. It was difficult to comprehend that this rather shabby, insignificant little man could produce such a vivid masterpiece. Leonie, who had discovered the full range of his talents, gave him a delicate kiss on both cheeks and invited him to say a few words.

This was inevitably an anti-climax.

"Messieurs. . . Mesdames. . . c'est avec le plus grand plaisir que j'ai produit cette peinture de Madame. . . "

Nobody listened to a word he was saying. Every man in the room was wondering if Leonie was his mistress. Was this history repeating itself – Catherine the Great and her faithful Potemkin? 'Bold mind, bold spirit, bold heart.' Whilst every woman in the room wondered if Brackles could do the same for her.

Amelie alone was quietly confident. Brackles had already promised her that when Richard and Debbie had gone, he would paint her a second picture, identical to the first. Arnaud had agreed to let them use his office as a studio.

At this moment, Arnaud was taking a series of photographs of the painting and its Muse. The Grand Duchess was resplendent in red and gold – in total contrast to her official picture. Arnaud happily snapped away, knowing that one of his photographs would almost certainly appear on the front page of the *Nice-Matin*.

When he had finished his work, the guests surged forward to congratulate Leonie and examine the painting more carefully – particularly the small lion cub nestling at her feet.

"Comme c'est chic!"

Whilst everyone was commenting on the picture, another guest arrived unannounced.

Sylvie was quickly at Leonie's side.

"Inspector Grimaldi!" she said in a low whisper.

The atmosphere changed in a trice.

Conversation stopped. Ludo froze. Simon groaned; "Oh, not again!" Brackles downed a whole glass of brandy in one go. Debbie looked for an escape route; but there was none. She dug into her handbag and unearthed a pair of dark glasses. The Grand Duchess was glacial in her welcome:

"And what do you want, Monsieur?"

"I have come to bring you some good news, Madame."

"Good news?"

"Yes. We have found the man who murdered your son-in-law, Monsieur Gaspard de la Nuit. He has been arrested and last night, he was charged with murder."

There was an immediate outburst of speculation. Who could it be?

"I think you know the man, Madame. He is your lawyer – Maître Duclos!"

The inspector revealed the culprit with the same artistic flourish as a magician reveals the white rabbit hiding in a battered top hat.

There was a gasp of surprise; but then a sense of relief. At least, it was none of them.

Most of the people in the room knew Maître Duclos. Many of them had used his services. His name appeared frequently in the press. He was a well-known public figure.

Grimaldi continued: "I have suspected this man for some time. . . "

Raynes knew this was completely untrue.

". . . He has confessed. He has a very guilty conscience. He attempted suicide; but fortunately he did not die. It will be a pleasure to see him facing the juge d'instruction."

Leonie looked at Ludo.

"So you are now convinced that it was not my daughter who killed Monsieur Gaspard?"

"I never believed it was your daughter."

Another lie.

"Well, why did you arrest her?"

"I wished to bring the matter to a head. To see who would break. And it was him."

A note of triumph crept into the inspector's voice.

"He has confessed to everything."

"Everything?"

"Yes, everything! We have also found Monsieur Gaspard's clothes, his passport, his driving licence – in his house."

He turned to Ludo. "We have even found a book which you gave to your husband as a present."

Sylvie looked at Raynes.

Monsieur Richard had done his job well.

The buzz of conversation resumed.

With a voice a little less glacial, Leonie asked:

"Would you like a drink, Monsieur?"

"Un Campari, s'il vous plaît."

Whilst he was waiting for his apéritif, he inspected Leonie's portrait.

"A very fine likeness, Madame." He looked at the lion cub – and then looked again. "I see you both have the same eyes."

Leonie mellowed a fraction.

"That was Monsieur Brackles."

"Do you have a lion cub in the house?"

"No. It was just Monsieur Brackles' imagination."

The painter twisted his empty glass in his hands and smiled proudly.

"It is a very fine painting. Will you be exhibiting it in the Musée des Beaux-Arts?"

"No. I shall be hanging it in my shop."

"So your customers will see it." He stroked his moustache thoughtfully. "They will all want copies, Madame."

Leonie smiled.

"I shall be happy to sell you a copy. But perhaps Madame Grimaldi would find it *trop formidable* in her salon?"

The inspector nodded sadly.

"You may be right, Madame."

Sylvie delivered his Campari.

He turned to Raynes – with a superior, contemptuous smile.

"Ah, Monsieur Raynes? You are still here. And the murder is solved." He sipped at his apéritif. "I think we may safely say 'the best man won'!"

Raynes was unnaturally modest.

"It looks like it."

Grimaldi made an expansive gesture.

"We have proof. We have a confession. We have an arrest. What more could we want?"

"You have my congratulations."

Debbie would have liked to intervene in the conversation. To tell the French inspector that, but for Richard, he would have had no proof, no confession and no arrest. But she realized that it was better if she kept in the background.

Awkward questions might arise. However, she was much amused by what Grimaldi said next:

"An English lady. . . yes, an English lady. . . has told me that you have a great reputation as a detective in England. Perhaps she was exaggerating?"

"No," said Raynes, rather less modestly. "I think she was probably speaking the truth."

"It is difficult to solve a case in a foreign country. Especially when you do not speak the language."

Leonie was not happy to see Richard being belittled.

"Monsieur Richard has been a great comfort and support to me."

Inspector Grimaldi laughed. A very superior laugh. What was comfort and support when compared with the cutting edge of real police work? He said proudly: "You know, Monsieur, that in Nice we have an excellent reputation for catching criminals."

"And this was one of your own?"

"Indeed he was. I never liked the man. He even tried to bribe me."

"So I heard."

Grimaldi's eyes narrowed.

"You heard? From whom?"

This was dangerous.

Raynes quickly changed the subject.

"Well, you won't be able to blame him for Signor Calvoressco's death! He was nowhere near the Villa Rose that night."

"Signor Calvoressco committed suicide."

"Did he? I'm not so sure. I think you will find that the cause of his death was the same pills as those administered to Monsieur Gaspard."

"The doctors have told me it was suicide. They tried to pump him out – but it was too late."

Raynes spoke quietly: "I think you will find the drugs were placed in his evening meal. He dined on his own on Tuesday night."

Grimaldi looked angry.

"Are you suggesting that he was murdered in this house?"

Ludo, who was standing nearby, groaned.

"Oh, God! Not another murder!"

Raynes nodded.

"You should also be asking yourself who it was who helped Monsieur Duclos move Gaspard's body to the freezer. And then, later, brought him back to the pool."

"Monsieur Duclos said he did it all himself."

"Did he? Well, he's lying!"

Raynes was amused to find himself contradicting the confession that he had written.

"So who helped him?"

Raynes smiled.

"Well, I don't want to cause Madame any more embarrassment, but Monsieur Duclos planted one of his friends in this house. Perhaps 'friend' is not the right word.

Shall we say 'a refugee from justice'? A criminal wanted by Interpol whom Monsieur Duclos imposed on Madame; and who is still living and working in this house."

Grimaldi was slightly unnerved by the authority with which Raynes delivered this information.

"Who is this man?"

Ernst – like Debbie – had been trying to maintain a low profile at the birthday party but he was still moving round the room and filling up numerous glasses with champagne.

"I think if you cast your eyes around this room, you may see someone who looks like a butler. . . "

Grimaldi stared round the grand salon. His eyes lighted on Ernst. He stroked his moustache thoughtfully.

"I have not seen this man before."

"No, you wouldn't. On the day the body was found, Monsieur Duclos ordered him out of the house so that you wouldn't meet him. He was the man who disposed of the freezer."

Grimaldi realized that Raynes now had the upper hand.

"How do you come to know all this, Mr Raynes? Have you been continuing your investigations when I told you not to?"

Raynes was completely disarming.

"I have done absolutely nothing, Inspector. But people speak to me. They tell me their suspicions. I think you will find Ernst a useful witness against Monsieur Duclos – and perhaps even a murderer in his own right. But, at all times, he was acting under orders." Richard turned to Leonie.

"Madame was asked to give him a job. She did not know his background. She did not know his papers were false. Is that not true, Madame?

"It is quite true, Monsieur."

It was not true – and even Sylvie knew it was not true. Leonie was quite aware of the man's background. But she had been glad to employ someone who was quite ruthless and could be relied upon to protect her against people like Gaspard. He had his uses. But he was certainly under the lawyer's control. As they all were. . .

Raynes continued: "I think you will find that he poisoned Signor Calvoressco on the Tuesday night. Simply – but very effectively. Because you were busy dealing with Maître Duclos, you failed to give this second murder the serious attention it deserved. But. . . " He shrugged his shoulders. "It was a mistake anyone could have made. Even a second-rate English policeman!"

Grimaldi was conscious that, in a few short minutes, Raynes had managed to upstage him. Without having read Monsieur Duclos' confession, he seemed to have a complete grasp of the case – highlighting a second murder and a second suspect.

Richard was delighted to see the French inspector knocked off his perch. In fact, he wondered if he could take his embarrassment one step further.

He had noticed that the Frenchman was looking round the room, clearly wondering if there were any more dubious characters to be found in the Villa Rose. He noticed that Grimaldi had at last caught sight of the woman in dark glasses standing in Raynes' shadow, trying not to be noticed. The inspector recognized her blonde hair. Her nose and chin seemed familiar.

Richard looked at Debbie with a mischevious smile and then turned back to Monsieur Grimaldi. He said casually:

"I don't think you've been introduced to Madame Raynes."

Debbie took off her dark glasses and gave the Frenchman a dazzling smile.

"Bonjour, Inspector. I hope Madame Grimaldi had a splendid vacation. . . "

Raynes smiled.

This was the perfect moment for the coup de grâce.

He said quietly: "I think we may safely say the best man won."